The hunger, the obsess...

TH...

Bestselling author Andr... enthralling and sensuous... ...y of a brother and sister, locked together in a vampiric circle of bloodshed and remorse, desire and shame. They are two souls sharing one body, one obsession, one savage secret. And soon, others will know everything about them . . .

ANDREW NEIDERMAN

Andrew Neiderman's acclaimed novel *Pin* was nominated for the Edgar Award and adapted into a feature film. He is the bestselling author of many popular novels of horror, suspense, and psychological terror. *Don't miss* . . .

Playmates

In a backwoods farmhouse, a mother and daughter are "adopted" by a strange, demented family.

Sister, Sister

They were Siamese twins with very unusual gifts. No one knew how unusual . . . until it was too late.

And now available in hardcover from G. P. Putnam's Sons . . .

The Solomon Organization

A secret society of men offers sympathy and support to a divorced father. But sympathy turns to terror—when his ex-wife is assaulted and his daughter kidnapped . . .

Also by Andrew Neiderman

THE NEED

ANDREW NEIDERMAN

BERKLEY BOOKS, NEW YORK

FOR MY DIANE,
MY RAISON D'ÊTRE

THE NEED

A Berkley Book / published by arrangement with
the author

PRINTING HISTORY
G.P. Putnam's Sons edition / March 1992
Berkley edition / May 1993

ISBN: 0-425-13662-0

A BERKLEY BOOK ® TM 757,375
Berkley Books are published by The Berkley Publishing Group,
200 Madison Avenue, New York, New York 10016.
The name "BERKLEY" and the "B" logo
are trademarks belonging to Berkley Publishing Corporation.

PRINTED IN THE UNITED STATES OF AMERICA

10 9 8 7 6 5 4 3 2 1

PROLOGUE

I AWOKE WITH blood on my hands. I smelled it and felt the warmth trickle down my fingers and settle at the center of my palms. Obviously, it was still fresh. The realization turned my spine to stone. I couldn't sit up; I could barely breathe.

Never before had Richard left blood on our hands. He had always taken great care to wash away any trace of a kill. He was a meticulous person by nature, the type who never left so much as a dresser drawer slightly open or a towel unfolded.

I had no doubts as to why he had left the blood. It was part of his revenge. He wanted to drive home his act and have me confront it from the moment I had returned. I sat up slowly, my heart aching with anticipation. All was quiet; all was still.

I wiped my hands on the blanket and, with fingers trembling, reached over to snap on the lamp on the nightstand. Richard had not only turned off the lights before his kill, but he had also drawn the drapes so that no moonlight would spill through the windows. I knew he had wanted Michael to think it was still me, to think it was my hands crushing him and squeezing the life out of him. I knew the way Richard thought and how exquisite he could be when it came to tormenting his prey. Of course he thought he had much more reason to behave that way this time.

I could hear his laughter inside me: a long hollow peal of laughter reverberating down into the depths of whatever soul we still possessed.

"No," I whispered without turning back to look beside me on the bed. "Please, no."

I took a deep breath and turned to witness Michael's shattered face. I recognized him only by the wave of his blond hair. It still lay softly over the top of his forehead, only now his spilled blood ran through the strands. His beautiful face, a face I had compared to Richard's in its classic handsomeness, had been battered until the nose bone collapsed and the cheekbones caved in. His mouth was open, the lower lip stretched below his lower teeth so the gums showed.

I tried to deny this gruesome sight, closing my eyes, but when I opened them, his corpse was still there, the bleeding coming to an end as his life trickled out and away. I dared not look under the covers at his naked torso. I knew how vicious Richard could be and how he enjoyed attacking other men in their sex.

Despite Richard's efforts to prevent me from doing so, I cried. On this bed Michael and I had pledged our love endlessly. Endlessly we wove our illusions and dreams into magical moments I had not thought possible for someone like me. No one had made me feel more feminine, more beautiful, more alive than Michael. He made me want to be a woman and from the start I knew how that threatened Richard. My mistake was I did not do enough to hide my feelings.

I caught my breath and sat up. For a moment when

I looked into the mirror above the dresser, I thought I saw Richard's reflection gazing back instead of my own. I hated him more at this moment than I thought possible. He must have seen that enmity in my eyes, for his image faded quickly.

I rose from the bed and went to the bathroom. I wouldn't let him escape, I thought. He cannot retreat into the deepest depths of our being. Not now, not ever again. I snapped on the light and stared into the mirror, bringing my face close and gazing intently into my eyes, looking behind them until I was sure I saw Richard looking out. I willed him to look out, forced him to hold his gaze on mine.

"You've gone too far this time," I said. "You had no right and I will not forgive you."

He looked skeptical, which only angered me more.

"Look out at the world through my eyes for the last time, for you will never see the light of day again," I promised.

He dared smile back.

"I swear," I said in a cold whisper. "I take an oath on our mother, on our entire race, never to permit you to hunt again, to live again. I'll drown you in me."

And then, to emphasize my determination, I closed my eyes tightly and willed him to sleep. He fought, clamored, chastised and swore, but in the end, he succumbed and when I opened my eyes again, he was gone. I studied my face to be sure.

Then I turned and looked back at Michael's broken body and our broken love.

Why hadn't I done this before, before Richard had had a chance to act? It was my fault, my fault!

"I'm sorry, my love," I said. "But there is little more

that I can do now but deny my very essence. And I will. I died when he killed you, and he killed himself."

I glared back in the mirror, and then I dressed and left Michael's apartment to prepare myself to go to the police and make my confession.

ONE

"I HAVE COME to confess," I said.

Detective Mayer sat back in his imitation black leather desk chair and smiled skeptically. He had crystalline green eyes. I had thought him a handsome man, and if it weren't for his being the policeman pursuing Richard, I might very well have pursued him as a lover.

As it was he had been pursuing me without ever knowing it. Now I was about to tell him, and he looked like he wouldn't believe a word I said.

"It's your brother I expect to hear that from," he replied, smiling impishly. Steven Mayer had one of those faces that looked washed in the waters of the fountain of youth—reddish blond hair and eyebrows, a sprinkling of freckles over the crests of his cheeks, and smooth, creamy skin. He had come from New York and begun his career as a bodyguard for celebrities. Then he decided he liked Los Angeles so much he would stay. At twenty-eight he became a police detective and had begun quite a successful career for himself, most notably tracking down the Rodeo Drive slasher. He was not married; he liked Italian food, Jane Fonda and Charles Bronson, loved *The Phantom of the Opera* and read Robert Parker detective novels religiously.

Richard and I always made it our business to learn about our adversaries. It was part of the nature of who and what we were and still are, even though I was about to put an end to it.

"I am my brother," I said.

He raised his eyebrows and leaned forward. At six feet three, he stood broad and impressive with a graceful, muscular body I could close my eyes, inhale and see. My imagination was as good as a probing X-ray machine. The desk he sat at, some standard requisition police department furniture, looked a size or two too small for him. He crossed his wrists on the top of it, and I couldn't help envisioning him bound and naked, waiting to see what I would do next to bring him to a pitch of excitement that bordered on exquisite torture.

"Having a little trouble with your script, huh? You mean to say, you're your brother's keeper."

"No, I said it correctly. Richard and I are one in the same person."

He kept his smile, but I could see the curiosity growing in his eyes. He sat back again.

"That's quite a trick."

"It isn't a trick; it's a natural phenomenon."

"A what?" He started to laugh.

"Think," I said quickly, punching the word at him. "Think hard. In your vigorous pursuit of my brother and in your investigations of the gruesome murders you have labeled the Love Murders, you have never seen Richard and me together in the same place at the same time. In fact, no one ever has," I said. His smile, although still imprinted was more like breath on a glass window, fading.

"So?"

"We are not two distinct people," I said.

"Let me understand this." He learned forward again, lifting a pencil to use as a pointer. "You are sitting there and telling me you become your brother? What are you, a transvestite?"

"No. I didn't say I dressed up as a man and impersonated my brother. We metamorphose, physically change from female to male, male to female."

He stared at me a moment, deciding whether or not to laugh.

"You know," he said shaking his head, "I understand that you movie stars are a little crazy, that it comes with the territory, but this kind of talk goes a little further, don't you think?"

"I didn't expect you to understand or believe me immediately."

"Oh, no? Well, let's be thankful for the little things."

"But when I'm finished, you will understand and you will believe," I said firmly.

"Is that right? What are you going to do, change into your brother right before my eyes?" he asked, now smirking.

"No. I am not going to let Richard reappear again. I am going to keep him buried within me. That's actually the killing I want to confess to. The others . . . form a trail leading to credibility. It means I must end my dual existence, no longer permit Richard to hunt; but I am ready to do that. I am ready to deny myself and in doing so, destroy the essence of myself."

"What will all your loyal fans do?" he asked, his face deadpan.

"They will find another face to idolize. It was only a matter of time before they would anyway. It's the nature of the business. The public is fickle, but I assure you, I am not worried about that anymore." I sat back.

"I will not sign another autograph; I will not make another movie. Clea Cave will disappear as quickly as the smirk on your face, once you understand."

He shook his head. Then he stood up and went to the window in his office that looked out upon the Hollywood Hills. Richard had intended to do away with Steven Mayer because he was "getting too close," and here I was about to bring him as close as he could possibly get without becoming a victim.

"So, you want to confess. Confess to what? Or should I say, which one?" he asked turning sharply. He looked angry about it. I realized how much he had wanted to get Richard and how much he admired me. Another idolizer, I thought, not without a certain mental fatigue. But the pained look in his eyes made the woman in me soften. I even sensed my interest growing. It was so hard to depress the desire.

"Let's begin with last night's," I replied, my voice nearly cracking.

"Last night's?" His face brightened again. "You mean that homicide over in Westwood? The publicist? What's his name . . ." He looked down on his desk. "Michael Barrington. Him?"

"Yes." I was unable to keep my eyes from filling with tears.

"Forget it, honey. This guy was strangled and mangled, and from what forensics tells us, the man who did it had fingers made of steel and hands like pliers. Why just the depth of the trauma in his windpipe . . . hell, it was crushed. Now I bet you have a helluva handshake, but . . ."

"I didn't do it. Richard did it and he's very strong."

"Just what I thought," he said sitting down quickly. "Now you're making some sense. When did you first learn your brother had killed this man?" He was poised to write some revelation.

"When I re-emerged and found Michael dead."

"Re-emerged? Re-emerged from where?"

"From Richard," I said. He stared at me and then lowered his head.

"Listen," I said. "I will begin at the beginning and when I am finished, you will understand. I promise."

He looked at his watch.

"Yes, it will take some time, but it will be worth it," I told him. He sat back to contemplate me.

"All right, I'll listen, but after you're finished, I want you to tell me exactly where to find your brother."

"After I'm finished, you'll know where to find him," I replied.

"So let's hear it," he said, as he put his hands behind his head and leaned back, willing at least to humor me.

"Actually," I began, taking the small book out of my purse, "I wrote a diary and got Richard to do the same. I thought we should keep some sort of record, a history, so to speak, even though no one else in our race has done so to my knowledge." I took out one of my cigarettes as well.

"Race?" He leaned over to light my cigarette. I took a deep puff and blew the smoke straight up. I smoked these perfumed cigarettes imported from Egypt, a present Richard received from one of his victims, claiming he had drawn her life force out of her with a single kiss.

"I'm an Androgyne."

"Come again?"

"An Androgyne. Let me explain it to you the way it is explained to every one of us. In the beginning God did not create man and then, when man was lonely, create woman. He made us first," I added, unable to keep an arrogant tone out of my voice. I couldn't help it. Whenever I have a conversation with one of the inferiors, I automatically become condescending. It was something I blamed on my mother. She brought me up believing we were superior.

"He made you first," Detective Mayer repeated. His head bobbed, his eyes were wide and the corners of his mouth tucked in tightly, creating a small dimple in his left cheek. I saw myself pressing the tip of my finger tenderly into that dimple, but then Richard invaded my thoughts with one of his own, and I witnessed his sharp finger cutting through the cheek and then ripping the man's face apart. I couldn't help but grimace.

"You all right?"

"Yes, yes. Anyway," I continued, taking refuge in the mythology, "unlike any other creature He had created, He gave us the power to change sex. He truly created us in His image, for God has no sex; he can be either male or female, just as we can."

"I have enough trouble being just a male. You know—shaving. I was thinking I would look good in a beard. What do you think?" He turned his head to show me his profile. "A goatee?"

"I realize your need to be humorous, Detective Mayer. It's a form of protection. As long as you treat me as if I were crazy, you don't have to face what will be terrifying." He stared at me and then straightened up in his seat again.

"Okay, so you had some introduction to psychology at college. Where did you go to college anyway?"

"Alcott in Massachusetts. My mother wanted me to stay away from Hollywood."

"She had the right idea. She was a model, right? A very successful model—Janice Cave. I saw some of the print advertisements she did in the fifties."

"All Androgyne are beautiful. We are the most beautiful creatures on earth, perfection."

"Suffer from terrible modesty, I see. Look, so you're an Androgyne, and you can change from female to male and male to female. Exactly how do you do this? A pill? Magic words?"

"After our initial conversion, our power comes in thought and concentration, our ability to seek the male viewpoint or as males to seek the female viewpoint. Then it happens.

"For me, it's like passing through a dream. I am in the womb again. I am in darkness, surrounded by warm and soft walls. I start to turn, to stretch and experience movement as if for the first time. Suddenly, I am sliding toward a small light. It grows larger, brighter. I draw closer. Then, I experience a repetition of orgasms until I explode into my new self, opening my eyes to discover changed hands, a changed torso. I look into the mirror and see my second self and wonder where I've been for a moment, until it all returns to me. My thoughts trail slowly behind the physical metamorphosis like smoke, you see. They arrive late."

Detective Mayer stared at me, his mouth slightly open.

"Where can I get some of that?" he finally asked. "Sounds right up my alley."

"I imagine any so-called normal male or female would want to be like us, to experience life the way we experience it. You can't imagine how much sharper all our senses are and how that reflects during the making of love. Every time we do, it's like the first time—explosive, truly ecstatic."

"You say any so-called normal male or female, yet you don't look any different from anyone I know, except of course, you're beautiful. I'm not going to deny that, and seeing the kind of following you have and the kind of box office your films command, it would be ridiculous to deny it anyway."

"You're right. No one looking at us, not even a physician examining us, can tell who or what we are. There is nothing that physically distinguishes us from your kind. Yet there is something about us that only we can discern. One Androgyne can look at another and know."

"How come?"

"None of us have been able to explain it. A friend of mine . . ."

"Also an Androgyne?"

"Yes."

"Are all your friends Androgyne?"

"No. We're clannish, but we're not obvious about it."

"Of course not," he replied, still humoring me. "You were saying . . . a friend?"

"William. He once told me his mother said it was something in the face, some message telegraphed in the blink of an eye. But others have theories ranging from telepathic thought to high-pitched sounds only we can hear."

"His mother? I take it you . . . what did you call yourselves . . . Androgyne . . . have normal parents then?" He sat back. "What am I doing?" he said turning to an invisible witness and raising his arms in protest. "You know, I'm as crazy as you are. I'm listening to this and asking questions . . ."

I ignored him. "We have mothers and fathers, but they're one being. And the concept of monogamy is alien to our very being. And then there is the pursuit of prey."

"Prey?" He leaned forward. "What do you mean, prey?"

"That's what I'm here to describe." I put out my cigarette.

"Please do."

"The place for me to begin would be the time of my first menstruation, when it finally came over me to metamorphose," I said. He sat back, his face suddenly caught in a web of seriousness—his eyes no longer smiling, his mouth no longer twisted in derision. His skin was taut and his shoulders stiff. He looked like he was holding his breath and I didn't blame him. I didn't blame him one bit.

"We were living in Los Angeles. As you already know, my mother was working as a model, doing magazine advertisements and some television commercials.

"There were a number of Androgyne scattered throughout the area, although we didn't move here specifically to be amongst them. They are literally everywhere in the world, moving amongst the inferiors, undetected, unnoticed, and not remarkable in any obvious way. Once we move into an area, however, it doesn't take long for the rest of our kind to locate us or us to locate them.

"We had a home in Brentwood and I attended junior high school there. As a preadolescent, I was gangly, uncoordinated and far from graceful, somewhere between a tomboy and that neutral state inhabited by females who have not yet developed anything sexual about them."

"Somehow, I'm having the most trouble believing that part," Detective Mayer said. He couldn't help flirting.

"Nevertheless, it's true. Are you going to let me continue?" I asked petulantly.

"Oh, by all means." He folded his arms across his chest and sat back.

"I was always a good student, friendly, outgoing. Other students invited me to their houses and parties. I had many friends and a few close girlfriends, but all that began to change the day Alison entered my school."

"Alison? Another . . ." He waved his hand.

"Yes. From the moment she stepped into the home-room, I knew she was one of us. She looked about the classroom, sifting through the curious faces, just the way all of us did when we first confronted a new environment, and settled on me. Our gazes locked; she smiled and we knew.

"My other friends, the inferiors . . ." His eyebrows went up. "Sorry. It's just habit. The normal girls . . . grew immediately jealous of the close relationship Alison and I quickly developed. Right from the start that first day, we were side by side almost everywhere. We were inseparable. I ignored any invitation that didn't include Alison, and I brought her into any conversation or activity that involved me. Those who were close to me before became resentful, and soon Alison and I found ourselves ostracized. But the fact that it didn't seem to matter to us both annoyed and intrigued my old friends. Soon they relented and drifted back, accepting Alison almost as much as I did."

"Considerate of them, or should I say stupid?"

"No, they weren't in any danger. Not yet anyway. Alison was closer to her first menstruation. She had long, light brown hair, rich and thick," I said, recalling. I couldn't help smiling at the memory. "It was already at the state an Androgyne's hair would be, for most of our physical characteristics were extraordinary. It was why so many of us became models, actresses, entertainers. I knew that Alison's hair took almost no preparation. Like my mother's, it would always look fresh, neat and healthy," I said. "She would make up things to answer questions from her admirers, tell them she used an egg shampoo or whatever."

"That wasn't fair. Why didn't she explain how God created you guys first and then . . ."

"Her complexion had the same qualities, richly healthy, as smooth and as clear as alabaster," I continued, raising my voice and flashing the fire in my eyes at him. "Remarkably, there were never to be any of the adolescent skin problems for us Androgyne. It gave credence to the belief that we were indeed God's favorite, God's perfect creations."

"Wait a minute. Wait a minute. Christie Brinkley isn't one of you, is she?"

"No."

He pretended he had been holding his breath.

"Okay. I just had to know. Sorry."

"I have to tell you about Alison. It's important to your understanding of all this."

"I'm sorry," he repeated. "Go on. Please."

"She was two inches taller than I was, with a body that had already begun to develop its feminine curves. But she also had a look in her eyes that suggested a more mature sophistication. She was quieter, more thoughtful, and balanced in a way when it came to boys that made most of us envious. There was a definite sense of control about her, control over herself as well as over others." I sighed.

"I will never forget the day after Alison's first conversion."

"Conversion?"

"When she changed from female to male for the first time."

"Oh. Of course. I forgot."

"I had gone with a few friends to the pier in Santa Monica. It was a magnificent spring day, the sky almost cloudless. The ocean was peppered with sailboats and motorboats, some of the sailboats so still against the horizon they looked painted there, like tiny splatters of white against the light blue canvas. My three friends and I were wandering about, playing the carnival games and watching the young men play volleyball on the beach.

"I had called Alison that morning to ask her to come along, but her mother, Beatrice, told me Alison wasn't feeling well. There was something in her voice that made me suspicious. She wasn't very specific about what was wrong with Alison. Usually she spoke to me eagerly in a friendly tone, inquiring about my mother and our lives; but this particular morning she was abrupt. Soon after I cradled the phone, my other friends arrived and we went off to Santa Monica."

"Nice there," the detective said. "I like sitting out on the patio at the Cafe Casino and . . ."

"It was a busy day at the pier," I said pointedly. Now that I had actually begun, my need to tell my story had become almost as overwhelming as sexual desire. I would force him to listen if I had to, I thought.

"Yeah, it's a busy place."

"As usual there were tourists from all over the United States and many places in the world. Many were sunbathing. Most were wandering about like we were, taking pictures and generally people-watching. There is a cement bike and roller skating path along the beach that runs south for miles and miles. This day there were veritable traffic jams.

"We walked alongside the bike path, wandering aimlessly, one or the other of us providing a continual monologue about other friends or family, talking about television and movies, dreams and wishes. When one of us took a breath, someone else picked it up immediately. We were like relay runners passing words between us, afraid of any intermittent moments of silence. The stories and fantasies were woven into a fabric that each of us

wrapped around herself. Secure in our cocoon of friendship, we giggled, we sang parts of songs, we stopped to
stare at a handsome young man in a tight bathing suit,
his tanned sleek body glimmering like polished stone.

"Two of my friends, Paula and Denise, had experienced their first menstruation months before. They had
well developed bosoms on the way so their bodies had
already made the transition from asexuality to femininity.
As the young man moved about in the sunlight, his narrow
hips turning this way and that, his suit snugly drawn over
his buttocks, I saw their faces redden, their eyes narrow. I
could almost feel the quickness in their breath. The shell
of their sex had opened and their imaginations turned
their fantasies into soft fingers exploring the wet, fresh,
throbbing essence within."

Detective Mayer blew through his teeth and loosened
his tie.

"My other friend, Gretta, babbled about renting roller
skates and kept asking us why were we just standing
around when there was so much to do. Hers was a different sort of energy, an energy searching for form and
meaning, a loose explosion of desires and wants dif-
fused, spread widely about, groping for some purpose.
Finally we relented and headed toward the rental skate
concession. It was then that I first saw him."

I paused to light another cigarette. Detective Mayer
was impatient—a good sign.

"Him? Who?"

"I knew immediately that it was Alison; that she had
undergone her first conversion."

"She had become a boy?" he asked, grimacing.

"Yes. Instinctively I was afraid for her, afraid that these
other friends would see the resemblances and somehow
discover the truth. I was shortly to discover that there

was nothing to fear, that the inferiors lacked the sensitivity and the insight. If they saw resemblance between the male and female identities of an Androgyne, they did not find it remarkable. People everywhere had people who resembled them in some way or another, and there were relatives, etc.

"For me, of course, it was different. My heart hesitated and then began beating madly. When he smiled, it was Alison's smile—warm, loving, vulnerable. His hair, although much shorter, was the same rich texture and color. He had Alison's hazel eyes and small, but congruous nose. All his facial features were in perfect proportion to one another, just as any Androgyne's were. Like Alison, his cheekbones rose just under his eyes, deepening them, drawing attention to them. His skin was darker, but just as healthy and clear. I thought he was an inch or so taller.

"Of course his shoulders were wider, firmer, and although he had Alison's narrow waist, he had thicker hips and far more muscular legs. He was wearing a cutoff pair of khaki shorts and a beige athletic shirt, so that the tone of the muscularity in his chest and arms was easily discernible.

"Standing there in the shadows of the roller skating concession, he wasn't all that different from so many young, handsome men on the beach at first sight. The girls looked at him and giggled, but none of them saw anything extraordinary about him. As we drew closer, my heart began to pound.

" 'Hi,' he said. The girls looked at him and at me, curiosity mixed with envy. I could read their thoughts in their eyes: Why had he chosen me to speak to when there were two others in our group who were obviously more desirable? His eyes sparkled with excitement. I sensed his great need to confide in someone his own kind. I could almost feel the frustration.

" 'Hi,' I said.

" 'You going to roller skate?' he asked, the hint of disappointment clear in his voice. My friends looked at me. Paula started to order the skates.

" 'None for me,' I said suddenly. His smile widened. 'I'll see you guys later,' I added. I didn't look back when he and I started away. I knew just how shocked they were, and I didn't want to hesitate long enough for them to ask questions. He said nothing to me until we were a good distance from the roller skating concession. He gestured toward the ocean and we crossed over the beach toward the water.

" 'I had to come find you,' he said. 'As soon as it happened, I had to come find you.' "

"Meaning, the conversion?" the detective asked quickly.

"Exactly. 'Alison,' I said turning to him.

" 'No, Nicholas,' he replied. 'It's funny how the name just came,' he said. 'I asked Beatrice about it and she said my identity was always there, latent, waiting. I just knew that was my name.'

" 'You must tell me everything,' I said excitedly. 'I want to know every detail.' "

"Who wouldn't?" Detective Mayer remarked. He leaned toward me, my story having captured him.

" 'I will,' he told me. 'I want to; that was why I came looking for you as soon as I could. I'm just bursting with excitement. And it's so strange, so thrilling.' He stopped and turned to me."

For a moment I wondered if I could go on describing the event. I pictured Nicholas standing right before me and the vivid memory seized my breath.

"What happened?" Detective Mayer asked impatiently.

"He said, 'When I look at you now, I see you in an entirely new light. I see things about you I never had noticed and I feel so different about you. I'm even a little embarrassed,' he added and laughed.

" 'Don't be,' I told him. 'When my time comes, you'll be the first to know about it too, and I promise I'll tell you every detail.'

"He nodded, the smile folded into his face, his eyes already gazing out at the sea as if the memories and the words were inscribed on the sheet of blue sea water.

" 'You knew,' he began, 'when Alison's period first began.' I nodded, already fascinated because of the way he made reference to Alison as a separate being, you see. 'She was frightened, at first,' he said. 'She knew what it meant, what was soon to come. She went to Beatrice and Beatrice told her to be patient.'

"Then he turned to me and laughed." I assumed Nicholas's posture, the way he threw back his head and lifted his arms.

" 'Be patient. My God, can you imagine going to sleep every night and wondering if tonight was the night she would have the urge to become male and then become male?' he asked."

"Yeah," Detective Mayer said, "I can see why he or she . . . whatever, would be a nervous wreck."

"I told him I thought about it, of course, but knowing it was impending . . .

" 'Yes, exactly,' Nicholas replied. He continued. 'So, deliberately, frightened of what would happen, she forced herself to think only feminine thoughts . . . concentrated on new ways to do her hair, her makeup, thought about new dresses, thought about boys, did everything possible not to think like a male, everything to avoid male thoughts.'

" 'But could she do that?' I asked. Two children, no more than five, a boy and a girl, went running past us, laughing at the way they splashed one another as they ran through the water. For a long moment, Nicholas watched them. His eyes were already filled with a fully mature Androgyne's hunger. The soft, innocent children of inferiors were akin to a delicacy. To stroke them and hold them close was a titillation, like running the dull edge of a knife across the throat of a lamb or a calf."

"Jesus," Detective Mayer said.

" 'Oh, no,' he told me, 'she couldn't prevent the inevitable. One night, perhaps the third night into her menstruation, she had her first male thought.' He blushed after saying this and I knew it was a special moment. But there was more, something else."

"What?" Detective Mayer demanded.

" 'She thought about you,' Nicholas told me, 'about kissing you . . . on the lips . . . '

"For some reason I couldn't quite fathom, the thought of Alison kissing me passionately on the lips did not disgust me. I was rather flattered. 'Then what happened?' I asked him.

" 'She started envisioning other girls,' he said, 'thinking about their bodies, their lips. One morning, on the fifth day, she hesitated to put on any lipstick and she knew, it was coming. Then, last night . . . '

" 'Yes?' I demanded. I was barely breathing. All the sounds of the other people . . . the laughter of children, the shouts of friends, the music from stereos and convertible car radios faded. It was as if Nicholas and I were the last two people on the face of the earth.

" 'She thought about being a male,' he replied. 'First, she thought about his face and how it would differ from her own, his hair shorter, his eyebrows thicker. She lost the graceful turn in her neck and the smoothness in her shoulders,' he said putting his hands on his own shoulders, 'and then she felt the tightness in her upper arms and the firmness in her chest and stomach. Her waist was wider and her buttocks larger.

" 'She thought it was only something going on in her imagination, like any other fantasy . . . becoming this movie star or that, this rock star or that; but then her hands moved over her thighs and suddenly, she felt it . . . Nicholas had emerged; he was hard, excited, throbbing,' he said softly.

"For a moment after he told me this, I couldn't speak, but I remember every detail about that moment. Terns circled above us, hoping for us to toss out some food. Off in the distant sky, a commercial jet began to climb to its flight path.

" 'What did you do?' I finally asked him. He shook his head and continued walking.

" 'I screamed,' he told me. 'Beatrice came to calm me and it was over . . . my first conversion.' He stopped and took a deep breath.

" 'How do you feel now?' I asked him."

"Probably had a bad hangover, huh?" Detective Mayer said.

"No. He told me he felt good. He felt great . . . excited. 'I feel like running along this beach for miles and miles and then . . . taking off my clothes and running into the sea. Afterward, I'd like to lie on the sand and wait for you,' he said.

"He made me promise we would always be friends; we would always trust one another and love one another. But I turned away from him. He sensed something was wrong.

" 'What is it?' he asked. I wondered if I could get him to understand what I had felt.

"I felt so immature. Here he had gone through his conversion and I was still like a little girl."

"Some little girl," Detective Mayer said. "Let me understand this. You were feeling sorry for yourself because you hadn't yet changed into a boy?"

"Yes." The detective did understand. There was hope. He shook his head and leaned back in his chair.

"I was not yet complete. It would be like all your friends had become men, but you remained a boy. How would you feel?"

Detective Mayer nodded, thoughtfully.

"So what did you do?" he asked.

"I told him to go on off and explore. I knew he was anxious to do so. Then I ran off before he could see my tears.

"I didn't find my friends. I went home and locked myself in my room, cursing and crying over my slower development. Finally, my mother came to my door and knocked softly. When I opened it, she saw my bloodshot eyes and we talked.

"She embraced me and comforted me and told me again how it had been for her just before she had had her first conversion. She had been lonely, too; she had felt left out and freakish. She kissed away my salty tears and we went out for pizza.

"Later, when we returned, Alison called. It was so strange hearing her voice after seeing her as Nicholas. It seemed like I had dreamt it all. But she talked about Nicholas, in the same way he talked about her, as though he were someone separate, someone we both knew.

" 'Nicholas was so upset you left him on the beach,' she told me. 'He wanted to spend the day with you, share everything with you.'

" 'When did you come back?' I asked her.

" 'A little while ago,' she replied.

" 'Where? On the beach?' I asked.

" 'No,' she said. I heard the hesitation in her voice and realized."

"Realized what?" Detective Mayer asked.

"He had gone on a hunt. We were only thirteen and just discovering what it meant to be physically and emotionally excited. Naturally, I was very curious.

" 'Tell me,' I asked her, my voice in a whisper, 'is it as wonderful as the others say it is?'

"She hesitated and in that silence, I could hear my heart pounding.

" 'Yes,' she said. 'It is.'

"That night I fell asleep dreaming about Nicholas, his smile, his soft eyes, the graceful way he walked over the sand. Before I awoke, I envisioned someone beside him. At first, I thought it was me, but as the vision cleared, I saw it was someone else, someone entirely different . . . another male . . . for the moment faceless. But even in my sleep I understood that face would soon be my own."

I paused. Detective Mayer stared and then sat forward.

"Would you like a cold drink? I have some Perrier in the fridge."

"Yes, thank you."

He went out and returned with a tumbler of the sparkling liquid. I watched the bubbles dance and then sipped some. He went to the window again. I liked the way his shoulders pressed against his jacket and I couldn't help seeing myself stroking him and running the palms of my hands down his chest to the small of his stomach. Was there ever anything as delicious as a man brought to the height of his sexual excitement?

"Do you want me to go on?" I asked.

"There's more?"

"A great deal more. I'm coming to myself now."

"Oh, then by all means," he said and returned to his seat. He gestured for me to start.

"It happened one day at school, just the way it happened to ordinary girls. I was sitting in English class, working on an essay assignment when I suddenly felt the warm wetness and knew it had started. I excused myself and went directly to the school nurse's office. I had been prepared for it, but she gave me a pamphlet about menstruation and let me lie down in one of the small rooms until I felt strong enough to go back to class. I pretended that I couldn't and she called my mother to fetch me.

"I ran out to the car. Janice was with Nelson, her agent, another Androgyne, someone I had learned had strange tendencies, preferring male lovers when he was in his male state. When I had first learned about him, I found the idea distasteful, even disgusting, but that was before my first conversion. Afterward, it was just as my mother had predicted: My viewpoints changed and suddenly nothing sexual, no form of passion was distasteful. I could understand and tolerate anything.

"I got into the back of the blue Mercedes, closing the door quickly behind me. Janice turned to me and reached over the seat to take my hand into hers. For a long moment, we simply stared at one another, her eyes mirrors of my own excitement. I could see how happy she was for me. Nelson laughed nervously.

"He was tall and thin in his male state, with a peach-tinted rectangularly shaped mustache and sweet potato red hair that he kept long in the back and swept up and then flat in front and on top. Janice called him 'a dandy.'

He was arrogant, but bright, and she said he was a very good agent, guiding her career carefully.

" 'The nurse wanted me to return to class,' I explained, 'but I just couldn't do it. My heart won't stop racing.'

" 'I know. We'll take you directly home,' my mother said.

"I wanted to know if it would be the same for me as it was for Alison, time-wise that is. She told me it was different for everyone.

" 'It happened to me the same day,' Nelson said without turning back. He liked to smoke cigarettes in this long, thin, seashell cigarette holder—only it extended the length of his cigarette so far that it looked absolutely comical. If he smoked and faced someone, he had to stand well back. But it was an heirloom, handed down from generation to generation of Androgyne, beginning somewhere in the early nineteenth century.

" 'The same day!' I exclaimed.

" 'My mother first thought that proved how much I wanted to be in the male state,' he said. He turned around and winked. 'Later, she reversed her opinion,' he added. He liked to joke about himself.

"But I was terrified, even after hearing Alison's story. There were also other stories, stories about Androgyne who died during the first conversion—hearts gave out. There was no definitive explanation for it, except to say the excitement overwhelmed them. Of course, I was worried it would happen to me. I couldn't imagine living through any more excitement than I felt at that moment.

"Janice told me to relax. She said I was perfectly healthy, strong. Everything was as it should be.

"I pressed my cheek against the car window and looked out at the scenery rushing by, wondering how the world would change for me. It was one thing to hear it from Alison's point of view, but another to experience it myself. A thousand questions I had never asked streamed through my mind on an assembly line of curiosity. Would colors change? Shapes? Do men see the whole world differently . . . see things as harsher, tougher, crueler? Would I be, as Janice liked to say, less intelligent when I was in my male form?"

"Now just a minute," Detective Mayer said. "On behalf of all males, I would like to protest."

"My mother claimed men were weaker, had less tolerance and perseverance. 'They can't endure calamity and hardship as well. You'll see; you'll understand,' she told me."

"Well," Detective Mayer said, "maybe there's some truth to that, but . . ."

"However, once, when I confronted her in her male state as Dimitri, I asked her if she still held these beliefs. Dimitri smiled at me in the same coy way, his eyes sparkling with an impish light, and said, 'Men pretend to be weaker only to gain a woman's sympathy and understanding. We like to be babied, held like children in our mother's arms and protected by the same warmth forever and forever, even when we're ninety. But it's a pleasant deceit. Women expect it, want it. Someday you'll understand all this. It's instinctive, especially for the Androgyne.' "

"Smart fellow this Dimitri, who was your mother?"

"In her male state, yes. Anyway, we arrived at our home and I ran quickly to the front door. Janice said something to Nelson and followed me into the house. I went directly to my room and suddenly looked around distraught. For the first time, my room did not please me. The curtains were too dainty, too frilly; the light pink walls looked pale, weak. My canopy bed seemed too fragile, and although the scents of my colognes and perfumes were still pleasing, there seemed to be too much. It was overwhelming. The posters of some of my favorite rock and movie stars made the room look like the room of a juvenile. I went directly to them and started tearing them from the walls.

" 'What are you doing?' my mother asked, as soon as she came to my bedroom door.

" 'These pictures,' I told her, 'it's so stupid to have so many of them up.' I tore one after the other from the wall, not even taking care not to rip them. When I turned around, Janice was smiling and shaking her head. 'Well . . . they are stupid,' I insisted.

" 'Not to Clea,' she said softly, and I stopped crumpling them in my hands. I looked around the room that I had loved, had felt so comfortable and secure in these past years and then turned back to her. Tears streamed down my face.

" 'I can't help it,' I said. She came to me and embraced me, holding me to her tightly. When her breasts pressed against me, the sensation was different, more interesting. I was more aware of their firmness and the memory of her naked flashed across my eyes, her rose-colored skin turning creamy white as I visually traced the lines of her neck down over her neck bone to where her delicious bosom began to emerge, the cleavage dark, promising, her breasts perky, the nipples lifting as if to place themselves gently but firmly between the lips of her lover.

"Even her scent was different. It was stronger and reached places in my mind that had been dark and closed. I felt the light come, the thoughts and reactions stretch and enliven. What I realized was I was experiencing my mother through every sense of my being, something I hadn't done so completely before. Before this, I would admire her in a new dress or in a new hairdo and concentrate on one thing about her. Now, when I heard her voice, I heard it in the same way I felt her body against mine. There was sensuality in it, and the combining of her scent, her voice, and the touch of her brought a taste to my lips I had never before experienced. I held her longer than I usually did. She brushed the hair from my forehead and guided me to the bed.

" 'Get undressed,' she told me. 'Sleep, rest, wait,' she said. I stared up at her.

" 'It's happening,' I whispered. 'Faster, much faster than it happened to Alison.' I took off my clothing."

"This is getting kinky," Detective Mayer said, but I could see the excitement in his eyes.

" 'You are beautiful,' my mother told me and leaned over to kiss my cheek. I wanted to hold her against me forever and ever, but she pulled back and left me. I closed my eyes and envisioned Alison.

"We were changing for physical education class, putting on our mint green uniforms, the one-piece pleated skirt and blouse. She was beside me, talking. I could hear and see her in my mind as clearly as I could when I was actually beside her. She had opened her locker and was unbuttoning her blouse. She peeled it off her shoulders and her bosom quivered under the firm elasticity of her bra.

"I watched her lower her skirt and fold it. Then she turned to me in this daydream and said she just hated sweating in her undergarments and then putting them on after a shower.

" 'Don't you?' she asked. Before I could reply, she had reached back and unfastened her bra. Her small, developing bosom seemed to come folding out of her chest, the nipples a rich apricot.

"I felt like reaching out to touch them. In my mind Alison closed her eyes and brought her hands up behind her head, offering herself to me. I felt a warmth building from my ankles up. It was as if I were being lowered into a warm bath. I brought my own hands up to my face and felt the heat. Then I ran my fingers down my cheeks to my neck, slowly moving over my collar bone to my chest. My emerging bosom was gone, but I didn't open my eyes in shock. I thought only of Alison standing naked before me.

"My hands went to the small of my stomach and hesitated. My male organ had come the way a man's erection builds. Suddenly it was there, hard and throbbing, just the way Alison had described it happening to her. But I did not scream, as she had. I opened my eyes."

Detective Mayer's eyes were bulging. His mouth was wide open.

"Janice was out in the kitchen," I continued, "making a pitcher of lemonade. I sat up slowly and looked at the mirror above my vanity table and confronted myself. 'Richard,' I thought."

"Richard?" Detective Mayer said, recognizing something familiar now. I nodded.

"It was my first thought. I actually sensed Clea drifting away, falling inside me until the sound of her voice in my thoughts was completely gone and replaced by Richard's voice and Richard's thoughts. Clea had been there, but had left.

"I brushed back my dark brown hair, thinking I could use a trim. I stood up to study my muscularity, the trimness in my waist and the firmness in my hips and thighs. I thought I cut as handsome a figure as Nicholas.

"Finally, the exploration of my body completed, my narcissistic hunger satiated, I went to the bedroom doorway and looked out at Janice, who had just settled into a chair to thumb through one of her magazines. She looked up and then put the magazine down alongside her glass of lemonade.

" 'Welcome, my darling,' she said.

" 'Richard,' I told her.

" 'Richard,' she replied. 'I've been waiting for you.' She took my hand and led me to a closet in her room. There, as I always knew, she had clothing stored for me, anticipating my size and shape well. I dressed quickly, anxious now to go out and explore and experience everything from Richard's point of view. Janice understood.

"When I gazed at myself in the mirror, I saw the same excitement in my eyes that I had seen in Nicholas's eyes when we were together on the beach in Santa Monica and I understood why his senses were so heightened. I was like a lion cub anxious to test his new-found strength.

" 'Be careful,' Janice told me at the door, 'you must get used to yourself.' "

"I'll bet," Detective Mayer said.

"I could barely hold myself back from charging out the door. I took a deep breath, looked back at Janice, who smiled at me with a mother's pride, and then stepped out into the world, reborn. An Androgyne."

TWO

"EARLIER YOU SAID something about prey," Detective Mayer said. He leaned back in his chair and I could see that in his mind, he was putting in what he now would consider to be fruitful investigative time. He had no idea yet where this would lead him, but he had come to believe it would lead to an arrest.

"Yes. Once an Androgyne reaches a mature state, she is driven to feed on the inferiors in her male form."

"Feed? What are you, vampires?"

"Of sorts. We don't drain people of their blood, however. We drain them of their very essence, their life force. It keeps us young and alive."

"Do you live forever and ever like vampires? Are you . . . the undead?" He couldn't resist a smile.

"No. Once we experience change of life, menopause, we cease being Androgyne. Part of what makes us so dangerous, I suppose, is what I told you before—on the surface, there is nothing to distinguish us from you. We don't come at you with long, sharp teeth and faces as pale as death. We don't change into bats or wolves. Heaven forbid we couldn't see our images in mirrors. Our egos wouldn't survive. I can't think of anything I'd rather look at than myself."

Detective Mayer laughed. He shook his head and grew

serious again.

"So you feed on normal people, steal their life force. How did this start?"

"According to our theology, this situation did not begin until God became disgusted with people. Their sexual lust made them prime prey and it was ordained that we would forever be their predators. They do not know, but we exist now as part of their eternal punishment for original sin. At least, this is what every young Androgyne is told and it's what we all believe."

"How convenient for you. Somewhat justifies killing, doesn't it?" he asked. I shrugged. "What if you should have an affair with a so-called normal male? Isn't that dangerous?" he asked.

"Not if it's only an affair," I said, but I had to look away. Without realizing it, he had struck the heart of my story. Only I wasn't ready to give him everything just yet. He wouldn't understand; he wouldn't appreciate why I was here, confessing.

"If it's only an affair?"

"Yes. You see, it is peculiar to our kind that Androgyne can only become impregnated as a result of lovemaking with another Androgyne. There is absolutely no danger for us in having sexual relations with the inferiors. Supposedly, we cannot fall in love with them. It is something that should be repulsive to us in the same way it would be repulsive for the tiger to fall in love with the lamb or want to protect the lamb against other tigers."

He nodded, but stared at me for a moment.

"I think you have a different story to tell me. Am I right?"

"Yes." I was impressed. He was a perceptive man. I reached for the small diary I had taken out of my pocketbook.

"What's that?"

"I told you, I got Richard to write a diary."

"It's in his handwriting?" he asked, unable to contain his excitement over a solid piece of evidence.

"Yes. I'll read from it and explain it."

"Okay." He got up from the desk and went to a file cabinet. "You mind if I start to tape a little of this? There's a lot to remember, and I think you would rather I did this than invite a secretary in to take notes."

"Yes, by all means, use a tape recorder."

"Thanks." He produced a small recorder and set it up in front of me on his desk. "Whenever you're ready," he said. I looked down at the first page. My fingers trembled so I squeezed the diary harder. Richard had never intended to share his thoughts with anyone but me. In some ways, this was even more of a betrayal than coming here and confessing. I felt him cringe inside me and even thought I heard a hollow "no!" reverberating down the caverns of my soul. But I ignored it and pushed on when I recalled Michael's broken body.

I sat back, subtly taking on Richard's demeanor, sitting as he would sit: straight, arrogant, head up, neck taut. Detective Mayer widened his eyes with interest. My heart began to pound in anticipation.

"Even from the start, I sensed that there was something about Clea that would make her different," I began. *"She didn't have the same attitude most Androgyne had about the inferiors, but oh how I came to despise them, to despise them for their vulnerability. Sex overwhelmed them. They had little of our balance and control. Few, if any, could ignore the bait, even if something told them it was part of an entrapment. Young girls ruined their lives by becoming pregnant as teenagers. Grown men violated oaths and hurt the women they loved.*

"They tried desperately to sublimate their insatiable appetites. They put their sexual urges into art and literature, into clothing and films, even into architecture. But all of it only postponed what was often inevitable. The wisdom of age was no antidote either. I have seen elderly men teased, tormented, titillated to the point where they would act like little boys for the favor of a kiss, a touch, a full embrace. Rich men spent lavishly on women to keep them at hand, and women, supposedly wiser, made fools of themselves chasing after younger men."

I paused to take a breath. When I read about Richard's abhorrence of normal people, I couldn't help but fill my voice with his sardonic and acrid tone.

"He does sound bitter. Yet you wouldn't know it from meeting him. A more charming man, you can't find," Detective Mayer said, half in jest.

"Richard uses his charm as a weapon. He'll kill you with it if he has to," I said and I meant it. I returned to the diary.

"And so the inferiors were always perfect prey for us. To take pity on them was pointless; but to care for any one of them on a level we would care for one of our own was not only unexplainable, it was sinful. I had hope that Clea would understand it was mainly because of that, that I took the action I took. I never sought her forgiveness, only her understanding. There was nothing for her to forgive me for; rather, something for which she should have been grateful."

I paused again, my throat closing.

"What is he talking about there?"

"You will see," I said, forcing back the tears. "Be patient, please."

"All right. Go on."

I took a deep breath and continued. *"But this all came*

later, after both of us matured into what even our broth-ers and sisters called beautiful and handsome Androgyne, prime representatives of our race. Janice said we had androgynous charisma. It seemed only natural for the others to gather around us, to look to us for our insights and wisdom and direction.

"I sensed this the first time I went out for a hunt, that very first day. Alison as Nicholas had sought out Clea immediately. He needed someone to talk to; he needed support and reassurance, like an infant who had just mas-tered walking needed continual reinforcement and com-pliment. He lacked my special inner strength.

"I didn't, as I had promised, call Alison to have her or Nicholas meet me. Instead, I walked to the tennis courts on Highland Street, not far from our apartment. Two young women, easily in their early twenties, were completing their game. I heard the peal of their laughter and, even before I reached the park, I immediately discovered a new power, the power to envision, to anticipate with a remarkable visual accuracy, based entirely on a sound or a scent, for it was part of the Androgyne's nature that when she metamorphosed, she intensified all her senses.

"This is what made our lovemaking so special for us and so all-consuming for the inferiors. To fuel our height-ened being, we had to absorb their sexual energy, to exhaust them, even to the point of death, to start their hearts pounding so fiercely, they moaned out of a strange hybrid of pleasure and pain. It was an entirely new experi-ence for them.

"I told Nicholas that when we made love with an infe-rior, it was for them as if they were making love for the very first time, for the very first time experiencing the sexual excitement. It was just that new and thrilling

for them, so that even though they were dangerously surrendering so much of their strength, their very life force, they did not hesitate. It reinforced my belief that they were victims of their own sexual pleasure.

"This super-sensitivity we possess is something the inferiors feel. It's part of what excites them about us, tempts them toward the flood. All this I learned that very first day."

"Excuse me," Detective Mayer interrupted, "but does he indicate dates there by any chance?"

"No, but we were only fourteen at the time and since I am thirty-five now, you can assume it was twenty-one years ago."

"Twenty-one years ago," he repeated and made a note of it on his yellow pad. "Okay, what does he say he did?"

"Do you want to hear it in his words or do you want me to paraphrase?" I asked, unable to hide my annoyance. I didn't think he appreciated the literary value of Richard's diary, how well Richard captured details and images and how important that was toward an understanding of what and who we were.

"No, no, his words. You're doing fine. Read on." He clasped his hands together and sat up straight like a little boy in grade school promising to behave. I turned back to Richard's diary.

"Why I chose one female over the other was not immediately clear, but later I understood that one had more sexual energy, a greater appetite and hunger. Some of them, even I had to admit, come remarkably close to our own capacity for erotic fulfillment."

"Big of him to say so," Detective Mayer interjected.

"I turned into the park," I continued in a louder voice, *"already focusing in on the light-haired girl. She had a smaller bosom, lean, well-shaped legs and a narrow*

waist. I thought she was far more graceful than her ostensibly more voluptuous partner. She seemed inexhaustible, growing stronger and more energetic as their game wore on, whereas her girlfriend huffed and puffed and pounded the court with heavier steps. Her movements were abrupt, jerky. She lacked the fluidity of motion that the one I heard called Cynthia possessed."

"Cynthia?" Detective Mayer confirmed. He wrote that in his yellow pad, too.

"Cynthia reacted to me far more quickly. As soon as there was a pause in their game, she spun around as if she could actually feel my gaze upon her. Later, that was exactly what she would say. I thought she put it rather nicely. 'You touched me with your eyes,' she said. Perhaps I had; perhaps, even we are unaware of what form our senses take when we are on a hunt.

"She met my gaze. I saw a slight trembling in her lips just before she smiled. Wherever the doorway to the erotic impulse is in the inferiors, it was opened. She embraced herself just as would a young woman who had been surprised naked. Her girlfriend called to her, but she was deaf to anything but the music between us. I saw that; I felt the power. Despite my young age, I was already the recipient of centuries of androgynous experience. I understood instinctively that when we metamorphose, we instantly inherit all that wisdom; and that knowledge and experience shows. Inferiors don't think of us as younger, even if we are years younger. All they see is the sophistication and it blinds them to anything else.

"It is as if our sexual history is our disguise, brought out and draped over us to cover the deadly, truer motive beneath. 'Like the Venus flytrap,' Janice once said, 'we lure them to us and then snap down over them, drowning them in a sea of pleasure.' "

"Damn," Detective Mayer said. His shoulders shook with the chill that crept up his spine.

"It's probably ironic that we are so curious about their weakness and our power over them, but we're constantly asking ourselves what it is about them that makes it happen. Mary, William's female self, once told me she had discovered that pleasure, just like pain, had its saturation point."

"How old is this William?" Detective Mayer asked, his eyebrows raised. "Where can I find him?"

"William passed on ten years ago."

"Passed on?"

"Mary could no longer metamorphose. Now she resides in a nursing home. Her mind has crumbled, but when she was in her prime, she was very wise, a prophet of sorts."

"I'll bet." Detective Mayer smirked and crossed Mary and William off. "Okay," he said, looking up.

I read on.

" *'Think of this,' Mary said. 'You like vanilla ice cream, let's say, so you eat a pint and you're full, satiated. What if another pint and another pint is forced into you. Suddenly something you loved becomes poison. Inferiors don't know when to pull back. They go beyond the saturation point . . . it's why they are overweight or hypertensive . . . why their bodies are abused so. I have never hunted one that wanted to stop making love, even though I knew she was at a point where she threatened her very own existence. It is their greed, their lust, that actually gives us the power to feed.*

" *'Actually,' Mary concluded, reminding me of our religious beliefs, 'we serve God. We make His poetic justice possible. It's why he put us here, so never feel guilty about what you do.'*

"I didn't feel guilty, although I will admit now that I did suffer some remorse the first time when I took Cynthia that day. But maybe I was simply overwhelmed by my own powers. I suffered less and less of it with every succeeding hunt. Clea's problem is that she never entirely purged herself of remorse over the things we do, and I have come to see that as a weakness, a fatal weakness for an Androgyne."

"Wait a minute," Detective Mayer interrupted. "I don't understand something. Your so-called male self can disagree with your female self?"

"Of course, we're two different people. Don't people disagree with each other?"

"But it's the same brain at work, isn't it?"

"Yes and no. A part of our brain is reserved for him and a part is reserved for me. Men and women don't think alike about many things. And you can't blame it entirely on hormones," I emphasized.

"Furthest thing from my mind," he said. "Get back to Richard's description of his meeting this Cynthia," he said, his voice full of hope.

"Cynthia turned back to her partner, but her concentration was ruined. No matter how she tried, she couldn't stop looking at me, and it reflected in her game. Soon her partner became discouraged as well. She said she was tired and suggested they bring their exercise to an end. Cynthia was very anxious to do so anyway.

"I was sitting on the bench placed there mainly for those waiting to use the court next. She wiped her face with a towel and came out to greet me. Her friend, still on the court, looked up with surprise.

" 'You play so well,' I said. 'It was a pleasure just sitting here watching you.'

" 'Thank you.'

"From what well I drew the words, I do not know. When I asked Dimitri about it during one of our father-son type talks, he said it was part of the androgynous instinct. 'The right words come to us just as the right actions come to a spider. Words are the web we spin. Of course, it isn't just the meaning of the words; it's in the way we speak them, the nuances in our voice and tone, the way our expressions complement the sounds. It's why we seem ageless, I suppose,' he said, sipping his bourbon sour and smiling with that arrogance I had inherited. 'A fourteen-year-old androgynous male would appear as sophisticated as a thirty-five-year-old cosmopolitan inferior.' "

Detective Mayer whistled through his teeth.

"Talk about your precocious teenagers," he quipped.

I didn't look up from the diary.

"It was the way I appeared to Cynthia, but how she appeared to me was something new and exciting, too. I did not see each and every one of her beautiful physical characteristics separately. The softness in her light brown hair was the same softness in her almond eyes, a softness I anticipated in her breasts. The quiver in her voice was the quiver I felt later on in her flesh and in the dark, cool area of her inner thighs. The moment we touched, I felt the pulse of her heartbeat everywhere along her body, wherever I placed my lips, be it on her gently curved neck, on her smooth shoulders, or on the small of her stomach.

"I have read the thousand and one analyses of sexual pleasure written by various inferiors. They talk of erogenous zones, places on the body that are more susceptible to a loving caress. Perhaps for the inferiors, such a thing is true. But what distinguishes us from them is the way our entire bodies become erogenous. Our fingers, the

palms of our hands, even an arm grazing against the body of an inferior become as electric and as erotic as the so-called erogenous zones on an inferior. I am sure they sense this. It's why merely holding hands with us begins to make them hot with passion."

Out of the corner of my eye, I saw the detective unbutton his collar.

" 'Cynthia,' *her friend called, but she no longer heard her.*

" 'Do you live near here?' *I asked her. I was sitting back on the bench, my arms spread over the top, my legs apart. I knew how confident I appeared, how relaxed I was. Her gaze traveled all over me. I saw the way her eyes moved quickly, like someone who had been starving for the sight of someone like me.*

" 'Just down the hill a block or two.' *She nodded toward it as if directing me where to go.*

" 'Cynthia!' *Her friend sounded more desperate.*

" 'She's not your roommate, by any chance, is she?' *I asked.*

" 'No.' *She laughed.* 'Just a friend. My roommate is at work.' *She turned back impatiently.* 'What do you want, Debbie?'

"*Her friend studied me from the distance, trying to determine if I were someone she knew too.*

" 'You're still going to the Blue Moon for a beer, aren't you?' *she asked, the doubt already in her voice.*

" 'No. I want to shower.'

" 'But you said . . . '

" 'Do you live nearby?' *Cynthia asked me, ignoring her completely now.*

" 'I live everywhere,' *I said. She laughed, a nervous, thin laugh. Something instinctive was warning her, but she was turning deaf ears. I sensed it and it filled me with even more confidence. 'But I'd like to see where you live,' I added. I stood up.*

" 'What's your name?'

" 'Richard. Obviously, you're Cynthia,' I said. She laughed again. Her friend was coming toward us. She anticipated it and turned on her.

" 'Talk to you later, Debbie,' she said.

"We walked out of the park quickly. Debbie stood gazing at us, her face filled with surprise and confusion. Neither of us looked back. As we walked to her apartment, I wove words just as Dimitri said we did. For Cynthia, the world around her, all other reality, became blurred and faded. She was mesmerized, but as much by her own lust as by my powers. In fact, William once said, 'We have no powers, not in the supernatural sense. What we have is an ability to turn them on to themselves, to unleash the pure animal strain within them, something they have tried to keep chained and controlled since the day of creation. It's ultimately why they began wearing clothes, why they created that ridiculous fiction about the devil and hell and eternal fire, why they formed government and made laws, why they have police forces and judges.' He laughed talking about it. 'Why they censor their own books and movies and plays, rushing about frantically to keep from speaking words and showing pictures that will . . . will do what? Do they ever really consider? They know they have a tendency toward lust.'

"William looked out at the blue sky above the ocean in his illimitable way, pronouncing his words like some biblical prophet. 'We feed on their desire to be fed upon,' he concluded.

"My first feeding was as much as I dreamt it would be. Never once did Cynthia pause to consider that she had brought a boy, much younger than herself, into her

apartment to make love. It wasn't the way I appeared in her eyes. Dimitri explained that older women, women past their menopause, women with much diminished sexual appetites, would see me as what I appeared to be . . . a good-looking thirteen- or fourteen-year-old boy. Of course men, men who weren't gay, would see me as that as well.

"But it was far too late for Cynthia. I learned little about her. She tossed out small facts about herself as if she were tossing off her clothing. She worked in a bank as an assistant teller. She had come to Los Angeles like so many others, dreaming of being discovered for the movies, but she had quickly realized that wasn't to be her destiny and she found work, one thing or another . . . receptionist, typist, clerk, and now this bank job."

Detective Mayer continued scribbling.

"She giggled nervously after everything she said. I understood that her words were her last ditch effort to protect herself. It became an incessant babble, the mind's way of protecting the body perhaps. But even as she spoke, her breathing quickened, her face and neck reddened, her lips became moist and her eyes small. She fingered the buttons on her tennis blouse, unbuttoning one and then buttoning it. I sat looking at her, my eyes burning through the endless gibberish like two small blue tips of candlelight burning through cellophane.

"She offered some disguise, some pretense intended to hold off her own lust and my obvious intentions. She was just going to shower and freshen up and then we would talk some more. But my words were now in my fingers. I began with that button on her blouse and peeled her clothes away from her like one unwrapping a gift, slowly at first, and then, because of the anticipation, going faster and faster.

"*Although my lips on hers brought neither of us any pain, it was like pressing your lips up against cold glass. We seemed stuck together. Everywhere my naked body touched hers, it was the same. At every contact point, I was drawing out her energy. I could feel her heart thumping through her soft breast.*

"*When our lips finally parted, she gasped, her eyes beginning to reflect the confusion. It was pleasure and yet . . . something had already begun within her brain, a tiny siren, a barely audible alarm, yet she didn't want to pull back. She made no effort to retreat, and when I brought myself gracefully between her legs and lifted her into position, she threw her head back and moaned with pleasure, forcing, I know, all other impulses down, shutting the door on any warnings.*

"*There are some wonderful writers, artists, musicians, creative people among the inferiors who have come dangerously close to perceiving our existence by looking into themselves. One once wrote that only at the point of death was it possible to truly feel the ecstasy of life. Faced with losing it, it throbbed and pulsated with a clarity never before experienced.*

"*Surely that was what Cynthia felt the moment I entered her and my thrusts began to draw the life force from her like some pump lifting the oil from its subterranean stream. I saw the pleasure building in her face, her eyes brightening like orbs of crystal that had captured the sun. She seized my hips to drive me even harder than I was driving myself. I saw that every orgasm she experienced was built on the preceding one. She was climbing toward heights even beyond her own imagination. Every pore in her body opened. She looked up at me and pleaded for me to do more. She was nearly at the top and needed just to be nudged a little bit farther.*

"The energy that traveled from her body to mine made me feel more alive than I had ever felt. She had no need to plead for any extra effort on my part. I wanted more and more and more of her. I had her taste on my lips without touching her. My fingers tingled with the touch of her breasts even though they were clutching her shoulders. I understood I was drawing the essence of her into myself and it filled me with the ecstasy the Androgyne must reach before they experience orgasm.

"It came and almost immediately afterward, I saw her begin to dim. First the light faded from her eyes, and what were once crystal looked more like gray-black coal. Her rosy lips paled into the lifeless hue of day-old dead worms and the crimson that had been in her cheeks and neck sunk into her now whitened flesh, dying out like an echo.

"Her grip on my hips loosened until her hands fell off my body and her arms dropped beside her. Because her mouth was still opened, I heard the death rattle in her throat. Suddenly her body quivered and was still.

"I dismounted, dressed, and left her lying there looking like a once beautiful lily pressed and dried between the pages of a book. My body was still electric, every part of me tingling, the taste of her still very strong on my lips, the scent of her still pungent in my nostrils. I knew I was carrying her off with me, that I had absorbed her like some sponge, and the process of digesting and assimilating her into me had just begun."

"Christ," Detective Mayer said grimacing, "what a disgusting description. But I don't understand, did he strangle her to death, suffocate her? What?"

"You don't understand," I repeated. "I told you, we draw out the very essence of life, the energy, that which makes your heart beat. We do just what Richard is describing: absorb you."

He shook his head.

"We need it. It's what keeps us young and alive. That's why I said we feed upon you."

Detective Mayer stared at me, still not fully understanding.

"Listen," I said and read on.

"Never did the world look as bright, did colors seem as vivid, did the breeze feel as warm, did the sky look as blue as it did when I stepped out of her apartment house. I filled my lungs with the air and walked away feeling more powerful and alive than ever before.

"Now I was eager to talk to one of my own, and for the first time, regretted that I couldn't draw Clea out of me and keep myself intact at the same time. I wanted to confide in her, to be a brother to her and have her be a sister to me. But she was asleep, somewhere deep within my androgynous being, waiting for her time.

"However, in that moment I understood something, something that was very exciting to me. There would be a moment when we would pass one another during the metamorphosis. She would be emerging and I would be submerging, but we would cross and in those seconds of transition, perhaps we would confront one another and look at one another and understand who we really were.

"Shakespeare, one of the greatest inferior authors, wrote, 'The eye sees not itself, but by reflection.' But inferior that he was, how was he to know that our eyes can be turned inward and even if only for a split second, we would see who we truly are."

I sat back to catch my breath, for whenever I read those words, they flashed Richard's face before me and made me relive the moment he was describing.

"Are you all right?" Detective Mayer asked.

"In a moment."

"Let me get you something else to drink . . . coffee?"

"Yes, please. Just black."

I sat back and closed my eyes. The moment I did so, I heard Richard calling. I tried to ignore him, but his voice echoed through every organ and traveled through my blood until he reached the chambers of my heart.

"You can't do this. You need me. Call me, seek me, do it now," he pleaded. But I drove him back and pressed my palms against my ears.

"Hey, hey, are you all right?" Detective Mayer said, returning.

I gasped and nodded. He handed me the coffee.

"Take it easy, relax. We've got time."

"Not as much as you think," I said between sips of coffee. "Richard will keep trying to return, to prevent me from confessing."

"Let him return. I'll handle him," the detective said with an inferior's stupid arrogance. I shook my head. They will never be able to overcome us, I thought. Richard was right about that.

"You want to go on, or . . ."

"No, I'll continue," I said firmly. I was determined to crash through the wall of skepticism and stupidity. I drank some more coffee and then turned back to Richard's diary. Detective Mayer sat down again, his pen poised above the yellow pad, his face masked with sympathy, but his eyes betraying his eagerness to achieve something concrete and make his precious arrest.

"Janice had metamorphosed into Dimitri before I returned. Wisdom and experience told her I would need to share my experience with the male viewpoint, a father figure."

"Excuse me," the detective said. "You're saying his

mother, your mother, turned into a man, just like you say you turn into Richard, correct?"

"Yes."

"Now clear something up for me here, if you please. Is this Dimitri your father? Richard's father?"

"My actual father was an Androgyne I had never met, nor ever would. For one thing, Janice was not positive as to who he was."

"How many guys did she sleep with the same week?" Mayer asked.

"It's not that," I replied. "An androgynous female does not become pregnant in the same way an inferior female does. Because of our ability to metamorphose, the male sperm could remain dormant in the female Androgyne for some time and then suddenly fertilize an egg and start the development of a fetus. A female Androgyne could make love with a dozen different androgynous men in the interim."

"Sounds like roulette. Also sounds like you guys don't care whether you know who the father of your child is or not. Am I right?" the detective asked.

"Since we don't live together as man and wife and since the male has no obligations, it doesn't matter.

"Of course, once an androgynous female becomes pregnant, she can no longer metamorphose until months after giving birth. The gestation period is the same and the birth is the same as it is for the inferior females. Any physician can deliver the child, and in no way will the androgynous infant appear androgynous to the nurses or doctors. Earlier in this century and before, it would prove to be difficult for an androgynous female to give birth as a single, unmarried woman; but with the radical changes in morality that have taken place in the inferior society, it no longer proves to be a problem. Before this, androgynous men, even perhaps the very one who impregnated the female, would pretend to be the husband and father.

"But to answer your question more fully, let me say every androgynous male is a father and every androgynous female is a mother, so I had no difficulty considering Dimitri as my father, nor did Richard."

The detective nodded, his eyes glistening. He was confused, but intrigued. I knew that he was still humoring me, but his skepticism was beginning to melt. Until it did, his doubt like a block of ice imprisoned his realization of how significant this all was.

"Richard continues," I said and read. *"Dimitri smiled knowingly when I entered the house. He was in the living room reading the evening paper and waiting for me.*

" 'There is no need for you to tell me,' he began. 'It went well. I can see it in your eyes.'

" 'Yes, it went very well,' I said, unable to contain my excitement any longer. He laughed as I rushed into the room. I didn't sit down. I paced back and forth, describing how I had heard her laugh, envisioned her body, and pursued. He sat back, listening attentively, experiencing it all vicariously, reliving his own first hunt through mine. 'There was never any hesitation on my part,' I said. 'I knew just what to do, what to say. I felt . . . felt as if I had rehearsed the part, the dialogue and action for hundreds of years, even thousands . . . '

" 'You have,' he said, growing serious. 'Through your ancestors, and as I can see, you have proven to be a descendant in whom they could be proud.'

"I nodded, happy for the compliment, but he sensed something in my face.

" 'Yet something troubles you about it?'

"There was that moment of remorse. I described my

feeling when I looked back at her, a corpse, her bed already serving her as a coffin, the bed sheet her shroud. She looked as if she would decay right before my eyes. Perhaps that was why I rushed away.

" 'Their deterioration is very rapid after our feeding,' Dimitri explained. 'In time you will be able to tolerate it. Some of us even enjoy seeing it,' he added and I sensed that he had become one who did.

" 'Enjoy?'

" 'There is an added sense of power when one realizes that he has done this . . . he has caused this whole process to begin. But for now, you are like a young boy who has shot his first deer . . . thrilled with the kill, but still trembling from the realization that it was you, and solely you, who has made the kill. It will pass quickly,' he assured me. 'And now,' he said, standing, 'I know you are very hungry, right?'

" 'Starving.'

"He laughed.

" 'Janice has prepared something for us. We'll have dinner and you'll describe the rest of it to me . . . how you felt making love, how she was . . . all of it, every vivid detail.'

" 'Yes, I want to do that,' I said. 'I have this need to talk and talk about it.'

" 'I understand.' He put his arm around my shoulder and pulled me to him. After Janice had metamorphosed into Dimitri, he had showered and put on the new Giorgio cologne he purchased on Rodeo Drive in Beverly Hills the day before yesterday. I rather liked the scent and thought I would use it myself whenever Clea became Richard. 'I'm proud of you,' he said, almost in a whisper. 'It will be a wonderful life. You will see.' His eyes watered with happiness.*

" 'There is so much I feel I have yet to learn, so much I have to know,' I told him.

" 'Yes, yes. And you will, and quickly too. Unlike the inferiors, you do not have to duplicate a foolish experience in order to appreciate why it is foolish. You do not have to learn it all for yourself; you benefit from your ancestors and that is a large part of what makes you so superior to the inferiors.'

" 'I know,' I said. 'It's something I already understand.'

" 'Good. Come, let's eat.'

" 'But tell me, Dimitri,' I said, 'will all that I know become something Clea will know too?'

" 'Some of it, yes,' he said. 'But I can't tell you to what extent. It differs for each Androgyne.' His eyes became small, his gaze penetrating. He searched my face as if he were examining it for any visible signs of Clea's soon to come emergence. Satisfied that she was still submerged beneath my identity, he smiled. 'But don't let any of that worry you. I assure you, Clea is as capable as you are and she will be someone in whom we will all be as proud.'

"I nodded and followed him into the kitchen, but something told me it wouldn't be exactly as he predicted. Perhaps it was Clea, deep inside me, already challenging some of my feelings and thoughts, for we were different; perhaps more different than the counterparts of any Androgyne. I couldn't help being afraid for her.

"And, when I say I was afraid for her, you must understand . . . of course . . . I was afraid for myself."

I looked up from the diary, the tears burning my eyes. For a long moment, the detective stared. Then he sat back.

"This parent, mother, father, whatever, encouraged Richard to kill, congratulated him on it?"

"Of course. From Janice's point of view, it meant she had a normal child."

I looked away.

"But you didn't like it," the detective said, seizing upon my hesitation, "did you?"

"No."

"Well, wouldn't your people consider you a freak, a failure then?" he asked with that impish grin, a grin I was beginning to despise.

"Yes. Once my weakness became clear, they tried to help me. We care for each other a great deal."

"Did they help you?"

"Yes and no. You will understand when I tell you the rest of my story," I said.

He stared at me a moment.

"Would you agree to my having the police psychiatrist sit in?" he finally asked.

"You haven't believed anything I've told you, have you?"

"I believe your brother is a psychotic killer, yes. And maybe the realization has affected you too."

I sat back. I could hear Richard's arrogant, "I told you so." Perhaps the only way I could get this man to believe me was to metamorphose, but once I did that, Richard would be in control and he would never permit me to return.

I closed the diary and put it back into my pocketbook. Then I stood up.

"What are you doing?" the detective asked.

"I don't want to waste any more of my time," I said.

"Now wait a minute," he called. I didn't pause. I opened the door and left him and walked quickly out of the police station, fleeing from Richard's confident laughter, which trailed behind me like cans tied to a terrified dog's tail.

I knew it was just a matter of time before he would encroach upon my thoughts and creep into my consciousness until I was thinking more and more as he.

Then, instead of my burying him inside me forever, he would bury me inside him.

THREE

I DROVE HOME, speeding up the Pacific Coast Highway as if I were being pursued. I even gazed into my rearview mirror from time to time as if I expected to see Richard driving our Mercedes sedan, his front bumper practically touching the rear bumper of my 580 SL convertible. I had the top down and the wind had its way with my hair.

The beaches were crowded and the ocean was calm, the white caps foamy and inviting. When I stopped at a traffic light, I could hear the happy peal of children's laughter until it was devoured by the heavy beat of rap music preceding the line of oncoming traffic. A van with two Mexican teenagers rolled by, both of them struggling to get a clearer view of me.

The light changed and I continued toward Malibu. Heavier traffic slowed me down. The frustration continued to build, closing up like a fist just under my breasts, tightening harder and harder until I could feel the tension travel down through my stomach and into my legs. Richard was in a rage. He was like a man thrown into solitary confinement, pounding on the dark, heavy walls of his cell, screaming threats.

"Be still, my love," I whispered. "I'm putting you to rest. It won't be much longer."

I turned off the highway and climbed the mountain

road that twisted like a corkscrew up the mountains to my house that overlooked the coast. My property had a gate and was walled in with hedges ten feet high. I pressed a button on my dash and the gate swung open slowly, gracefully, or as Richard had written, "like the Pearly Gates."

Of course, the sedan was where I had left it in the morning in our three-car garage, right beside the white '58 Thunderbird, Richard's toy. I got out quickly and headed into the house. It was Sylvia's day off so there would be no one to interrupt or disturb me.

I had a plan.

I must remove everything that belonged to Richard, cut him out of my life as skillfully as a surgeon cuts away a cancer. If I had nothing that reminded me of him staring me in the face, perhaps I could succeed in keeping him buried.

I went directly to his room and pulled out the suitcases from the closet. Then, without folding them neatly or taking any great care, I began to yank Richard's clothing off the racks in his walk-in closet and stuff them into suitcases. When there were no more suitcases, I ran out to the kitchen storage room and located some garbage bags. I returned with them and continued to stuff his shirts, pants and jackets into bags. I filled one with all his shoes and then I attacked his dresser, pulling out the drawers and emptying their contents on the floor. When I had it all dumped, I got on my knees and began stuffing the garments into bags.

A small packet of letters I had never seen had fallen out of one of the drawers. It had been buried under his socks. A lightning chill shot up my spine when I picked them up because I recognized the handwriting.

"Can't be," I muttered. "Can't be."

An echo of laughter reverberated through the chambers of my heart.

"No!" I threw the packet back to the floor and stood up. I didn't want to look at it, didn't want to read any of it. I would ignore it, I told myself. The laughter sounded again, more ridiculing, more challenging than before. I shook my head and backed away.

"No."

"Yes," Richard whispered in the back of my mind. "You have to know. Pick up the packet and read. Do it."

I had to show him I could resist him any time I wanted. I took a deep breath and plucked the packet off the floor as quickly and as sharply as a bat snatching an insect out of the darkness. Then, without letting my eyes fall on it, I dropped it into a garbage bag, holding it out as if it were something that could contaminate me.

That done, I went around the room gathering up Richard's artifacts, tearing pictures off the walls, even valuable art he had bought in Laguna Beach. I gathered up his collection of pewter and crystal figures, all replicas of mythical creatures and wizards. There was a pewter castle with windows made of crystal, the centerpiece of a collection he had begun during his trip to Carmel five years ago. The collection itself took up nearly an entire garbage bag.

After that I went into his bathroom and collected all his soaps and colognes, his after-shave lotions, his razor and hair brushes. I threw in his monogrammed towels and washcloths. I left nothing in the cabinets, not even the top to a tube of toothpaste because it had been his toothpaste.

Finally, I stood back and perused his room. He had a room as large as mine with windows that looked out over the ocean. Unlike me, he had never brought a lover here. He was very particular about his things, especially his personal things. He would never let anyone use his hair brush or even wipe his hands with one of his towels. He couldn't tolerate anyone so much as stepping into his room, much less crawling into his bed or using his bathroom, and he forbade Sylvia to come in to clean it. That was something he did himself.

Everything had been kept immaculate and neat, so I knew it would enrage him even more to see the room as it now was—garbage bags filled and strewn about, drawers upside down on the beige carpet, cabinets left opened, hangers dangling and on the floor of the closets. I thought that once I got rid of all of his belongings, I would close the door of the bedroom and keep it closed. Since Sylvia never entered it anyway, she would never become suspicious.

Suddenly, I was very tired. The emotional strain of going to see the detective and confessing, the trip back and the frantic pace at which I had attacked Richard's personal effects had exhausted me. I decided I would take a little nap before doing much more. Right now, lying down on my soft mattress and silk sheets and covering myself with my downy quilt was too inviting a temptation to resist.

The final step in excising Richard from my life, I thought. The hardest part was behind me. The rest would be easy in comparison.

I needed a hot shower and a nap.

I went through the house to the other wing, to my suite of rooms. Our house was a large hacienda with stucco walls and Spanish tiled floors punctuated here and there by beige Berber rugs. Almost every room had a Casablanca fan and windows looking out over the magnificent views of the ocean and mountains. Our furniture was an elegant Southwestern style; wood and glass, Aztec designs and Indian prints of mauve, blues and whites. There was an airy, open feeling in every room between all the windows and skylights.

Other members of the androgynous community loved visiting and sleeping over. From time to time, we had wonderful pool parties, inviting only our own kind. Depending on our mood, either Richard or I would be on hand to play host. One time, while a party was still in progress, we metamorphosed. I felt he should be there to enjoy it too.

When we were younger, we were always like that— thoughtful of each other. What had happened to change it? Was it only love, jealousy and fear? Or were we suffering from something that would eventually attack all Androgyny, a disease involving the conflict of identities, a disease as deadly as anything that could attack the inferiors?

I was almost across the house when the phone rang. I stopped in the living room and lifted the receiver of the brass phone that was on the table by the patio door. It was Alison. She was at the gate.

"Buzz me in. I've brought someone to see you," she said in her usual demanding fashion. Ever since her first conversion, she had been developing more and more of an arrogance. And then, after my conversion, she became jealous of me. But she was confused by her own conflicting emotions. She loved and envied me at the same time. Janice had told me androgynous females don't compete with each other the way the inferior females do.

"We're not petty or vicious. We don't gossip and turn our feminine cunning on each other out of envy. That's because we have a distinct sense of confidence. We don't ever feel insecure about ourselves, no matter how many other beautiful women are in the same room. We know we are beautiful."

"Oh, Alison, why didn't you phone first? I was just getting ready to take a shower and a nap."

"I did phone, but all I could get was your stupid answering service so I decided we would simply chance it and drive up. We were nearby anyway."

"Who's 'we'?"

"Am I going to have to carry on a conversation at the gate through this dumb speaker phone?" she asked petulantly. I sighed. Like me, Alison had become an actress, a wonderful actress, only everyone in the business complained about her temperament. Fortunately, for both of us, we had yet to perform in a film together.

"All right. You can come in, but just for a little while. Okay?"

"After your fifth or sixth yawn, we'll leave," she said. Few of the Androgyne I knew had a skin as thick as Alison's. Almost everyone else would have seen I wasn't in the mood for company and left. But not Alison. And contrary to what we all expected, Nicholas was very much the opposite—sensitive, polite and never sarcastic. In fact, he occasionally complained about Alison, wishing she would try to work on some of her negative traits.

I pressed the number six which opened the gate and then went to the kitchen to get something cool to drink, anticipating that Alison only would demand it anyway.

She came bursting in, sweeping the air before her as if she were making an entrance to a grand ballroom in the midst of an expensive and impressive affair. She wore a light blue bandanna over her peach-tinted hair, a frilly white blouse and pink pleated peasant skirt with pink leather sandals. Her cerulean eyes were bright with energy. Alison could drive depression out of a room, literally blow away gloom with a peal of her laughter, the light of her smile, the music of her voice; and if anyone around her dared remain despondent, she would abuse them as though they were deliberately spoiling her happiness. As far as she was concerned, no one had a right to be unhappy in her presence.

Entering behind her was a young girl, perhaps no more than twelve, with a look of curiosity and wonder that reminded me of myself. It took only one glance for me to realize she was an androgynous child, perhaps only months, if not only weeks away from her first conversion. I could see she would be a very beautiful woman and an extraordinarily handsome man with big dark, piercing eyes, firm lips and an almost Oriental bone structure to his cheeks and chin. It would be the kind of face that would drive an inferior female mad with longing, a face of mystery, yet full of erotic promise.

As a woman her face would have that metamorphic quality even some beautiful inferior females had, a face that changed in little ways from time to time: blue eyes becoming green, a mouth that tightened and relaxed, a smile that sometimes appeared inscrutably beautiful, as innocent as a child's, and then suddenly curled into a licentious leer.

Being forced to confront an androgynous child on the verge of becoming fulfilled took my breath away. It stirred me deeply, forcing me to recall my own exuberance when I stepped up to the threshold of my dual existence. Immediately I began to reconsider my recent actions. I pressed my face toward the fire. My cheeks glowed; I felt as if I had a fever.

"You don't look so good, Clea," Alison said, a mixture of surprise and glee in her voice. "I don't understand how you could have lost your heart to that ridiculous boyfriend."

"You have to have a heart to understand," I replied quickly.

That struck the girl as funny, but as she laughed, her eyes swung around the room. She had the sensitivity of an Androgyne and knew something was terribly wrong.

"Isn't she the sensitive one?" Alison said to the young girl. The young girl nodded and gazed reverently at me. If there was anything I didn't need right now, I thought, it was being forced to entertain another admirer, even one of our own kind. "Clea, I brought Denise to meet you. She's not only one of your greatest fans, she's a worshipper," Alison added, her voice dripping with envy. "Her mother says that the walls of her room are covered with your photographs and movie posters."

"Oh?" I smiled at the young girl, who smiled back but who also looked at me with confusion in her eyes. It made my heart beat faster. She saw something in me that Alison was not yet aware of. This young girl had some extra power, some superior insights, I thought. "Well, I'm very pleased to meet you, Denise. Do you live nearby?"

"Venice Beach," she said. There was a note of compassion in her voice. She knew I was suffering.

"You know of her mother," Alison said. "Diana, the psychic. Anyone who's anyone consults her. She tells me even Donald Trump makes it a point to stop to see her whenever he's on the West Coast."

"Anyway," Alison continued, "I was having a session with her when Denise appeared and we started to talk. When I realized our conversation was entirely about you, I thought it would be nice if I brought her to see you. I thought you might need a bit of cheering up," she added, pointedly.

"That's considerate, but . . ."

"Well, Denise," Alison said quickly, "here she is in

the flesh, Clea Cave, one-time Academy Award nominee." Alison would never forgive me for receiving that honor, I thought. She flopped back into a papasan chair, throwing her body loosely over the big circular cushion. "Ask her anything you want."

Denise and I stared at each other.

"I think you're embarrassing the girl, Alison," I said quickly. "Would anyone care for some lemonade?" I started to pour a glass.

"Of course," Alison said.

"Thank you," Denise said.

Alison's eyes began to narrow. I saw the way she was studying me.

"Are you sure you're all right?" she asked softly when I handed her the glass of lemonade.

"I'm fine."

"And Richard?"

"Sleeping," I said pointedly.

I handed Denise her glass of lemonade.

"Thank you."

"Please, sit down," I said indicating the settee. I sat across from her and Alison. "Do you intend to be an actress, too?"

"I was thinking of becoming a television journalist," she said.

"Someday, Denise Byron will anchor the national network news," Alison declared. "Her mother told me and her mother ought to know."

"I don't doubt it," I said smiling at Denise. "I can see she already has the poise, and she looks like a very bright girl."

Alison looked from me to Denise, her eyes growing sharper.

"Thank you," Denise said.

"Well, you said you had questions you would love to ask Clea if you had the opportunity to do so," Alison said. "Now you have the opportunity, so ask away."

"Perhaps Clea is not in the mood to be pestered by a fan," Denise replied, her eyes on me. "Maybe I can come back another time."

"By all means," I said quickly.

"What do you mean? That's ridiculous. I drove all the way up here, came up that ridiculous road . . . why anyone would choose to live like an eagle . . . I insist you ask her at least one question, Denise," Alison said firmly. "To tell you the truth," she added turning back to me, "I was curious as to what she would ask myself."

"You had better ask the question, Denise," I told her. "Otherwise Alison will nag you to death all the way back down the mountain." Denise smiled.

"All right. What is the most disadvantageous thing about fame?"

"What a good question," Alison remarked. "Only, she could have asked me the same one."

"I don't think we would have the same answer, Alison. You feed on fame. To me, it has been a burden."

"Oh, poor thing. Look around, Denise. See how she suffers in this slum with only three expensive cars in her garage and only two or three hundred thousand dollars' worth of clothing, not to mention the hundreds of thousands of dollars in jewelry, gifts from rich admirers."

"Fame," I said turning more to Alison than to Denise, "robs you of your opportunities to be yourself." My words struck like arrows. Alison held her smile, but it turned cold.

"You are tired, aren't you, darling?" she said. She put down the glass of lemonade and stood up. "The police haven't bothered you about Michael, have they?"

"People knew we had seen each other often."

"More and more often lately."

"Yes."

"Were they just here?"

"No. I was there," I said. I looked away.

"And?"

"And what?" I replied swinging my eyes back at her.

"What did you tell them?"

I looked at Denise, who was now studying me so intently that I felt I was being examined by a doctor. When I gazed at Alison again, I realized what she had done. She couldn't have brought Diana up without making me realize what she was trying to do, so she brought the psychic's daughter, who, I now realized, had inherited whatever gifts of prophecy and analysis her mother possessed.

"I'm sorry," I said, "but I am exhausted from the ordeal. Perhaps you should come back some other time."

"What did you tell them?" Alison demanded. "Did you tell them about Richard?"

"They already know about Richard. You know as well as I do that he's been under investigation."

"That detective—Mayer—he questioned you?"

"Yes."

"Do they intend to arrest Richard and charge him with Michael's murder?"

"I don't think they have enough evidence," I said. All through this exchange, Denise eyed me intently. "I'm sorry," I said, rising, "I really must take a hot shower and rest. I'm sure you understand, Denise."

She nodded, knowingly.

"You shouldn't try to handle this all by yourself," Alison advised. "It's times like this that your friends serve you best."

"I appreciate that. I'll call you soon. I promise."

She smirked and then stood up.

"All right, we'll leave." Denise rose from the settee. Alison looked around again. "Sylvia's day off?"

"Yes."

"Are you sure you want to be left alone?"

"For a while."

"Is Richard going to wake up soon?" she asked quickly, almost as if she had intended to catch me in a lie.

"I don't know," I said. "Maybe."

"Have him call me when he does wake up. I'm eager to speak with him. Will you write a note now so you don't forget?"

"Yes."

Alison smiled.

"Okay, Denise. Let's go flying down this stupid hill, risking our lives at every turn."

"Good-bye," Denise said. "I'm sorry we burst in on you at the wrong time."

"That's okay. Please do come back soon." I followed them to the door.

"Oh, let me just run to the bathroom," Alison said. "I'll be only a minute, Denise."

I turned to tell her to go to mine, but she headed quickly down the corridor, back toward Richard's room. Had I left the door open?

"This is a beautiful house and I love the views," Denise said. "Have you and Richard lived here long?"

"Nearly ten years." I gazed nervously toward the corridor.

"What's your next movie?"

"What? Oh, I've just received a script entitled 'Winter of the Virgin Dead.' It's rather a good love story involving vampires."

Denise laughed.

"What an invention, vampires," she said. "Silly, but fascinating, don't you think?"

"Yes. Please give your mother my regards. I meant to see her myself lately. Now I'm sorry I put it off."

She nodded. "I'll tell her. She's a big fan of yours too."

Alison returned and I saw from the look on her face that I had left Richard's door open. She had looked in and seen what I had done.

"Okay," she said not revealing what she knew. "We'll leave you. Don't do anything I wouldn't do," she added, disguising a threat with a jest. She embraced me. "Please, call me. I want to help you," she whispered. We kissed each other on the lips.

"Good-bye, Denise," I said.

"Good-bye," she replied and they were gone.

I turned away from the door, trembling. Somehow, Richard had snuck past me and called out for help and now that Alison knew, she would return with the others. They wouldn't let me betray Richard, for I would be betraying them.

If Richard didn't greet them when they returned, they would kill me.

And if Richard did greet them when they returned, I would already be dead.

I took my shower and had my nap. When I awoke, I was confused for a few moments. Every so often reality and illusion would become indistinguishable. Memories seemed more like dreams and dreams seemed like memories. Michael's death had been the subject of my nightmares so often, it was hard to believe it had really happened. And just as horribly as I had envisioned it!

I had no problem imagining the details. Richard had

written them in many different ways in his diary and of course had described it to me in his last letter. It was clear how he would be, how he would act, and what he would do. I knew and I didn't stop it. Why didn't I? Was I incapable of it? Perhaps Richard was always in control. Perhaps he was still in control and now was simply toying with me, letting me think I could destroy him.

As if to prove his power, I felt the urge to go to that garbage bag and draw out the packet of letters I had been too terrified to peruse. I rose from my bed, still reluctant, but taking the steps anyway, the steps that led me back to Richard's room. I stood in the doorway and looked over at the sack lying limply by the dresser.

"No," I cried weakly, my tears escaping freely now. I shook my head. "Please, no. Don't let it be so."

I tried turning away. I would get dressed, I told myself, and go to Antonio's for dinner. There would be people I knew, people who could distract me and help me to forget. But I had to rid myself of this one bag filled with Richard's things. I had to take it out and drop it in the garbage can, otherwise, it would call to me all night and I would never sleep.

Cautiously, I entered Richard's room. It was almost as if I expected him to step out of the bathroom wearing one of those expensive silk robes I had crushed under his other things in one of the garbage bags. Suddenly, I could imagine him standing there, smiling gleefully, yet so handsome I was helpless to resist.

Slowly, deliberately tormenting, he would untie the robe and pull it away to reveal his manly body.

"It would be the ultimate act of love," he whispered. "Come to me, Clea. We would merge in passion unlike any moment of passion ever experienced by our kind. It would be innovative, entering sexual frontiers not even dreamed of by our people. Touch me, Clea. Touch me," he pleaded, bringing his hands to his hips and coming forward.

"No . . . please." I had my eyes closed and could see myself starting to back away.

"Clea, I long to make love to you."

"But if you did, you would destroy us both, Richard. It would be a form of suicide," I cried quickly. He blinked and thought, his passion cooling as he realized what I said was most likely true.

That hesitation was enough. The vision of him popped like a soap bubble and was gone. I covered my face with my palms and caught my breath. As I lowered them, I confronted the bag that contained the packet of letters. It was no use thinking I could rid myself of them without looking. They would haunt me forever. Resolved, I stepped forward and fell to my knees by the bag. I dipped my hand in and drew out the packet.

"Why?" I asked them as if they had the power to respond. Of course, the answers lay within the rubber band. I stripped it off quickly and unfolded the first letter.

Dear Richard,

    After you read this, you might not want to have anything to do with me again. I realize that is the risk I take, but after thinking it all over, I've decided it would be even worse if you made your own discovery and believed I had betrayed you. I swear that is not so, and I pray you will understand that we are driven by passions we often cannot control. You have told me this often yourself.

    Yes, I love you and want you and even need you, but I find I love Clea as well and need her too. You and I do have something special, but I would be lying if I didn't tell you Clea and I have something special as well.

You once told me we can expand the boundaries of our capacity to love and that we are complex creatures. You taught me not to be afraid of my desires and that passion was not wrong if it was a deep and sincere passion. I'm hoping you have that same open-mindedness you demanded of me and you will not hate me for revealing that Clea and I are lovers also.

Forgive me for loving you both.

Michael

I threw the packet down, the tears streaming down my cheeks. I felt Richard holding his breath inside me, waiting to see my full reaction. I knew what he was expecting— he was expecting me to hate Michael for what he had done and to be grateful that Richard had killed him. He would claim he had done it for both of us.

But I knew better.

I shook my head.

"You tempted and seduced him just so you would bring me to this moment," I said, my words so filled with anger, I sounded more like a snake hissing them. I looked down at the remaining letters. "I don't care what's in the rest of these letters. It wasn't Michael's fault. How could it ever be an inferior's fault?" I asked him and smiled. "For as you have written many times, they don't have our cunning. No, Richard, this was obviously all part of your despicable plan and I still intend to make you pay."

I could feel him start to laugh inside me again, so I ended it quickly.

"I loved him more than I love you," I cried and his fetal laughter was quickly aborted. I could feel him shrink back like a shadow being pressed into a corner as light expanded in a room.

I dropped the packet back in the garbage bag and tied the bag firmly. Then I rose and thought again about going to Antonio's. Just as I turned to go to my own room and get dressed, I heard the buzzer. Someone was at the gate. Had Alison returned with a few of the others? I hesitated to press the button on the intercom and the buzzer rang again and again. I finally did it.

"Yes?"

"Hi. Hope I'm not interrupting anything," Detective Mayer said.

"I was just about to get dressed to go out to dinner," I replied. "What do you want?"

"Actually, dinner is a great idea. Do you have a date?"

"A date?" I couldn't help smiling at the term. "Hardly a date. What do you want?"

"To apologize and ask if we could continue our talk." I heard him laugh.

"What's so funny?"

"I can never get used to talking to people through these dumb metal boxes."

"All right." I sighed. "I'll buzz you in. Come up to the house." I pressed the button to open the gate and waited for him to arrive at the house.

When he did, I opened the door to let him in. Before he could say another word, I gestured toward the bar.

"Make yourself a drink and get comfortable. I was just about to dress."

I realized I had greeted him in one of my more diaphanous robes and I was nude underneath. His eyes widened and a smile of appreciation began at the corners of his mouth.

"Thank you," he said. He made it sound as if he were thanking me for giving him this unadulterated view of my body. I turned quickly and headed for my bedroom.

I chose one of my Valente originals, a blood red dress with a tight, sleeveless bodice, v-neck collar and pleated skirt. The waist had a jeweled belt sewn in. It made my

hips look even more narrow. Tonight, I would wear my
hair down, I thought. A few quick strokes with my brush
made it lie obediently down my neck and over my shoulders. I put on a wet, red lipstick and just a little eyeliner.
Then I sprayed some cologne over my bosom and turned
away from the mirror.

When I did so, I caught Richard's image flashing at
the end of mine. I looked back. His face dissolved into
the glass. Sometimes, that could happen: We would get
a glimmer of our second selves sparkling across a mirror
like a meteor flickering across a night sky.

He would do all that he could to prevent me from
doing what I had to do.

The detective was looking at my album on the long
glass table. He turned the pages slowly, drinking in each
photograph with care, committing some of them to memory, I imagined. He looked up when I appeared and froze
as if he had confronted a ghost.

"Something wrong?"

"Wrong? Hardly. I just didn't realize how beautiful
you were in person. I mean before, in my office, under
those conditions, I . . ." He stumbled about, searching for
a graceful way to express his own awe. It wasn't the first
time I had had such an impact on a man, of course, but for
some reason, I enjoyed the delicious torment the detective
was experiencing. My beauty confused him and made for
obstacles he would rather not have encountered. "Well,
let's just say, I didn't look at you as I would look at a
beautiful woman."

"It was all business? Like a physician examining a
pretty girl, but keeping his mind on track by telling himself she is just another patient, that's just another heart
I hear beating, and she has just another small intestine
suffering spasmodic pain?"

He laughed.

"Something like that. I was admiring your photographs. Where were the ones of Richard taken? The ones at the end of this album," he said indicating the polished black leather album before him.

"Ixtapa, Mexico. He likes to go off on these holidays from time to time. A hunt under the sun, he calls them in his diary."

"Yes, that diary. Well," he said, sitting back, "I must confess I didn't just drop by for a chat."

"I didn't think you had." I headed for the bar.

"Can I make you something?" he asked quickly, jumping to be gallant and gracious.

"What are you having?"

"A scotch and soda."

"I'll have a vodka and orange juice," I said. He slipped around the marble counter and took the orange juice out of the small refrigerator. I sat on the cushioned stool and watched him make my drink carefully. For a man who considered himself cool and collected, analytical and strong, the detective was behaving like a flustered fan. I couldn't help smiling at him.

"Anyway," he said pouring the vodka in, "I did some checking." He handed me my drink.

"Thank you."

"You're welcome, especially since it's your booze. So, as I was saying, I did some checking and the murder you described in Brentwood occurred more or less the way you described it."

"The way I read it from Richard's diary," I corrected.

"Yes. I mean, the girl was seen going off with a young man and she did work at a bank, and . . ."

"Yes?"

"Well, the medical examiner has her down as dying

from asphyxiation, but it was as if all the oxygen in her blood had been sucked out. There weren't any traumas. Her breathing passages were clear and there was no evidence of anything having been kept over her mouth and nose."

"I told you what happens," I said dryly and sipped my drink, my eyes peering over the glass. He drank some more of his own.

"Well, that's part of what I wanted to clarify. When you say Androgyne draw the life out of their victims . . ."

"Our bodies become like sponges, like magnets, like vacuum cleaners," I added.

"And there are no wounds, no cuts or stabs in the prey?"

"No need."

He shook his head and then smiled.

"It's only in the male form though, that you . . ." He gestured with his free hand, making a small circle and then popping his fingers into the center of the imaginary ring.

"That's right." I smiled seductively and leaned toward him. "You're relatively safe with me."

He swallowed.

"I don't know about that." He came around the bar. "Okay, suppose I buy all of what you are telling me. My first question is why are you doing this, betraying your own kind? And my second question is when do I get to arrest Richard?"

Although the detective's questions were quite predictable, I grew anxious once he put them into words. I turned toward the front door, wondering about Alison and whom she might have spoken to by now. The detective caught my glance.

"Are you expecting someone?"

"Eventually." I swung back to face him. He was only inches away now and I could smell his manly scent beneath his cologne and aftershave lotion. It stirred my heart and quickened my pulse. I could actually taste his lips on mine without touching them. My eyes closed as if we did kiss.

"I can tell you this," he said barely above a whisper. "It would break my heart to see you change into a man."

I smiled. I liked him. He held onto his sense of humor, clung to it like a castaway clung to driftwood. It kept him from drowning in the sea of cynicism around him, the cold, dark ocean of blood, blood of the raped and murdered, the suicides and psychopaths, as well as the innocent victims who wandered into the path of that tide.

"Whenever I meet anyone who interests me, I don't rush to metamorphose." I ran my right forefinger up his tie and over his chin to his lips. He didn't back away. He was practically mesmerized. How easy it is, I thought; how easy it has always been.

"And . . . what does Richard say to that?" he asked.

"To what?"

"To your dragging your feet to metamorphose?"

I pulled my hand back abruptly and swallowed the remainder of my drink.

"He gets upset," I replied and put the glass down. I got off the bar stool. "I'm hungry."

"Can I take you to dinner then?"

"Do you know Antonio's in Pacific Palisades?" I asked heading for the door.

"No, but . . ."

"I'll drive," I said. I opened the door abruptly and waited. He smiled and rushed forward.

"Aren't you going to turn off your lights?" he asked as I started out behind him.

"No. I don't want anyone stumbling over anything," I replied. He looked puzzled, but amused. It made me laugh.

"We poor cops ain't used to riding around in Mercedes convertibles," he joked as I opened the car door. "But, anything for the force." He got in quickly. "Nice Thunderbird," he remarked looking over at Richard's car.

"It's Richard's. I never touch it."

"That's another question," he said as I backed out of the garage. "And I'm still aware you haven't answered my other two. But after you metamorphose, will you and Richard still have the same fingerprints?"

"Of course not. There will be nothing physically identical, just resemblances. I thought I told you that."

"Well, I . . ."

He grabbed hold of the door handle as I shifted down and accelerated, driving the car so quickly out of the driveway, it looked as though we were going to ride right over the precipice across the street.

"Hey . . . I'll have to give you a speeding ticket, if you don't slow down."

"I like driving fast," I said turning into the hill to descend. "It's only when we come face to face with death that we understand what it is to be alive. Trust me," I told him and sped downward, deliberately going faster than I had ever gone before. When I nearly failed to negotiate a turn, I slowed down, realizing any suicidal tendencies could very well be engendered by Richard.

The detective was grateful. He looked sincerely terrified. I had to be sure he understood.

"I'm sorry," I said. "It was Richard."

"Richard?" He shook his head and looked back as though he thought I meant Richard had been on the road. "Where?"

"In me. He was trying to kill us."

"Trying to kill us?" He started to smile.

"Yes. And believe me," I said, turning to him, "he'll try again."

FOUR

"TELL ME," THE detective said, leaning toward me, "what happened after you first became Richard and then he became you again? How did it change you?"

We were sitting at my table in Antonio's. It was a corner table out of the view of most of the others, although it was on a landing raised above the main floor. Vincent Antonio had designed his restaurant with a simple, but elegant decor: red satin drapes over the small panel windows, white tiled floors and synthetic gray stone walls. The small cast iron tables were covered with white silk tablecloths. The seats were cushioned. There were wall lamps and a very subdued set of crystal chandeliers. All of the tables had candles in red or yellow glass sleeves.

The music consisted of choral pieces like the *Carmina Burana* or arias from famous Italian operas. People who dined at Antonio's kept their voices down. It wasn't like the typical open, bright and noisy California restaurant with bright Southwestern colors.

I smiled at my detective. Ever since our arrival, waiters and waitresses, and Vincent Antonio himself, had been falling all over themselves to please me. Mayer had become every inch the moth hovering about the light of my smile. He enjoyed basking in my celebrity.

"You're sure you want to hear all these nitty-gritty details? Most men, inferior men, would be bored."

"Try me," he said, lifting his wine glass. He peered over it as he drank. I could feel his mind poised like the mind of a marksman taking aim. Where was all this leading? What exactly was he trying to find out? I was beginning to enjoy the intellectual tennis. My serve.

"All right." I took a deep breath and recalled. "I awoke the morning after my first conversion aware that Richard had been in my room and that what had once been solely my room was now our room. Yet, I did not resent the changes he had made. Things that he had removed were things I now saw as part of my preadolescent childhood. Although the room was distinctly less feminine, it hadn't been turned into something solely masculine. It was truly androgynous.

"My closet had been divided into two parts with Richard's clothing on the left and mine on the right. Without having to check first, I knew which drawers in the dressers were his drawers, now containing his socks, his underwear and T-shirts.

"Some of my things, mementos of junior high school experiences, stacks of perfumed letters I had received from my girlfriends, dolls and dolls' clothing were placed on the floor of the closet toward the rear. It didn't anger me, for I felt as if I had grown up overnight. When I looked at myself in the mirror, I discerned changes in my face, especially in my eyes. There was a new look of sophistication, a glint in my gaze that suggested a first-hand knowledge of intimate experiences."

"But weren't they Richard's intimate experiences and not yours?" he asked quickly. He was snappy in his return, hoping to make a point.

"I told you we can share things, most things. In truth

my metamorphosis had turned my eyes into two windows, and when I looked in the mirror, I thought I could see through them, see down a stream of history that flowed from the beginning of time. Images and visions of beautiful Androgyne passed before me. I saw men and women passionately embracing one another, turning and fitting themselves every which way to reach for some ultimate ecstatic moment. I sensed that I had inherited much knowledge and experience and this awareness aged me in moments.

" 'Experiences, wisdom, poetry,' Janice would tell me, 'link us together like some long, thick, but invisible umbilical cord.'

"In my newer, more powerful and far more vivid imagination, I envisioned this rope of flesh pulsating with the blood of a thousand Androgyne. Spaced along its surface from its origin outward were the scars marking where each Androgyne had fed on the cord; and out on its forward section, extending into infinity, were the nodules marking the birth of what would someday be new Androgyne."

The detective grimaced.

"Where did you get these grotesque images?" he wondered aloud and then turned to his wine as if seeking comfort in its warmth and flavor.

"My ability to conjure such images didn't surprise me. All of my senses had been heightened, enabling me to bring to life every aspect of my environment.

"When I looked at Richard's things, I saw him. In everything he touched, in all that was distinctly his, he had left a print of himself. His face, his eyes, his smile and laugh were all about me. Even though he now was submerged within my identity and being, the essence of him was still present with sufficient intensity to give me the understanding that everything I had once had, everything that had been solely mine, was now his and mine. My world had truly been split in half, and I sensed that I would no longer feel complete unless I could somehow share what I had with him."

"Let me ask you something," the detective said. It was a poorly disguised attempt at something spontaneous. I knew he had spoken with some psychiatric expert and come away with a number of questions to pose, but I didn't mind at the moment. I was eager to meet the challenge, to see what sort of weak strategy he and his so-called specialists could come up with. "When you're not Richard, do you ever think as Richard or hear Richard's voice?"

"At times. All Androgyne do. It's like someone whispering in your ear. You'll turn around, forgetting for the moment that he can't be entirely separate from you, and you will look for him in crowds or among your friends. You might," I added smiling, "reply."

"And if someone hears you . . . an inferior?"

"I pretend I'm thinking aloud." I leaned toward him sharply and seized his hand. The abrupt movement took him by surprise and he nearly dropped the glass of wine he held in his other. "Don't you see," I said emphatically, "he haunts me."

He gulped down some more wine and I released his hand and leaned back again.

"Do you do the same thing to Richard? Speak to him? Haunt him?"

Good question, I thought. He was trying to see if I could have influenced Richard, perhaps have prevented him from killing Michael, or for that matter, any of the others.

I leaned back and gazed over the room. I didn't want the detective to see the tears that had come into my eyes. I drew them back, buried them under my lids and took a deep breath. Then I slipped my Ingrid Bergman natural smile over my face and fingered the silverware as I stared down at the table.

"No. It's not the same. The male in us is more insecure. He will need to reinforce his existence. Instinctively, he will know that he will be the first to go."

"Like this Mary who could no longer become William after she had had her menopause?"

"Exactly," I said, looking up sharply. He wasn't just toying with me. He was keeping track of all the details. I was impressed.

The waiter brought our appetizers.

"Good-looking shrimp," Detective Mayer remarked. "Not like the stuff I get at Mike's, a small bar and grill near the station. Sort of a hangout for us police types."

"I know your hangouts," I said.

"Oh?" He started to chew his shrimp and stopped. "You're not trying to tell me that there are . . . police who are your kind?"

"That's precisely what I'm telling you."

He resumed chewing, nodding thoughtfully.

"Why did you decide to have Richard keep a diary?"

"He was doing it anyway, in a sense."

"What d'ya mean?" He ate slowly, enjoying the succulent flavors. I decided he was a man of great passion, this detective. He submerged himself fully in his pleasures and was the kind of a man who would suck the meat clean off the bone.

"He was writing me letters." The detective stopped chewing.

"You mean sending you mail?"

"Of course not." I had to laugh. A couple at the table

just to the right of us looked our way. I saw they had the look of people who had grown bored with each other and whenever they went to dinner, tuned themselves in to other people in the hope of finding someone or something more interesting than themselves. Whenever I saw couples like this, I envisioned them as echoes dying out as they dropped through the dark and lonely caverns of time. To be married and lonely had to be a torment, I thought.

"I would awaken and find them waiting for me on the desk in our room. Naturally, I had no memory of their being written. I was supposed to destroy them after reading them, but I tried hiding them in a shoe box in our closet or in a pillowcase, or wrapped in my panties. Wherever I hid them, he discovered them and burned them. It was a game we played.

"Of course, there is one he didn't destroy—his last letter to me; for he hasn't yet returned to find it and burn it."

"Can I see it?"

"Eventually," I said. "I stuck it in his diary. It's after the last entry and it pertains to his latest . . ." I hesitated to use the word "hunt" in the androgynous sense, for I knew that Richard hadn't gone on a typical hunt to feed so he could live on. This was a pure act of jealousy and revenge.

"Tell me more about the letters," he asked.

"Like what?"

"I don't know. What did he write about?"

"In the beginning his letters were like the letters an older brother might write to his younger, but budding sister. Like most men, he saw himself as wiser and far more sophisticated when it came to male-female relations. After all, he had emerged and had been the one to go on the hunt and get the kill, so it was just natural for him to assume he knew more."

"He described all his kills, then?"

"Not all, some. The ones he found more interesting than others. Don't worry," I said, "I remember a lot of detail from those letters and I'll tell you some of it."

He nodded, a look of appreciation on his face.

"That morning after I awoke and made all the discoveries about our room, I found his first letter on the desk, placed right next to my schoolbooks so I wouldn't miss it."

"Let me ask you this," Detective Mayer said, "you say you have different fingerprints. Do you have different handwriting?"

"Of course. You still don't understand that we are two different people, two entirely different people."

He saw the anger in my eyes. He wasn't this dense; he just didn't want to understand.

"I'm sorry, I . . ."

"You're just like any other arrogant man: You can't accept the fact that God created something more wonderful than you."

"He created you. I accept that. I'm just having trouble accepting Richard."

"Um."

"Hey," he said, leaning toward me. "Don't blame me for not wanting to see you become a man."

We stared at each other for a moment and then I smiled. He was a little more complicated than he seemed to be, my detective.

"Getting back to the handwriting . . . I thought he had a fine, thin handwriting, in much more artistic script than mine. The ends of his words all had little sweeps at the base of the final letters. At first, that made it difficult to read, for the words seemed connected. But I quickly got used to it. I have his very first letter memorized. Do you want to hear it?"

"Very much." He leaned back, folded his arms just under his chest, and waited.

I closed my eyes. When I did so, I could hear Richard reading me the letter in his voice.

Dear Clea,
    Today you are beginning school as a woman. I can tell you that the boys in your class will be a little intimidated. They won't be pushing and punching and joking around with you in the same way. They will stand back and do things to one another to fight for your attention.
    Older boys, however, will approach you directly, expecting you to swoon. Many will try to take advantage of your innocence. Be alert and remember what they are after. It's not a conquest, conquering you; it's conquering their own innocence, their own insecurity. Men have always seen women as prey. It should come as no surprise then that the androgynous men literally hunt.
    I know this sounds like a big brother preaching to a younger sister, but I can't help but want to give you the benefit of my masculine viewpoint.
    Forgive me for my condescending tone.

                                              Love,
                                              Richard

"Love, Richard," I repeated, barely doing more than mouthing it.

I opened my eyes. Detective Mayer was staring at me intensely, his mouth slightly open.

"When you say that from memory . . ."

"Yes?"

"Your face, it seemed to change for a few moments." He shook his head. "Must be the dim lights, the wine."

"No," I said. "Richard was probably using the moment to reach out. It's as if I provided him with a window, a hole in the ice, and for a moment, he could come up for air."

I shook my head and sighed.

"I couldn't help it. The memory of that first letter . . . seeing his signature. You can't begin to understand, but when you ask if our handwriting is different . . ."

"Yes?"

"Don't you see? The sense of him being a whole, separate person was embodied in the way he wrote his name. It was so unlike the way I would write my own." My heart was pounding. Perhaps I was going too far, reminiscing too vividly. I felt like a suicidal person stepping up to a precipice and then pulling herself back.

"What did you do with that first letter?"

"I put it in the top drawer of the desk. A day later, it was gone."

"Maybe you had just misplaced it."

"No. Richard had emerged and found it. He told me so in his next letter and asked . . . no," I said pausing and smirking, "ordered me not to keep any correspondence."

"What was he afraid of?"

"Someone like you, perhaps."

"Or you," the detective countered. That was good; that was brilliant. I looked at him with different eyes. This man wore many faces. I was beginning to think that he lived within a prism and it wasn't possible to see clearly who he really was. Perhaps that came from his work, his need to win the confidence of those he questioned and suspected.

I wanted to warn him of the dangers, tell him that it was possible to lose track of who you really were. You could spend your whole life looking into mirrors, searching for the truth of your identity and seeing only one false face after another. Visual amnesia could terrify your very soul, for without a name, the soul would wander aimlessly from door to door, never sure which one opened on home.

The waiter, a dark-haired man with a face as pale as an unlit candle, brought our food. His lips were so red, I was sure he had painted them with a trace of lipstick. I could see he made the detective uncomfortable. Mayer sat back and looked the other way while we were being served.

"So many of your kind are not sure if they want to be male or female," I told him when the waiter left us. "Why should you be surprised at learning about the Androgyne?"

"You're right. Did you see that guy's fingernails?"

"Maybe it's a woman." It wasn't, but I wanted him to wonder.

"Christ. You sure this place is sanitary?"

I threw my head back and laughed.

"Sexual deviation doesn't make its home in filth. Some of the fags, dikes, homos, gays—whatever term you want to use—are the most immaculate people I know."

"I suppose," he said and cut into his veal. I dipped my spoon and fork into my angel hair.

"What are you thinking about or remembering now?" he asked.

"Why?"

"You've been sitting there, smiling and twirling your angel hair for nearly a minute."

"I was remembering rushing to school to see Alison the day after Richard had emerged and hunted.

"Of course, she knew instantly. We simply stood there, staring into one another's eyes. The corridors were usually so noisy in the morning: students rushing in from their buses, lockers slamming, people shouting to one another, teachers monitoring the halls and demanding less roughhousing and noise, bells ringing. Yet, we heard none of it; only our own voices.

" 'His name is Richard,' " I said. She nodded, her eyes filled with happiness for me. 'But tell me,' I asked her quickly, 'did Nicholas leave anything for you to read?' You should have seen the look on her face, the envy.

" 'To read?' she said. 'What?'

" 'A letter? Advice?'

" 'No.' She was practically in tears. Of course, I regretted telling her immediately, but how was I to know? Of course, I thought that everything happening to me had happened to her."

The detective nodded, chewing harder.

"I told her Nicholas would surely leave her notes or letters, too, but instinctively I knew he wouldn't. I knew that what had begun between Richard and myself was unique, even to Androgyne; and I sensed that I should be more discreet about it. The others wouldn't understand and might even feel threatened by it."

"Threatened? Why threatened?"

"Unusual or uncharacteristic behavior might lead to discovery, exposure. There was and has never been any doubt what would happen then."

"What?"

"Your kind would hunt us down, exterminate us. Consequently, we don't tolerate deviants in our race."

He nodded, thoughtful. Then his eyes brightened. I knew what he was going to ask.

"What about you?"

"It's complicated," I replied. I finally lifted my angel hair to my lips. "But after a while, you will understand and appreciate why I am doing this."

"I appreciate it already," he kidded. "This food is fantastic. I've got this Italian buddy whose mother makes the best baked lasagna I ever ate, but even she can't make food like this. I mean it's not what you would call authentic Italian. It's . . . it's . . ."

"Gourmet," I said.

"Yeah, gourmet." He ate from his pasta side dish, rolling his eyes to indicate how much he enjoyed the food.

"Anyway," I continued, "right from the beginning, I felt a great need to protect Richard. There would be secrets between us, secrets I would share with no one until I had met William, because I sensed he was no threat."

"What do you mean? Why wasn't he a threat?"

"He was in the autumn of his androgynous life. The spirit in the blood had slowed down. He rarely went on hunts anymore. The change was more for the sake of visiting himself than anything else. And he had taken a sort of grandfatherly interest in me. There was no competition between us.

"Not that competition is bad, you understand. It's natural, good. Young Androgyne are like two wild horses, challenging each other's endurance, speed. It sharpens them both."

"So this envy of Alison's didn't damage your friendship?"

"Hardly. She wanted to know what sort of advice Richard had given me. I told her it was advice to the lovelorn. And then I added, 'the nerve—him giving advice to me as if men know more than women when it comes to sex.'"

"I bet Alison liked that."

"Very perceptive. She loved it. Once again, we were allies.

" 'Nicholas wouldn't dare impose his views on me,' she declared.

"I told her after a while, Richard wouldn't either.

"We laughed, pressing our shoulders against each other. Mr. Thornbee, a math teacher on morning hall duty, saw us together. His gray-black eyebrows lifted and the wrinkles in his forehead deepened into dark incisions. His lower lip looked much smaller than his upper to me because he had a small chin and a face that looked as though someone had squeezed it between a powerful forefinger and thumb while it was forming.

"Although he was nearly sixty-five and almost asexual to me, I sensed a male's interest and curiosity in the way he looked at us now. Something dormant had been stirred in him. Perhaps it was only the memory of what it had once been, but it was enough to bring a flush to his face and a brightness to his eyes.

" 'Girls,' he finally said and then paused as though he had forgotten why on earth he had said it. 'I . . . you had better get a move on if you don't want to be late for homeroom.'

" 'Oh yes. Thank you, Mr. Thornbee,' I said. There was something in the way I turned my shoulder and gazed back at him that brought a smile to his lips. Alison sensed it too.

"Then we both swept our hair back and walked down the corridor, side by side, strutting with so much androgynous confidence that those who stood before us stepped back to let us pass, remaining some distance behind us. It was almost as if they could sense there were four of us and not two moving through the school hallway."

I went back to my food. The detective sat staring at me for a few moments, his face locked in a gentle, almost loving smile. It was as if he could feel what it was like to be a young girl and have a close friend, one with whom you could share your thoughts and feelings, your fears and dreams. You could pass your most intimate thoughts between you as easily as you could pass lipstick. That was a wonderful thing, a wonderful time. Free of inhibitions, we marched brazenly into each new day, unafraid of being naked, eager to do whatever we could to bring the quiver of ecstasy into our flesh.

After a moment Detective Mayer emptied his wine and sat back.

"This has been one of the finest meals I have ever had," he said.

"It's the company."

He laughed.

"Maybe." He looked about. "I like this place; I really do. I didn't think I would when we first came in, but now . . . it sort of wears on you like a new pair of shoes. You break them in and never want to give them up. It's that way with everything that's new I suppose."

"Very much so. William put it another way. He said, 'Be careful how you lose your virginity, for you will feel that exact moment first, each and every time you make love after.'

"Freud said it another way," I continued. "He said there are four people in every love affair, the woman the man first fell in love with and the man the woman first fell in love with, as well as each other. Do you understand?"

"How the hell did you get all that out of my new pair of shoes?"

"Everything, one way or another, relates to sex. Did you ever have a foot massage?"

"No."

"Well, if you did, you would see how slipping your foot into a shoe that fits comfortably is a very erotic thing."

"Jesus."

"Take your shoe off," I said.

"Huh?"

"Go on. Take off your shoe and sock and give me your foot under the table."

"You're kidding." He looked around to see if anyone had overheard. Even if anyone had, they wouldn't have shown it. "Should I?"

"Do something dangerous, Detective Mayer. Go for it," I taunted. He thought for a moment and then leaned down to slip off his shoe and his sock. I felt for his naked foot and placed it in my lap. Then, slowly, I began to massage his sole. He closed his eyes.

"Oh man," he moaned. "I never would have believed it could feel so good."

The detective insisted on paying for our dinner. He claimed he could write it off on his expense account.

"Despite my exposing my very sole to you," he punned, "this is an investigation."

"Every time a woman and a man make love or merely caress, it's an investigation," I told him.

I didn't drive straight home after we left Antonio's. First, I took him up the coast, driving very fast so that the wind whipped around us. The moonlight was so bright on the water; it was like a long finger of fire burning from the beach to the horizon. About ten miles north of Malibu, I pulled off the highway where there was enough room on the shoulder of the road to park and gaze out over the water.

"Beautiful night," Detective Mayer said. "Makes me want to be young again, a teenager on his first date. You don't live any longer than normal people, do you?" he asked.

"No, and as I explained, the male counterpart lives even less than a so-called normal male."

"Why wasn't it the other way around? As I remember it, God made Adam first and Eve only when Adam was lonely, right? How come the female half of you guys gets to live longer?"

"I don't know," I said. "It's just the way it is. You don't have all the answers for your kind, do you?"

"Hey, don't get testy. Just asking. Mind if I smoke?"

"Not in my car."

He shrugged. "It's all right; I'm trying to stop. So," he said, "tell me more about those early days, when you first became Richard."

"Those early days," I said and smiled. I understood why he wished he could be a teenager again. There was such excitement in every discovery, in every change.

"My first menstruation and subsequent metamorphosis had hastened my female development, just as Alison's had hastened hers. During the next five days, I thought I could actually feel my body growing and molding."

"You're kidding."

"No, I'm serious. In fact, one night I awoke because there was a tightness in my chest that made it hard to breathe. I began to panic and sat up quickly with a small scream. It was Dimitri who came to my door. He had just returned from a hunt in San Diego."

"San Diego? Why San Diego? Wasn't there enough prey for him here?" the detective asked, sounding surprisingly bitter.

"He had met someone and the pursuit took him to San Diego. Hey, we just don't go after anybody, you know. Confident predators are selective, choosey. Why eat hamburger when you can have steak?"

"Well, what does the male Androgyne look for in prey—big tits, long legs, pretty face?"

I shook my head.

"Just like all the others, you measure a woman in terms of what you see on the surface. Your dicks make you blind, dull your perception. You lack insight. I suppose that's why I've come to appreciate some of my gay men friends. Unobstructed by a normal male's hormones, they look at the whole woman, see her potential as a person rather than only as a good lay.

"But to answer your question, male Androgyne see the essence of the woman, her life force. Sex is only a doorway through which we enter the heart and steal the fuel that makes it beat. Can you understand that?"

He looked skeptical and confused in the light of the moon, but there was something in his eyes, a twinkling that confused me for the moment. He laughed quickly.

"I'll think about it. Hey, some of the things you've been telling me take a little digestion," he said rubbing his stomach. "Like that gourmet meal. You don't just chew and swallow."

"Very good."

"Go back to your story. You had screamed."

"Yes. Dimitri came to the door and flipped the light switch. Then he rushed into my room. I was drenched in sweat, my nightgown clinging to my skin. I looked up at him and tried to take deep breaths. Of course, he knew immediately what was happening."

" 'Stay calm,' he said and sat beside me, taking my hand into his. 'It will pass,' he said reassuringly. 'You will be all right.'

"I told him I had had a terrible nightmare. A giant hand had taken hold of me and was squeezing me." I laughed.

"What's so funny?" the detective asked.

"Dimitri said, 'Perhaps it wasn't a nightmare. Perhaps God is molding you this very night.' "

"Doesn't sound like a nightmare; sounds like a nice way to explain it," the detective said. I was surprised at his reaction, but continued my story.

"Dimitri smiled and leaned forward to kiss me on the cheek. I could smell the scent of the woman he had been with. Her perfume, her hair spray, her very essence was pungent. He was still in the process of absorbing her and that was what was keeping him from metamorphosing back to Janice."

"You mean . . . the woman from San Diego that he . . ."

"Yes. He saw that I was soaking wet and told me to get up and shower and change into a clean, dry nightgown.

"I nodded and went into the bathroom. When I drew the wet garment over my head and gazed at myself in the mirror, I saw that my bosom had developed and my waist had narrowed. I turned and noticed how much tighter and curvier my buttocks had become."

"This happened overnight?"

"Yes, and because these were changes that would come gradually to the inferior females, the sight of them frightened me at first. It was almost as if I had been transferred to another female form."

"Understandable."

"But as I turned about and considered myself, I grew more and more conceited. I was perfect; I was beautiful. I thought I was even better looking than Alison. Perhaps I was the prettiest androgynous female there was. The very sight of myself took my breath away," I said and smiled, recalling the memory of those first images. The moonlight on the ocean glittered. I stroked my hair and took a deep breath, sighing like a lovesick teenager; only, I was in love with myself.

"Well, as far as modesty goes, you're not much different from any other female, I suppose," Detective Mayer said. I ignored him because I was still lost in my reverie. "Hello?" he said drawing me back.

"When I awoke the next morning," I said, "I felt taller, fuller, and far stronger. I had a ravenous appetite and ate two portions of scrambled eggs. Janice wasn't at all surprised, although she had no memory of what Dimitri had said to me the night before."

"Why not? It was her as a man, right?"

"She wouldn't remember," I snapped.

"All right, all right. I'm sorry. So you woke up in this beautiful body. Then what?"

"What Richard had told me in his letter would happen began to happen that day at school. The boys in my class buzzed around me like flies longing to light on a piece of cake. They approached and pulled back, found reason to touch me, drew closer and then snapped away as if they sensed I could clamp down on each and every one of them and claim them forever. I couldn't go from class to class without one of them coming up beside me to say something. Before the day was out, I realized I had become the object of some game they were playing. They were competing with one another to determine who would win me over first.

"Of course, Alison had been having a similar thing happen to her. She had already had a conversation about all this with her mother.

" 'We don't want to bring undue attention to ourselves by becoming snobs,' Alison said. 'But we have to be careful about our relationships. Beatrice says that we are like newborn colts, unsteady on our feet, unsure about our strength. The adolescent still in us wants us to have normal teenage relationships, but we can't have them. The longing will pass quickly,' she assured me. I remember we were sitting by ourselves in the cafeteria . . ."

"Now wait a minute. Hold on," the detective said turning to me. "You told me Androgyne are only deadly in their male form, right? I mean, you don't make love to a man and . . . suck the life out of him, do you?"

"No, but we have a greater sexual capacity, a greater sexual appetite and things can happen sometimes, if we don't control ourselves."

"Things? What things?"

"I'm getting to it," I said.

"Wait, wait, just tell me up front. These things, they can be deadly to the man with whom you are making love?"

"Yes."

"Shit. And I had such great plans for the night."

"But not always deadly," I said, laughing. I was beginning to find him delightful, my detective.

"Okay. Go on."

"Something remarkable but insidious had been occurring all that week—the girls who had been our friends were drifting away. Actually, it was more like they were standing still and we were pulling away. Things that made them laugh, things that titillated them and things that annoyed them were suddenly very insignificant to us. We no longer sympathized or agreed, nor had we any interest in doing the things we had all done together before.

"Like two foreigners who had just entered the school, we sat alone, speaking in our own language, while our old friends watched us, their eyes changing from confusion to anger and finally to indifference, returning once again, to mirrors of themselves. For us, they no longer existed. We were too involved in our own discoveries. And we were light years ahead of them when it came to emotions and desire.

"Before Richard's genesis and my subsequent maturation, I had fantasized being this boy's or that boy's girlfriend. I had often dreamt of being desired by older boys just the way I was being desired now. The feelings weren't completely gone, although they were weakened because most of the older teenage boys looked immature to me."

"There goes your and Alison's normal adolescent years, huh?"

"Almost. There were two senior boys, Paul Slattery and Jimmy Burton. Both boys were well over six feet, Paul being six-four and Jimmy, six-five. They were the school's basketball stars.

"Before our conversions, like most of the junior high girls, Alison and I, too, had gone to the games and watched them lead our team to victory. We, too, had stood by in the halls and gazed longingly with fantasy eyes as they walked by with older girls, laughing, seemingly living on another level, worlds beyond the level we were on. They were the heroes, the movie stars, the celebrities of our school, respected and adored by so many, even by some teachers.

"They were handsome and bright, each on his way toward winning academic scholarships as well as athletic, both often likened to someone like Bill Bradley, a Rhodes scholar who had become a professional basketball player and then a senator from New Jersey.

"Although I no longer idolized them the way other girls my age did, I sensed their power and freshness in a new and more involving way. They weren't as handsome and glamorous as they were delicious. Their health and sexual prowess turned them into a delicacy. I was drawn to them the way someone might be drawn to a gourmet meal, not that I had become cannibalistic in a literal sense. Rather, I had become sensitive to their masculine richness. I craved them the way someone with a weakness for sweets might crave a chocolate.

"Standing between them and very close to them, I was able to drink in the scent of their bodies and vividly imagine the taste of their lips. Whenever one or the other spoke, I concentrated on his mouth, feeling myself drawn to his tongue. Each had a way of accenting something he said by bumping his hip or shoulder against my hip or shoulder. What they said didn't matter. I heard only the rhythms in their voices and nodded and smiled at the proper times.

"Their faces looked so shiny and soft. I felt as if I could dip my fingers into their cheeks and scoop out their tongues. No matter how I tried to avoid it, all my images were grotesque, a mixture of sex and violence. And, unfortunately, the same was true for Alison."

"Why unfortunately?" he asked.

"One day, shortly after my conversion, I found Alison talking to them after school. Instinctively, I sensed some terrible danger in the intimate way she had wedged herself between them, rubbing her hips against theirs, stroking their arms and chests, tormenting them with her eyes. Even all the way across the hall, I could feel the heat and sensed something happening within myself.

"It was like . . . like a claw scratching at the inside of my chest, digging its way out and I thought if this was happening to me only gazing at her with the boys, what could be happening to her?

"I rushed to her side and pulled her away, but neither Paul nor Jimmy would give up pursuit. They followed us, trying to get us to stop and enter a conversation. Alison glared at me when I turned back to drive them away.

" 'Why did you encourage them?' I demanded.

" 'I didn't,' she protested, but her voice was deeper and I had the distinct sense that Nicholas was emerging. It was the most frightening thing."

"You mean right there in the school hallway?" the detective asked almost in a whisper.

"Yes. When I looked at her face, I saw almost imperceptible changes taking place: the metamorphosis of her eyes and mouth, even the faint traces of a beard and mustache. My heart began to pound. Paul and Jimmy were right behind us."

"What did you do?"

"I pulled her into the girls' room, thinking if I could splash her face with cold water . . ."

"Yes?"

"But the boys were under a spell. It was after school, no one was around . . . they followed us into the bathroom. I tried being annoyed, but Alison thought this was funny and even more exciting. When I looked at her hands, I saw the fingers had thickened and there was distinct hair over her wrist, darker, coarser."

"It was happening?"

"Yes, Nicholas was emerging."

"What did you do?"

"I thought if I drew the boys from her, I might stop the metamorphosis, but I succeeded only in accelerating it. I tried being nice to them, reasoning with them, promising them we would go someplace with them if they would leave the bathroom. That stimulated them further. Paul turned to me and Jimmy drew Alison into a booth."

"And . . ."

"I realized it was too late. Something terrible was about to happen. I thought quickly, driven by a need to protect the Androgyne. I talked Paul into leaving the bathroom with me, promising to go for a ride with him and clearly suggesting that I would agree to park somewhere and have sex. He was so excited about it, he nearly walked through the door.

"I looked back once before we left. Alison's ankles were already thicker."

"Good grief, you mean she was changing into a male in the booth while she was with this boy?"

"Yes."

"But wouldn't he realize it?"

"He was mesmerized by now and would see what he fantasized. At least that's the way it's been explained to me. Men are like that you know; Pygmalions always sculpting their Galateas and making love to the images rather than the women, and then, when they realize the woman is just a woman, they grow depressed and start sculpting another image."

"And women don't do that, I suppose?"

"They do, but men do it more. Men are more in control of visual images in this country—advertisements, magazines, film and television. They make composites: take the lips of this model, the breasts of this actress, the legs of another . . . and create their dream girls."

"Yeah, yeah. So you left this boy making love to his dream in a school toilet. What did you do?"

"I succeeded in getting Paul out of the building. We went for a drive and I asked him to stop to get me an ice cream. When he did, I slipped away and rushed back to the school, but it was too late."

"Too late? Why?"

"The janitor had already discovered Jimmy's body. His head had been submerged into the toilet and he was drowned. An autopsy later also revealed his neck had been broken."

"Jesus. Why? Why did she do it?"

"She didn't. Nicholas did."

"Why?" the detective asked.

I took a deep breath and turned to him.

"For the same reason essentially that Richard killed Michael."

"Barrington? The publicist?"

"Yes. He was my lover."

"But . . . you couldn't stop it?"

"I thought I could," I said softly, tears now putting everything out of focus. "But I was wrong, I was arrogant and that's another reason why I came to you to confess."

FIVE

MY DETECTIVE DID not badger me with questions. He waited for me to get myself together and then start the car so we could return to my home. The tears that had streamed down my cheeks blew off into the wind as we sped up the Pacific Coast Highway. Before we reached the hill leading up to my house, he spoke.

"I don't think I fully realized until now just how much emotional and mental pain you are in," he said. "I must apologize for not taking you as seriously as I should have from the start, but I'm sure you can appreciate how difficult that was for me," he added. "I meet all sorts of people and hear all sorts of stories. Last week, I met an alien from the planet Rudor in another galaxy. He killed people for their fingernails."

I didn't appreciate his attempt at humor and he saw it.

"Anyway," he continued, "I'm sorry if I appeared insensitive."

I didn't offer any forgiveness. At the moment his feelings were not very important to me.

"So," he said shifting in his seat, hoping to shift out of his own discomfort as well, "does the male part of an Androgyne always get jealous of the female's lover and kill?"

"No, not always."

"But that's what happened to Nicholas, right?"

"You have to remember he was still very young then and just learning how to control his emotions. Even though, as I have told you, androgynous teenagers are far more sophisticated than ordinary people at their age, they are still in some state of adolescence. Nicholas just . . . just lost it," I said. I hit the button for the gate and watched it open. In the brisk breeze, the shadows cast by the moon swayed. The twisted, mangled contours looked like the odd but significant shapes on a Rorschach test.

"He just lost it? I'll say."

"Alison felt horrible about it afterward. I found her behind the school, just wandering about aimlessly. Nicholas had retreated immediately after his actions, cowering down in her like some mischievous little boy who knew his mischief was soon to be discovered. Alison had some of the boy's blood on her hands, so I took her home quickly and scrubbed her fingers. Beatrice took one look at us and knew what had happened. She was very angry.

" 'I warned you,' she said. 'I told you to be careful and especially to stay away from boys in your own school. Didn't I?' She turned to me and said, 'Let this be a lesson to you, Clea, and don't be as impulsive as Alison is.'

"I wish she hadn't done that sort of thing," I said.

"What sort of thing?" the detective asked.

"Pit us against each other like that. Alison loved me and still does, but she resents me too."

"Did she have anything to do with Michael Barrington's death?" he asked quickly.

"No. Well, I shouldn't say categorically no."

"You're not going to tell me she was jealous, are you? And she talked Richard into doing it?"

As the lights of passing cars flashed on his face, I saw

his cynical smirk. I was sure it came from years and years of police work and having to confront all sorts of riffraff. It occurred to me that professions, jobs, the roles we play, all create masks in our faces, masks that fade in and fade out with an automation that dehumanizes us, makes us kin to machinery. Events or words trigger reactions that skip over thought and feeling. One moment he was feeling sorry for me and expressing a sincere compassion, and the next, he was mechanically denigrating me.

"No. What happened between Richard and me and Richard and Michael was different," I said as we drove in.

"How so?"

I parked the car and turned to him.

"I was falling in love with Michael. It wasn't just another sexual escapade."

"So? I don't understand. Why is that different?"

"Apparently, so was Richard."

"What do you mean?" He thought a moment. "You don't mean Richard was also in love with Michael Barrington?"

"That's exactly what I mean. Michael had been his lover too. Actually, I found out very recently," I added. "At first I did think it was just an incestuous jealousy." I laughed with a maddening chill that startled the detective. "You see, even Androgyne can be blind when it comes to emotions, especially if those emotions involve other Androgyne. I had thought Richard's motives were more sublime."

"Incest? More sublime?"

"In a sense, yes. I thought he was thinking of me; he wanted me all for himself. But no, he wanted Michael all for himself."

The detective shook his head.

"What happened to this built-in need to share?"

"Yes. What happened to it? I must confess, I didn't like the idea of sharing Michael with Richard, any more than he liked the idea of sharing him with me. The difference is, I wouldn't kill Michael over it."

"Are you sure?" Detective Mayer asked.

"What do you mean? Why do you even ask such a thing?"

He shrugged.

"Maybe you killed Michael after all and now you are concocting this story to cover your own guilt."

"But when I first came to you, you said it wasn't possible for me to have committed the murder. You said it had taken great strength to do the physical damage to his body."

"Uh-huh. That's because I was convinced then that Richard was not only the killer of Barrington, but had committed other murders too. But I also know that women caught up in some passion have been known to achieve great physical strength.

"Just yesterday, we had a situation. A four-year-old child was hit by an automobile in West Los Angeles and pinned under the rear wheel. The child's mother literally lifted the car off her body and pulled her out from under. Later, she didn't recall doing it, but there were witnesses who confirmed she had.

"I'm not saying you killed Barrington. I'm just showing you how everything is possible in an infinite universe," he added, now smiling coyly. "I'm going to need more concrete evidence that it was Richard who committed the murder and not you, of course."

"You'll get your evidence," I snapped.

"Will I?" He turned from me to the house and then looked at me again.

"You want to come in for an after-dinner drink?" I asked. Actually, by then the drink was a foregone conclusion. I didn't have to ask. Mayer's actions, his gestures, the look in his eyes were as good as a road map showing me the way to his motives and thoughts. Most men were like my detective: transparent.

"Sure."

We got out and walked quietly to the front door. I dug for the key in my purse, but when I put it to the lock, my hand shook. How strange, I thought. Why did I suddenly feel this anxiety?

The detective saw my fingers tremble and put his hand over mine.

"May I?" he asked. I gave him the key and he inserted it into the lock. But just before he actually turned it, a bullet came crashing into the door right between us.

"Down!" he cried pulling me toward the patio floor. He reached up and continued to turn the key so the door would open. A second shot splintered the doorjamb on our right. He pushed the door open and we quickly crawled into the house.

"Stay down," he said, holding his palm against the small of my back. Then he drew his gun and slammed the door shut. I felt ridiculous face down on the marble floor. He stepped past me, went to the front window, pulled back the curtain in the corner and gazed into the night.

"I don't see anyone out there," he whispered, but he kept searching.

I got to my feet and brushed down my clothing.

"Get away from that door!" he commanded. I moved farther into the house quickly. He looked out again. "What the hell . . ." He turned back to me, his eyes narrowing. "You don't look all that surprised," he said.

"I'm not." I put down my purse and went to the bar.

He returned his pistol to its holster and followed.

"What is this? Why aren't you in some kind of shock? We were just shot at! Twice!"

"*We* weren't," I replied as I took out the Sambuca. "I was and I don't think they meant to kill me. Although," I added, looking up at his confused face, "I won't swear to that."

"What do you mean they didn't mean to kill you? Who didn't mean to kill you?"

"The Androgyne. One of them anyway . . . whoever Alison put on it, I imagine," I added. "Rocks?"

"What?"

"Do you want yours on the rocks?"

"Oh." He looked back at the door. "Yeah, please. Is there a back door, a side entrance?"

"French doors off my bedroom right down this corridor," I said pointing. "They're the closest."

"I'll be right back. I want to look around."

"Should I say be careful?"

He found his way in the dark and slipped out of the house through my French doors while I prepared his drink. A few minutes later, he knocked on the front door and I let him in.

"Nothing," he said. He studied the door, found the hole made by the bullet, and then followed its possible trajectory and went to the wall opposite the front door. I put his drink on the bar and sat down on the stool behind it to watch him. He returned to the bar and came around searching for a knife. After he found one, he returned to the wall and dug out the bullet.

"Nine millimeter," he said holding it up. "Ring any bells?"

"Sorry." I shook my head.

He pocketed the bullet and returned to the bar.

"What makes you think whoever it was didn't mean to kill you?" he asked and sat down.

"I think they just meant to frighten me out of talking to you. Androgyne rarely kill their own kind."

He sipped his drink and shook his head, smiling. There was a twinkle in his eye.

"But isn't that what you're doing in a sense?"

"Not in a sense; in actuality."

"And you can live with that?" The smile left his eyes and was quickly replaced with an intense look, a delving, searching gaze that made me feel like some kind of specimen being studied under a magnifying glass.

"No," I said softly. "But I don't intend to live with it. I intend to die with it."

"Oh yes." He nodded. "I forgot." He looked back at the door again. "Want me to call this in, get some protection up here?"

"No point. I'm positive that whoever it was is gone by now. Besides," I added, "you're here and you're protection."

He took another, longer sip of his drink.

"I don't feel especially protective." He thought for a moment. "Maybe that wasn't your Androgyne. Maybe that was just some friend of Michael Barrington's seeking revenge. Another lover, perhaps."

"I doubt it." He had an impish twinkle in his eye.

"What makes you so sure?"

"I was enough for him; I'd be enough for any man, for when men make love to an androgynous female, they make love to every fantasy they've ever had or will have. We can be many things to a man. He has no need to go looking elsewhere."

"Unless he's looking to make love with another man," he said dryly.

"So what's your point?"

"It could have been one of his gay lovers. I just had a case like that. One of the men in a relationship was also heterosexual and in love with this woman. She drew him away from his gay lover, so his gay lover killed her. In this case maybe Barrington's gay lover thinks you killed him and wants to kill you."

"I don't know," I said. I had to admit that he was presenting a feasible possibility.

"On the other hand," he said, still smiling, "maybe he knew about Michael's relationship with Richard and was jealous of that and thought I was Richard coming home with you. He was aiming for me."

"You're the detective," I said.

"Exactly." He dropped his smile. "I find it hard to believe that you didn't know that Michael Barrington had gay lovers."

"Why?"

"Any man's sexual history, sexual preferences must be easily discernible to you. You claim you can provide any fantasy. If I buy that and buy your so-called androgynous powers, it would follow that you look with X-ray eyes at any man and see his sexuality like no one else can. Am I right?"

I scrutinized my detective for a moment. It was as if he were growing, changing, metamorphosing himself. And all because of his short, but obviously influential relationship with me. I shouldn't be surprised, I thought. I often had a dramatic effect on men and changed them in one way or another. The detective was getting more sophisticated, more perceptive. It was almost as if he were beginning to look at the world through my eyes too.

"Let me say I had my suspicions," I confessed.

"But you didn't want to believe them?"

"Probably not and that was a mistake, a weakness," I added quickly.

"Otherwise, you would have realized earlier that Richard was his lover too?"

"I imagine. You're getting good, Detective Mayer. Should I begin to worry?"

"About what? You're confessing everything anyway, aren't you? Or are you holding back something?"

"We all hold back something." I searched his face, running my gaze over it like the beam of a flashlight over the dark driveway outside. He didn't change expression. "There's something you're hiding."

"Yeah, but I'm not the subject here. Let's get back to you and Richard," he said quickly. I had plucked a string, touched a tender spot. He recoiled inside his detective's mask and switched on his investigative eyes as if he literally had a knob he could turn on his body and change channels as one would change them on a television set.

"Was Michael Barrington Richard's first homosexual experience?"

I smiled. "Hardly." He raised his eyebrows.

"Not you too," he groaned.

"I said we can be many things. It's not particularly my thing, but I won't deny that I have done it. It's in our nature to explore every aspect of love, every sexual avenue. Let me assure you, however, that I have never found a woman who excited me as much as a man."

"Thank goodness for the little things."

"But Richard's first homosexual experience was rather extraordinary. Care to hear it?"

"I feel like I'm in one of those twenty-five-cent peep shows," he remarked. Then he saw the look on my face. "Just kidding. Of course I want to hear it. Anything that's part of this investigation interests me," he added.

I went to fetch Richard's diary and returned.

"Perhaps you would be more comfortable on the sofa," I suggested.

"Yes. Mind if I have a little more of this?" he asked, indicating the Sambuca. "I think I'm going to need it."

"Top off my glass too, while you're at it." I waited for him to bring our freshened drinks. "Thank you." He sat beside me on the sofa and leaned back against the thick, soft arm. Then he held up his glass.

"Ready?" he said.

I sat back, turned the page, and began.

"Sometimes I am so disgusted with the hunt because there is little or no challenge. It's like a group of so-called hunters participating in a shoot-off, a thinning out of a herd. The dumb animals are assembled in some fenced-in area and the shooters just kill and kill and kill and after a while they get satiated and then nauseated. Shooting an animal without going through the hunt is like digesting food without having eaten it.

"I remember in my early days I would put on a pair of tight black jeans, so tight that my testicles were clearly outlined in the material and my phallus pressed against the zipper like some thick snake up against the glass in a cage. I'd slick my hair back and put on a black silk shirt unbuttoned to my navel. I would wear a gold chain and then I would go up to Hollywood and hang out on the streets.

"The parade of endless cars wove down the boulevard like an incessant, run-on sentence, a true circle in which the beginning and the end were indistinguishable. No one was going anywhere. It was the going that counted. Movement meant life, excitement, freedom. I saw from the way the young men and young women gaped and scrutinized other young men and young women on the

street that they were all looking for that mythical lay, the ultimate sexual encounter. It was truly going to be like shooting stupid buffalo, oblivious to the sound of the guns and the members of their herd falling around them—fat, easy targets, so ignorant of their vulnerability they took any pleasure out of the kill. One might as well shoot at trees.

"And that was the way I suddenly felt, even though car after car paused near me and young women shouted, pleaded, cajoled, some practically begging me to get into their vehicles. This was not really a hunt in any sense of the word. My all-consuming hunger had driven me to take the easiest path, but something else within me, something superior now demanded more, and a realization came over me with that same intuitive pleasure that had accompanied so many new discoveries, a realization that the deeper pleasure came not from the capture, but the hunt.

"It's in the hunt itself that we gain our strength, our wisdom. The challenge hones and sharpens our powers. We grow when we overcome adversity.

"There was no sexual challenge here. Sex for these young people had lost its magic. It had been reduced to a form of consuming. The parade of customized automobiles with their glaringly bright colors continued, their rap music thumping, making it seem as if we all stood on the shell of some giant heart, beating beneath us. Periodically, there was a pause in the line and girls or men would be drawn into one vehicle or another, sucked up like debris to be swallowed in a vacuum cleaner. Soon afterward they groped one another in the backs of automobiles, grunting and groaning, rushing to accomplish a sexual experience just so they could make their nights complete."

"About how old was he here?" the detective asked.

"Fifteen," I said quickly. Richard's words held my eyes to the page and I wanted to run them through my eyes and my brain and down the channels to my tongue and lips. I was obsessed with them. I felt my face glow as I read on.

"Disgusted with the sight, I fled to another part of the city, a quiet, residential area known as Hancock Park. The houses here, some veritable mansions, had been built with old Hollywood money. There were nineteenth-century French styles, English Tudor, colonial, a potpourri of architecture constructed at a time when wealthy people sought individuality.

"I gazed into some of the lit windows and saw, however, that many of these houses were dying from the inside out. The inhabitants, descendants of their wealthier ancestors, were unable to keep them up, yet they couldn't afford to move out and pay the higher rents or mortgages. Walls now had blanched squares where paintings once hung, paintings that had been sold to meet expenses. The gaping holes made me think of toothless old men and indeed the worn, crinkled rugs reminded me of the dried and wrinkled skin of old women. Many of the large rooms were underfurnished, their open spaces places for ghosts to hover and mourn the old days.

"Two houses down a young man emerged to walk his dog, a gray toy poodle who looked arthritic and waddled like a duck. When it saw me, it barked frantically, the sound dying halfway up its throat. It always amused me how animals sensed the danger in us faster than their inferior masters. Even birds flitted about madly when we approached. Cats raised their backs into humps and showed their teeth. Only snakes seemed unafraid, even friendly."

"Now why is it that I would have thought that?" the detective said with his usual sarcasm.

"It just so happens that there is a biblical explanation for that," I replied.

"In whose Bible?"

"Yours. With a different interpretation, however. It wasn't the devil who tempted Adam and Eve in the form of a snake; it was an Androgyne. We were there at the time, too, you know."

"So why would they like you if they were blamed for something you did?" the detective asked quickly.

"Because men hate them and they have no one else. They're lonely."

He started to laugh, but I raised my long, but graceful right forefinger and leaned toward him, forcing him to stare into my eyes.

"Don't ever underestimate the importance of loneliness, Detective Mayer. People, animals, will do anything to avoid it. It will drive them even to do things you would consider kinky or at least bizarre." His smile quickly faded. Had I struck a vulnerable place in his heart? What were his secrets? I wondered for the first time. I smiled. "Something sound familiar?"

"Go on, read the diary."

"I will," I said, "but first tell me what sort of an effect seeing all this—what should we call it—degenerative behavior has on you? Do you ever wonder about the deviants? Are you ever curious about their sexual behavior, about what it is that so fascinates them?"

"It simply disgusts me," he said. "The diary. Please."

I held my smile on him, keeping him uncomfortably in its glow like someone caught naked in a searchlight. He unbuttoned his collar and loosened his tie.

"Well?" he pleaded.

I turned back. My back stiffened into Richard's posture, my shoulders felt thicker, stronger. Despite myself, I couldn't prevent him from invading me in little ways when I read his words, but it was a sacrifice, a price I was willing to pay, even though I knew there were risks.

At any point during the reading of the diary, mouthing Richard's words and thoughts, I could metamorphose. His hold on me could grow so firm that I would fall before him as if he had my wrist in his strong hand and was twisting it, bringing me to my knees.

"As I drew closer to the young man," I read, *"I could make him out clearly in the illumination cast by the driveway lantern. He looked to be a slim, five-feet-eight or -nine-inch man with dark blond thin hair that lay haphazardly over his forehead and temples like the thatched crown of some monk. He was as pale as one who had kept himself inside copying manuscripts.*

"The same lack of concern for his appearance was evident in his clothing. He wore a faded, formal white shirt, the kind that required cufflinks. He had the sleeves rolled up unevenly, revealing narrow wrists, the left of which had an old watch in a rose gold casing strapped over it. His gray cotton pants were baggy and at least two inches too short. He wore old basketball sneakers with no socks.

"What attracted me to him were his eyes, magnified somewhat under the thick lenses in clear plastic frames. It seemed as if there was another man trapped within him, gazing out through those eyes, now early morning sky blue. He cracked a smile with his soft, thin lips when he saw me.

" 'You're lost, huh?' he said.

"I paused before answering, seizing his attention and holding him in my scope of gravity as if he were a moon and I a planet.

" 'No. I wanted to come here. I wanted to get away from the noise and the glitter.'

"He laughed, the sound seeming to echo within him as if the person who lived there repeated everything he did and said. His dog stopped growling, but eyed me hatefully.

" 'You got away from it all right,' he replied. He looked around, the smile frozen on his lips. Although he was amused I had come to his neighborhood to escape the activity and excitement, he looked proud of what he saw about him. It made me think again that there was someone else within him looking out, for his eyes betrayed a longing for the way things had been.

" 'You know anyone here?' he asked quickly, remembering I was there.

" 'No,' I said and found myself speaking as softly and as seductively as I would had I been in the presence of a beautiful inferior female."

"Oh no," the detective said. "I feel it coming."

"Do you want me to stop?" I asked him. My own heart had begun to pound in anticipation. It was beating with the intensity of Richard's heart, the thumping reverberating through my arteries and veins and echoing in every chamber in my body. It was as if I were shut up in a room of pipes and Richard himself was hammering on them. The clamor was maddening. I nearly dropped the diary and put my hands over my ears.

"No, but are you all right? You look . . . pale."

"Yes, yes." I took a deep breath, closed my eyes and drove the thumping down. Then I opened my eyes and smiled. "I'm all right." I turned back to the pages.

" 'I'm just taking Pebbles for his short walk,' the young man said. 'He's nearly seventeen years old and has lived here all his life.'

" 'I thought he looked like an old dog,' I said. I smiled at the dog, but as soon as I looked down at him, he growled again.

" 'He's not usually this afraid of strangers. Perhaps he smells the scent of your dog. Do you have a pet?'

"I laughed, a thin, high laugh that surprised even me.

" 'No. I don't have time for pets. Actually, most animals don't like me.'

" 'Really? Now that's interesting. Animals are instinctive and very perceptive, yet you don't look like a bad person to me. What's your name?'

" 'Richard,' I said. 'Richard Cave.'

" 'Cave? I knew a Caver, but not a Cave.'

" 'What's your name?'

" 'Gordon Lathrop Cardwell. The name makes me sound a lot richer than I am. Presently,' he added. He followed that with a short laugh and cleared his throat. 'Well . . . Pebbles and I will be on our way. Have a good escape, Richard Cave.' He nodded and started away.

"Now this was a challenge, I thought. I had found men attracted to me before. Some men admired me, or should I say, envied me and were in love with me the way they would be in love with an idol, a fantasy for themselves; but there were men who found me sexually interesting to them and who were confused themselves as to why that should be.

"Gordon Lathrop Cardwell didn't seem at all attracted to me. His sexual impulses were a normal male's or apparently subdued, stored away so long they were still in hibernation, despite his youth.

"Less than ten minutes later, when he returned, I was waiting for him. Just inside the stone wall and hedges in front of his colonial-style home, there was a gray marble bench. I was sitting on it when he turned in and Pebbles began barking again, this time his bark more shrill.

" 'Well, how do you do?' he said, but there was something in his eyes that told me he wasn't completely surprised, and in fact, was pleased.

" 'I hope you don't mind.'

" 'No, of course not. You know, you do look lost. Well, can I offer you something to drink . . . something soft, of course. Maybe call you a cab?'

" 'I was just sitting here admiring your home. I'd like to take a look at it,' I said, but when I looked at him, he could surely see that was subterfuge. He smiled and then sighed. It was as if I had just confirmed a suspicion he had been harboring for a long time, as if he had been expecting me. I must say, that threw me off a bit, and for a moment, I lost my androgynous confidence, my superior demeanor.

" 'Sadly, it's not what it seems to be anymore, but you're welcome.'

"The dog barked faster as if it understood what its owner had just proposed.

" 'Now, Pebbles, if you don't behave you're going into the garage. Okay, Richard,' he said, and I got up and followed him into his house. And what a strange house it was.

"There was only one piece of furniture in the long entryway, a dark mahogany table with a glass surface. It was set against a dull blue wall spotted here and there with family portraits in silver oval frames.

" 'Parents, grandparents, uncles and aunts, nieces and nephews,' he declared, gesturing briefly at the wall without turning to it and continuing on through the entryway until we came to the enormous living room, a room which still contained most of its original furniture: a dark blue velvet settee and couch, a pair of matching high back

French provincial chairs, marble tables, a hand-carved hutch filled with knickknacks, and a worn Persian rug. The room was lit by a single chandelier, some of its bulbs blown. At the center of the far wall was a white marble fireplace, obviously not used for ages. Now, a potted plant was set inside it.

" *'Living room,' he announced. I went in and sat back on the couch. He stood in the doorway, an expression of curiosity on his face now. 'Don't you want to see the rest of the house?' he asked, smiling as though he knew the answer.*

" *'Thank you,' I said. 'This is fine.'*

" *'Oh? Something to drink?'*

" *'Nothing.'*

" *'Oh?' He looked about as if he had come into the house for the first time himself. Then he turned to me and nodded knowingly, his expression growing very serious. 'So . . . you've finally come.' I tilted my head.*

" *'Pardon me?'*

" *'I've been expecting you, of course.' He laughed. 'I must confess, I expected you would look different . . . look older, but to be like the times, look like the times, I suppose. Well . . . I'll just put Pebbles in his room. He has his own room now. It used to be a den, but I don't use it and . . . ' His voice trailed off. 'Be right back,' he said.*

"The sound system still functioned. He put on some music.

" *'Movie soundtracks written by Percy Faith. I'm afraid I don't have anything more up-to-date, more to the taste of you young people,' he said apologetically.*

" *'This is fine,' I told him. 'I'm a lot older than I look.'*

" *'Of course you are. You're as old as . . . as death itself.'*

"How did he know that? I wondered. Who was this strange young man? Was he an Androgyne, too? Janice had told me that there were some Androgyne who were undiscernible, even to other Androgyne, because the androgynous part of them had, for some unknown reason, dimmed. It was the only disease we knew, our AIDS virus, our cancer—the thinning out and weakening of our androgynous being.

"Of course, no one but us would recognize it as an illness because the effect of the sickness was to make us more like the inferiors.

"Gordon stood back, reminding me of someone who stands outside a store-front window gazing in at the beautiful but expensive things, afraid to go in for fear he or she will lose control and spend much more than he or she can afford:

" 'You live all by yourself in this big house?' I asked. I couldn't believe that I was nervous.

" 'Yes. My mother was the last to go.'

" 'Was she from California?'

" 'No, Chicago.'

" 'And your father?'

" 'He was from New York by way of Chicago. That's where they met and got married,' he said, and I thought unless he is fabricating a family history, he is not androgynous.

" 'How did your father die?'

" 'Automobile accident. I was only twelve years old at the time. My mother suffered from congenital heart disease and died in her sleep. I came in to bring her some juice and she was gone. They say it's the best way to go.'

"My confidence returned. He was just another inferior, albeit a strange one, but just another prey.

" 'They're wrong. There are better ways to go,' I said provocatively.

"His laugh was thinner. The instinctive warnings had begun, I thought and then I thought, here's a man who might listen to them. Surely not all inferiors fall to our advances.

"But he didn't step back; he stepped toward me.

" 'What sort of work do you do?' I asked. What I really meant was 'Would anyone miss you?' I think he understood the question.

" 'I don't do anything of any consequence, I'm afraid,' he confessed. 'I clip coupons, live off some small family investments, just enough to exist, actually. I have no ambitions, no talents, no skills to speak of. I read, listen to music, occasionally take in a movie. In short, I take from others and give little or nothing in return. Every morning,' he continued coming closer to me, 'I feel guilty I'm alive.

" 'I've got this theory, you see, that there is a fixed number of living things in the world and something new can't be born until something else gives up. So you see, I'm holding back something new, something that might have talent or skill and ambition.'

"He was standing right before me now.

" 'That's why I'm glad you've come tonight. I've been waiting for you. I'm tired and the echoes in the house are getting so loud I can't sleep at night. I don't even dream anymore. I just . . . relive the day . . . in reverse.'

"How strange and wonderful his words made me feel. It was as if I had stumbled upon another holy purpose for our existence, as if I had been selected to do something significant, something few Androgyne were chosen to do.

"I lifted my arms toward him and he fell to his knees

*before me. Then he raised his soft blue eyes to me. I
took his glasses off and carefully placed them on the
floor. His naked eyes were smaller and wet with suffering. When I looked at his thin lips, I felt myself aroused.
My pants grew tighter in the crotch. He understood with
a perception that made me wonder again if he had some
extra sense.*

*"He unzipped my fly. I caressed his face, stroked his
hair and leaned forward to kiss him on the forehead.
When he lifted his face, I saw his tears.*

*" 'I'm afraid I'm not very good at this sort of thing,'
he whispered. He was already fondling me. 'Am I doing
it right?'*

" 'Absolutely.'

*" 'I've never had any real lovers, male or female,' he
explained. How he could carry on a conversation in the
throes of passion amused me. 'In fact,' he confessed,
'I've never really been with a woman, other than my
mother.'*

*" 'You've been with your mother?' I recoiled. Nothing
was more distasteful to an Androgyne than an incestuous
relationship with one's mother."*

"Well, I'm glad there is something that is distasteful to
an Androgyne," the detective said. I barely heard him. My
own breathing had quickened; the nipples of my breasts
had hardened and a warmth trickled over the small of
my stomach. I couldn't pull my eyes from Richard's
words.

" 'Why with your mother?' I asked.

*" 'It's another theory of mine . . . men struggle to
return to the womb . . . to the safety. Never were we
any more secure and comfortable. So,' he said sitting
beside me on the couch, 'do you mind if I call you
Mother?' He closed his eyes and brought his head back*

on the couch. Then he took my hand and brought it to his now opened pants.

"Strangely, he had no erection. I felt as if I were caressing grapes and a small piece of rubber hose. But when he turned on his stomach and lowered his pants, I saw a most exquisite pair of buttocks, soft, enticing, very feminine.

" 'I feel as if I am falling back through time anyway. I'll soon be an infant again, wanting to be fondled,' he said.

"I took off all his clothes, and he lay there like some young obedient child.

" 'Oh Mother,' he said and brought my hands to his penis again. It had hardened and I finally felt my androgynous hunger. It came roaring in over me, inflaming my skin. My lips became fuller, my tongue expanded and pressed against my teeth, the bottoms of which had become so sharp, they drew a thin incision along my own lower lip. The taste of blood sent a rush into my brain. I felt like roaring, like tearing through his chest and sucking on his very heart.

"He moaned like a baby and puckered his lips. I drew his life out of him with soft kisses first. He was so eager to surrender. I could actually feel his body dying from the bottom up. It was one of the most thrilling kills I had made during my short androgynous life. As his life left him and traveled into me, I grew larger, stronger and more demanding. I turned and twisted his body to fit it against me. I poked, drew, lunged into him and out of him and felt him shriveling in my arms, his body deflating like a balloon and suddenly becoming limp, empty, a shell of itself.

"In the end, I embraced him to me and did feel as if I were holding an infant in my arms. He died with a *baby's smile on his lips. I left him naked on the couch, his knees up, his arms bent, his small hands cupping imaginary breasts.*

"I ran out of his house, his dog still barking behind me. I don't remember how I got home. Perhaps I ran all the way. Suddenly, I was there.

"Janice was waiting for me, of course, and knew immediately what sort of experience I had had, for his essence still lingered in my eyes.

" 'Sex can be a torment for them, can't it?' I asked her. The taste of his turmoil remained on my lips.

" 'Yes,' she said, 'but it will never be for you.'

"We sipped some wine and sat in the darkness and talked until she had unraveled all the confusion. How wise and wonderful she was.

"I fell asleep that night, thankful I had been born an Androgyne."

I took a deep breath and closed his diary. The detective was very quiet, his eyes fixed on me, his body frozen.

"Are you all right?" he finally asked.

Was I? I wondered. My heart was pounding with a new intensity. Richard was climbing up out of me, clawing his way to the surface. If I closed my eyes, I could see his eyes on the backs of my lids staring into mine. My arms tingled because hair was pressing up and out of my skin. My breasts were diminishing and there was a terrific throbbing in my genitals.

"He's coming," I whispered. "I've got to stop him . . . please."

"What can I do?" the detective asked.

I opened my eyes and gazed frantically at him.

"Make love to me," I said. "Quickly!"

SIX

"WELL," THE DETECTIVE said, a smile spreading slowly across his face, "I have been asked to do many things in the line of duty, but . . ."

He stopped smiling when he saw the desperation in my eyes.

"You're not kidding, are you?"

I felt a tightening at the corners of my mouth. Richard's sardonic grin was coming. Quickly, I reached out and took the detective's hand. He stood up with me and without saying a word, followed obediently as I led him out of the living room to my bedroom. Even though he would not be the first man I had brought there, I felt a certain danger. It was as though I were exposing more than myself by permitting him to see my intimate things.

I had a king-size bed with an eggshell white cast-iron head- and footboard. It was an authentic antique, weighing nearly eight hundred pounds. There were hand-carved casings of mermaids and nymphs set along the head- and footboard. The bed was set against the far wall, but I could lay there and look out at the ocean when the red silk curtains were drawn open and the blinds were up. Because these windows had a western exposure, the bedroom was particularly bright in the late afternoon. At the moment the curtains were drawn closed.

I paused at the foot of the bed and turned to the detective. He looked confused, lost, unsure of himself. Sex could do that—turn the most confident men into awkward, bumbling buffoons. In their excitement they would pop buttons, take one sock off and leave one on, trip over their shoes; and if they attempted to disrobe me first, they always had trouble with fasteners and zippers. Few of the men I had known were graceful about their foreplay. Michael had been a definite exception: caring, soft, gentle, his fingers moving so softly they could have been made of air.

I stepped up to the detective and began to unbutton his shirt. He stood there, his indecision settling back to be replaced by his growing passion as he realized this was no dream; this was really about to happen. He fumbled with his belt buckle after I had opened his shirt and run my palms along his chest.

"Aren't you the muscular one?" I said. "I suspected so."

"Got to keep in shape for times like this," he replied. Standing in his polka dot boxer shorts, he did not cut as sophisticated an image as he might have hoped, but when he peeled off his T-shirt to reveal a firm ripple of muscle along his pectorals and deltoids, any thought of laughter was driven away.

I smiled appreciatively as I reached behind my dress and unzipped it. The dress poured down my legs and fell to the carpet. I stepped out of it as carefully as one would step out of a warm bath. Then I unfastened my bra, which had been so tight, it flew off me as if it had been a dove trapped and suddenly freed. I wore no panties.

The detective's eyes brightened with erotic fire, his smile lustful. But that was good. As his gaze traveled from my breasts down, I felt Richard slipping farther back. I sensed him groping, clawing, losing his grip and falling down the dark tunnel that twisted away from my identity. Darkness was overtaking him once again. I felt him sinking. His screams were drowned in the pool of my laughter, a laughter only he and I could hear.

"I feel like I'm about to step into a *Playboy* centerfold," the detective said.

"Let your fantasies run wild, lieutenant."

He raised his eyebrows.

"First time you called me that."

"Time to appreciate your rank," I said. He smiled. We both sensed that our love banter was drawing to an end. We would soon speak to each other through our fingers and lips, each embrace a sentence carrying us toward the climax.

I moved toward him, his smile now more a smile of awe than humor. I touched his lips gently and brought my hands to his hips, drawing his lower body to me first. He lifted his hands to my waist and for a moment, we stared into each other's eyes, tormenting each other with our contact. Then we kissed.

I pressed my tongue as deeply into his mouth as I could, running over his own. The aggressive move took him by surprise, and he gagged and pulled back.

"Easy," he said. "It's a long night."

We sat beside each other on the bed.

"You surprise me," I said.

"Oh? Why?"

"Most men don't have the control. They need immediate gratification." I laughed. "You'll hear the inferior women complain about their husbands. They'll say they don't want any foreplay anymore. It's mount, grunt, come and dismount. Some women don't even experience a single orgasm before their husbands are satisfied. They want to be loved, cherished, stroked, their sex shaped like artists shape clay, with tenderness and affection."

"Isn't that what you want?" He ran the palms of his hands over my ribs and lifted my breasts to bring my nipples toward his lips. He moved from one to the other, tasting, licking, nibbling. I closed my eyes and pressed my cheek to his head.

"I don't think anyone could shape you any better than you already are," he said. "Forget all this crap about metamorphosis."

I lay back so he could move his mouth down my body. I felt the blood rush to my face and the heat from that blood slide down over my neck and settle between my breasts, where I knew I had reddened.

As my own passion grew, my heart pounded nails into the door that shut Richard out. The essence of him flickered like a dying candle in the darkness, its tiny flame vulnerable to every rough breeze, everything and anything that moved past it too quickly.

I opened my eyes and saw the detective crouched over me, his head now between my legs. He turned me gently so he could run his hands over my buttocks and kiss the softness there. His hands were soothing but firm as he brought his fingers to the back of my neck and massaged. He was naked himself now and as he bent over to kiss me behind the ears, I felt his hardness press between my thighs, throbbing. The rhythm of that throb synchronized with my own pounding pulse.

I went to my knees so he could find his way, and I thought of Iago's line in *Othello*: "I am one, sir, that comes to tell you your daughter and the Moor are now making the beast with two backs." But the detective chose instead to turn me again and tuck my legs under his arms.

"You're so soft," he said. "There is nothing masculine about you."

"Not now. Thanks to you," I added.

He laughed and then he brought himself to me with impressive grace. I opened my eyes to look into his. He was studying me with an unusual detachment. All the men I had ever been with had their eyes closed at this point. In the darkness behind their lids, they searched for some ultimate moment which was surely about to come. But my detective was still a detective scrutinizing my face with his investigative gaze.

He moved slowly at first, and at first, because he was in such control of himself and was merely mechanical, I found myself losing interest, the passion and heat receding from my face and neck like a cooled thermometer. He sensed it and smiled.

"I just wanted to be sure," he said, "that I was making love to a woman, that you wouldn't undergo any metamorphosis while I was in the act and suddenly, I would find myself embracing another man. Richard might be stronger than you think."

"Is that why you turned me over?"

"Yes," he said. "Aren't you the little heterosexual."

I shook my head and smiled. Should I blame him for being so careful? I thought not; instead, I should be happy he had come to believe me and all that I had told him.

He brought his lips to mine and this time it was his tongue that pressed inward, demanding, and it was I who nearly gagged. I felt his body tighten and his grip on me intensify. He drove deeper into me, now thrusting with abandon.

Now his eyes were closed; now he was merely another man seeking physical ecstasy. I squeezed his waist between my legs and clung to him like a monkey. He was lifting me off the bed with his jabs. On and on he went as if the ultimate orgasm was just out of reach each time we came around. Our moans and groans became indistinguishable. My fingernails were digging into his skin, but he didn't flinch.

I had never suspected he would be so satisfying a lover. We were locked together so tightly in the erotic embrace, I thought our bodies would eventually meld; either he would absorb me or I would absorb him. I couldn't remember when I had experienced more than one orgasm with a man before. Even poor Michael spent himself instantly after my first, but the detective drove on and on bringing me to a second and third. It seemed odd for me to hear my own cries of pleasure.

Finally, he exploded, bringing his mouth to my shoulder and biting down as if he were more in pain than ecstasy.

I cried out one last time, and he loosened his grip and let his head slip down between my breasts. There he lay regaining his breath. I could feel his heart pounding against me, and surely he could feel and hear my own. Neither of us moved, each afraid to be the one to shatter the moment; each stunned by the magnitude of our sexual ecstasy as if we had gone too far and were awaiting some form of retribution: a heart seizure, some sharp, punishing pain.

I was the first to recuperate. I ran my fingers through his hair and stroked his neck and shoulders. He lifted his head from my bosom and smiled, his eyes so bright with satisfaction and pleasure, they were practically incandescent.

"For a while there, I didn't think I could get enough of you," he said. "I was afraid you had turned me into an Androgyne and I was going to consume you."

"You were wonderful, a delightfully erotic surprise."

"Really?" His male ego brightened, and he smiled from ear to ear. "I was good, wasn't I?" he bragged.

"Don't look so damn self-satisfied. I have been with other men who were just as wonderful, if not more wonderful," I said. It was a lie of course, but I couldn't stand the way he gazed down at me, seeing me as some sort of conquest. He laughed and rolled over.

"You complain about men, but I've never seen a woman who knows what she wants. If she satisfies a man and if he satisfies her, she accuses him of having too much male ego. If he is modest about his lovemaking, she accuses him of not loving her, of not being passionate or caring.

"It's women who make love a torment, not men. For men love has a conclusion. They know what they want and they seek it. When they find it, they're satisfied, but women . . . women are never satisfied. They're always looking beyond one orgasm for another, greater orgasm." He drew some shape in the air and cried, "The ultimate orgasm."

"Really?" I said dryly.

"Yes, but do you know what else I think?" he said, turning over to lean on his elbow. "I think women were designed that way deliberately. Because they are insatiable, they are always attractive and attracting. It makes for an endless pursuit."

"That assumes the man is always the pursuer."

"One way or another," he said, "we are. Believe me," he said confidently.

"And how did you get so wise so suddenly?" I asked, half smiling, half impressed.

"I always get philosophical after I make love. It probably stimulates that part of my brain. What about you? How do you feel right now?"

"You already told me," I said. "Unsatisfied."

He laughed and lay back, his hands behind his head.

"You're my first actress. Notice, I didn't say 'my first performer,'" he added.

"That's all right. You're my first detective. I had a traffic cop once though, one of those . . . what do you call them: CHIPs?"

"It's not the same thing," he said. "Plain clothes change a man." I laughed and he turned to me again. "How did you become an actress anyway? Were there Androgyne in the business who helped you, got you the breaks? Not that you needed any special favors," he added quickly. "I've seen your films. You're good and you look great on the big screen."

"That's another part of my story," I said. I turned to him. He looked very interested and for the moment he was able to put aside the fact that we were still lying naked beside each other, our bodies only inches apart.

"Tell me. Please. When did the acting start? High school?"

"It happened at college," I began. "As I told you, my mother wanted me to go to college away from here. Alison and I didn't have any other incidents while we were in high school; we had learned our lesson dramatically that afternoon."

"Oh yes. How did that end up?"

"There was an investigation, of course, but the police bought Alison's story; especially since the boy was so battered and had been so big himself. Alison couldn't possibly be a suspect. She told them she had left him in the bathroom and that was the last she had seen of him.

"They assumed it was some other boy, someone who had been jealous or something and had been following them. He came in after she had left."

"Did Alison follow you to your college?"

"No, she went to New York to modeling school and became an actress that way. We saw each other off and on, but we had begun to hang out with different sorts of people. My training was more classical. I majored in drama and took acting classes. She got right into print advertisement and television commercials."

"And you're a far better actress because of the way you went about it. Not that I'm a critic or anything, but I've seen you both in action."

"Thank you. In my sophomore year, I won a lead role in a Shakespearean play."

"Which one?"

"*Othello*. I played Desdemona."

"You? An innocent? You must have been a good actress from the start."

"Very funny. Actually, you're right. I did have natural ability. All my teachers thought so. They said I had an instinctive stage presence, that after I stepped into the lights, they could almost see my transition from reality into illusion. I absorbed my character and took on her gestures, her facial features, her demeanor. I never acted in a vacuum. Soon, they were using me as an illustration for other students.

" 'See how she always grasps a sense of place. See how she understands the importance of the dramatic pause. Slow down, feel your character, be like Clea.'

"Other girls envied and resented me, of course. I realized early on that it would be that way my entire life. There was one girl in particular at my dorm . . ." I paused and closed my eyes as I turned away from him.

"What? Why did you stop talking?"

"It was the first time I had used Richard in a vengeful, hateful way. He claimed he understood and he didn't mind being used like that, but . . . it just wasn't . . . wasn't . . ."

"Androgynous?" His smiled widened.

"Yes. Go on and laugh if you want, but we do live by a higher standard of ethics. We have a greater obligation to live and be moral."

"I remember. You're God's first, his chosen."

"Exactly. If we have base motives for our actions, then what we do is no longer pure and good and divinely ordained. We have been given a significant responsibility—to act out God's retribution. We are here to serve Him, not ourselves."

"Please, spare me the evangelism. I would have thought your kind avoided that."

"Just because we are what we are," I snapped, "it doesn't mean we're not religious in our own way."

"Okay. I'm sorry. You were vengeful and you took advantage of your androgynous powers and gifts to satisfy a selfish motive."

"Well, I did."

"Tell me about it. I'll be the judge," he said. The expression around his eyes tightened with sincerity.

"Her name was Ophelia."

"You're kidding. They named her after Hamlet's girlfriend, from Shakespeare?"

I was impressed with the detective's literary knowledge.

"Yes. That was part of it," I said, unable to hide my disdain. I was surprised that my hatred for her was still as passionate as it had been. Time had not cooled the heat from my hate, nor had my vengeful satisfaction relieved it.

"Her parents were professional actors, classical stage actors and they had named her Ophelia because they had ordained that she would be an actress too. They filled her with the belief that she had inherited whatever acting talents they had. A more conceited little bitch you couldn't find," I said through clenched teeth.

"But was she good?"

"What?"

"Did she have any talent?"

I blazed a look of fury at him and then turned away and gazed up at the ceiling.

"Yes," I admitted. "But nowhere near as much as she thought she had," I added quickly. "And she couldn't stand the fact that I did."

"What was her full name?" he asked in a detective's tone.

"Ophelia Delano, but she decided to change it to something with more star quality. So she called herself Ophelia Dell."

"Not bad. Ophelia Dell. It has a certain ring to it," he said nodding. "What did she look like?" he asked and instantly, her face flashed before me on the screen of my vivid memory.

"She had long, ebony black hair. She wore it down to her shoulder blades. Her dark eyes glittered like shiny black pearls. When I first set eyes on her, I thought she might be androgynous because she had the smoothest complexion of any inferior I had ever seen. But believe me, she was no Androgyne. I hated her mouth, the cute way it curled up in the corners whenever she was pretending to be pleasant and thoughtful or when she was flirting . . . tormenting some boy, I should say."

"A cock tease?"

"One of the worst." I laughed.

"What?"

"There was an expression, a saying: 'Ophelia cast her coquettish smile and gathered erections around her like someone casting peanuts attracted pigeons.' "

"Sounds like something you made up," he said suspiciously. I flashed a sharp look at him. How quickly he was learning to understand me, I thought.

"What if I did? No boy was good enough for her, you see, but she wanted all to be at her feet. She gave away kisses with the same reluctance girls used to have giving away their virginity. She had this thing . . . oh, how I hated it . . . of kissing the air between you or blowing a kiss.

"If ever men proved themselves mindless, spineless fools, they did with her—buying her gifts, spending lavishly to wine and dine her, calling, pleading, standing out in the cold rain or snow for a sign, a glimpse, or one of those kisses made of air. She tossed a gesture, a wave in their direction and they had orgasms," I said.

"It sounds," the detective said slowly, "like you were more jealous of her than she was of you."

"Me? Jealous of an inferior female?" I laughed. "Please. I'm just trying to give you an idea of how obnoxious she was so you can appreciate why I did what I did." He looked skeptical. "I don't care if you believe that or not."

"All right, all right. I believe you. How did the other girls in the dorm feel about her?"

"Most were fooled by her," I said. He smirked. "Well, what do you expect? They didn't have my insights and perception, did they? They thought she was so fine, so classy, so wonderful. They vied with each other for a compliment from her, for a chance to do something for her to win her favor.

"Flatterers came out of the woodwork. I'm sure she got to think she was a goddess; the others, the idiots, treated her as if she were."

"All except you."

"All except me, and don't think she didn't hate me for that as well as everything else . . . especially beating her out for Desdemona in *Othello*.

"Everyone sympathized and patronized her when she lost, of course. They blamed it on the director being so young and so infatuated with me. She even had the audacity to spread rumors that I was sleeping with him and that's why I beat her out for the part. Sour grapes."

"Were you?"

"Was I what? Sleeping with him?" He stared. "What if I was? I was still twice the actress she was."

The detective roared.

"Well, I was. She was too affected, too perfect. She lacked sincerity."

"Maybe," he said nodding.

"No maybes about it. Whenever she acted, I could see this almost imperceptible twinkle in her eyes before she did anything. She was thinking, following the book, don't you see? They were the correct gestures and all, but she was too mechanical. She was insincere."

"But only you could see it?"

"I'm positive others did too, but they were carried along by the wave of adulation and were afraid to criticize her, even after poor Mark Bini's death."

"Oh?" My detective was tightly in orbit around me now, locked in the gravity of my story and drawn to my every word, every breath, every sigh. He held his own breath and waited. When it seemed to him that I wouldn't go on, he lost patience.

"Who was Mark Bini? How did he die?"

"He was another drama student, barely twenty. He died tragically, brutally. I was very fond of him and he adored me, but he was hypnotized by that . . . that femme fatale. Mark was diminutive, but adorably so, all his features so fine as if he had been meant to be a toy, a replica of a beautiful young man.

"His hands were smaller than mine," I said holding mine up before me. "Can you imagine how tiny his fingers were? They looked like the fingers on a doll, with small fingernails—manicured fingernails," I added. "Mark was fastidious about himself—his hair always trim, his clothes pressed and clean and the colors coordinated.

"He was all of five feet one and about ninety-eight pounds. I think he had a twenty-two-inch waist."

"That is small."

"But his facial features were exquisite—a perfectly straight nose over straight, strong lips with a sharp, sculptured jaw. He had childishly innocent-looking deep blue eyes with long eyelashes most women would die to have.

"But despite his being petite, he had a most extraordinary resonant singing voice. I remember our director was almost in physical pain because he wanted Mark's voice in plays and musicals, but Mark was so diminutive next to any leading lady, it would have presented an undesirable comical picture. So, the poor boy was relegated to the chorus or secondary roles. Occasionally, he soloed at recitals. People in the audience would either stare in disbelief and admiration, or close their eyes and imagine a different person producing those melodic sounds.

"The girls saw him as cute, as something of a mascot. It was as though his smallness made him asexual, a eunuch. They didn't mind parading about in their bras and panties in front of him. Some even went bare breasted in his presence. They thought he was a bit effeminate because he remained in their company so much and so often."

"But you knew better?"

"Of course. How blind they all were. He was in sexual torment, his insides tied in knots. I was the one who discovered he wore jock straps to keep his erection caged. Can you imagine the agony he underwent just to be there, to inhale their perfumes and powders, to touch their soft lingerie and bathe in their smiles as they stroked his hair or kissed him in a sisterly or motherly fashion on the cheek?

"Why if one had forgotten her towel, she would call to him, not to another girl, to fetch one and bring it to her in the shower."

"They must have known what they were doing—toying with him like that."

"Maybe some did. Ophelia certainly did," I said, the heat coming to my cheeks as I recalled.

"She went further?"

"Beyond is more like it. She made it a game or . . . how should I put it . . . her own personal drama, classical tragedy. Suddenly, he was following her everywhere. No matter where she went, there was Mark Bini standing in her shadow, just behind her or just to her side, waiting for her to toss him a smile, a gesture, collar him with an affectionate word. She had him on a leash made of promises, shortening it or lengthening it on whim.

"He'd stand forever at her side while she talked endlessly to someone else without even introducing or bringing him into the conversation. Whenever she went to the library, he sat beside her or behind her, staring at her hypnotically, his eyes unflinching, his body frozen, but in tune with her every move. Should she get up, he would get up."

"What did you do, follow both of them around the campus?"

"I didn't follow them; I observed; I saw. Oh, maybe, sometimes I remained in a room or a hallway just to see what Mark would do or what she would do to him," I confessed, "but I didn't have to spend a great deal of time observing to see what was happening.

"One particularly freezing night she got him up and out of bed to come to the dorm to rub her sore shoulders, claiming only Mark's small hands could do it right. He came rushing over, not even taking the time to dress properly for the cold. He came down with a terrible bronchitis afterward and had to remain in the infirmary, but she didn't care. She didn't even visit him. Or send him a card!

"And then there was that time she had him put on her underthings. He was so infatuated with her, the thought of wearing her bra and her panties filled him with sexual pleasure. And then, when she had him dressed like this, she put rouge and eyeliner and makeup on his face. She even sprayed him with her perfume."

"And he ate it up?"

"He was in ecstasy. She was scantily clad herself all the time she worked on him, dressed only in translucent black panties and wearing one of her uplift bras so her breasts bubbled over at him when she bent over him to paint on the eyeliner."

"You must have been watching to know that."

"A few girls called me. There was a small crowd outside her room, peeping in the doorway. I was sure she deliberately left the door a little open so they could see. And when she had finished, she called us in and called to all the others on the floor to expose him to their ridicule and laughter."

"Didn't you say anything?"

"Whenever I did, the others thought I was being a party

pooper. I didn't want them to think I was jealous of her, of course."

"Of course. Well, this episode must have turned him off her. Right?"

"It did for a while, but she kept reaching for something more, something terribly dramatic, you see," I added in an affected tone of voice.

"So suddenly, she pretended she really liked him and he was no longer standing behind her in her shadow. She brought him forward and held his hand. She kissed him passionately on the lips. Once like a satellite circling her, he now became a comet crashing to her surface, pulled down and drawn closer with every touch, every kiss, every whispered word."

"Didn't the other girls think it was funny—this dramatic change on her part?"

"Yes and no. You see, she had decided on a role to play and for an actress to be successful, she has to be convincing."

"So she got the others to believe she really cared for him?" my detective said incredulously.

"Yes. They were so gullible. Anyway, it drove home any lingering doubts poor Mark Bini had.

"But of course," I said, sadly this time, "men are blind when it comes to women. Their fantasies are so bright they wash out reality and they no longer see anything but their own dreams."

"Not true for women as well?"

"I suppose. Men are just more . . . obvious about it and more easily made victims."

"Maybe. Where did this business with Mark Bini go?"

"To the final act, of course; but there was no curtain call this time. She had this poor boy believing that she would sleep with him if only . . . only he could demonstrate how utterly loyal and devoted to her he was. She wanted all her friends, her ridiculing friends, she told him, to see that what was between her and him was serious, meaningful, sublime.

"How? he wondered. What could he do? She need only name it.

"Something desperate, she told him. Something few men would do for the women they loved. And then she said, 'Or are you like Hamlet, a coward?'

"She had the audacity to recite 'To be or not to be . . . ' The implication was clear. Was Mark brave enough to sacrifice his life, if need be, or to find some way to demonstrate that he would?

"After all, she had come to believe what her parents had been drumming into her stupid head all her life—she was Hamlet's Ophelia.

"Do you know?" I said turning to my detective, "that afterward, she had the nerve, the insane nerve to stroll about the dorm with flowers in her hair singing mad songs as does Ophelia in *Hamlet*?"

"You said afterward. After what?" he asked barely breathing.

"Mark Bini cut his wrists in front of the other girls. They thought he was playing some game, joking as he usually did, but the blood that flowed was real. Then he went into one of the bathrooms and locked the door, claiming he would remain there bleeding until Ophelia came to him.

"So why didn't they bring her to him and end it?"

"She knew he was going to do it. They had planned and rehearsed the entire scene the night before. He expected her to come, of course, but she wanted to see just how far he would go if she didn't come."

"You're kidding?"

"She was writing the script as she went along, playing this role. In her mind she probably saw the faces on people in the audience—concerned, horrified, their eyes pleading.

"I knew exactly how she was thinking. She was the femme fatale. It was a hard role to play, but the audience must not like her at the end. All actresses have to play distasteful parts at one time or another, you see. Really good actresses, that is.

"This is what she believed or pretended to believe. She was on and off the stage so often, one never knew when she was acting and when she wasn't."

"Didn't the girls call for help once they realized she might not come in time?"

"First they found Ophelia. They thought that would solve it. But she delayed her arrival, putting on makeup, brushing her hair, choosing what to wear. In her mad mind she was preparing for her stage entrance, you see. Finally, when she did appear at the door . . ."

"Yes?"

"She really was on stage. All of us stood back in disbelief. She turned to us as though we were the audience and postured. 'Mark,' she cried, 'I know you love me beyond your own life, but love that is true cannot be bought at any price. You might as well come out.'

"Then she looked at the other girls and walked away."

"What happened?"

"It wasn't the way they had rehearsed it. She was supposed to cry and plead, and he was supposed to come out and into her arms. He was waiting for that.

"He was like a magician, a Houdini, locked in an airtight compartment, expecting everything to work as usual. Only it didn't. He lingered too long. Finally, everyone panicked and we sent for help. Maintenance men broke down the door and there he was, sprawled on the floor, his blood in a pool at each wrist, his tiny body now looking like the body of a baby bird that had toppled from its nest."

"How horrible. The other girls must have hated Ophelia for what she had done," my detective concluded.

"They wanted to, but she confused them with that mad act I described. Most actually felt sorry for her. How she suffered. There were some great scenes of waking in the middle of the night and crying, 'MARK! MARK!' The girls would gather around her as she bawled uncontrollably into the pillow, everyone comforting her.

" 'It wasn't your fault.'

" 'He went too far.'

" 'How could you know? And after all, you loved him.'

" 'We all loved him.'

"With real tears streaming down her cheeks, she would turn and thank them for their condolences and sympathy. It was going to be so hard going on with this on her conscience, but thanks to good friends and their support, she would manage.

"Soon, she was her old self again. Or should I say, 'selves.' "

My detective was silent for a few moments.

"How did you find all this out? I mean, the business between Ophelia and Mark?"

"She was proud of it."

"But she didn't express that to the other girls and from what you say went on between you and her, she wouldn't have told you. Right?"

"She didn't tell me. She told Richard and then he told me in his letters and diary," I said and smiled.

"You mean, you brought Richard out, turned him on her in a sense?"

"I thought it was time she had the acting challenge of her life," I replied.

"What happened?"

"It would be better for you to hear it in Richard's words," I said and got up to get his diary.

SEVEN

I RETURNED WITH the diary and, still completely nude, sat in the lotus position on the bed. My detective was sprawled out on his side, facing me with his hand propping up his head. He, too, remained completely naked. A more captured audience, I couldn't command. His eyes were fixed on me; he looked as though he were holding his breath. Then, he smiled.

"You look like you're settling in to read me a fairy tale. You remind me of my mother reading me to sleep."

"Did she always read to you completely naked?" He laughed.

"Not always."

"I assure you," I said, "this isn't a fairy tale." He nodded, closed his eyes and opened them in anticipation.

"For the Androgyne," I began, reading from the middle section of Richard's diary, *"arrogant women are a delicacy. Their arrogance adds a delectable spice. After all, it was exactly this vanity that destroyed Adam and Eve and drove them from Paradise. All Eve had to hear was that God was preventing her from eating from the Tree of Knowledge because he didn't want her to know she was as beautiful as he, and she rushed away to disobey the commandment.*

"*Ironically, the arrogance that should make a woman less accessible makes her vulnerable. The more pompous a woman is the more susceptible she is to flattery, and flattery is the poison with which assassins weaken their victims and get them to become careless and unprotected.*

"*Late one night after I had metamorphosed, I discovered a letter Clea had left for me on her desk. I read about Ophelia Dell and Mark Bini and Clea's outrage over what had happened.*

"*Before we had arrived at the college, Janice had made it clear that I must never hunt on or near the campus. She didn't want me to do anything that might bring attention to Clea. Whenever I did emerge, therefore, I went miles and miles away to prowl in some singles bar.*

"*But after I read Clea's letter, I realized how angry she was about what had happened and how much she wanted me to render the proper punishment. She didn't ask me specifically to do anything, but I read between the lines and understood why she had called me forth. After all, we had in a very true sense been created for just this purpose.*"

"Now I know what you people think you are," my detective quipped, "love vigilantes."

"Perhaps we are," I said without looking up. I read on. "*That evening I pretended to arrive at the dorms looking for Clea. Naturally, I drew a great deal of interest, especially after I entered the lounge and introduced myself as Clea's boyfriend. I knew it would be better to say that than to say I was her brother. A brother the police could trace; a vagabond boyfriend was another story.*

"*It was a rather big, luxurious lobby for a college dormitory—nicely carpeted, walls paneled, well lit with soft-looking couches and chairs, rich-looking maple and pine tables, one section set aside solely for television viewing. There were a half dozen or so girls watching television and a few sitting on sofas talking with boys. Ophelia was holding court on the right: Her disciples gathered around her and at her feet, listening to her describe a date she had had with a graduate student the night before. I had deliberately approached one of the girls on the periphery of that circle, introduced myself and asked for Clea.*

" 'We didn't know she had a boyfriend,' Ophelia Dell said after she heard me introduce myself. She laughed and looked at the others. 'We were all beginning to wonder if she wasn't gay.'

" 'Hardly,' I said and laughed along with everyone else, raising my eyebrows with insinuation, which caused Ophelia to look at me with sharper interest. She was a rather attractive young woman, and were I an ordinary young man, I most likely would have been captured by her beauty. But I sensed something dangerous about her: There was a fiery glint in her dark eyes, like a tiny diamond set in black onyx. I knew Clea thought Ophelia played with people's emotions, amused herself by tapping the keys that produced elation and then, without warning, began to tap those that produced depression. Clea believed that Ophelia was always performing. In her letter to me she wrote, 'Wherever there were two gathered in her name, there build a theater.' Something like that.

"Anyway, of course I saw beneath the facade. Ophelia Dell wasn't performing in the sense that she was consciously aware of what she was doing, how she was manipulating an audience. Oh no, she believed in her various personalities and unlike an actor, became these people. It's the difference between acting and schizophre-

nia. Ophelia could flit from one personality to another with the grace and ease of a trapeze artist flying from one swing to another.

"Clea, being a woman, missed this. She was blinded by a woman's natural jealousy of another attractive female."

"Now wait a minute," my detective interrupted. "You're not going to let him get away with that, are you? I mean, it's not true, is it . . . that business about a woman's natural jealousy?"

"It might be," I confessed. "But Richard forgets that men are also at a disadvantage when confronting beautiful women. Sex blinds them, makes them incapable of seeing reality."

"So from what you're saying, I should conclude that no one, male or female, sees the truth and understands who or what this person really is?"

"When it comes to an attractive member of the opposite sex, no. Unless of course, he or she wants to be forthcoming."

He smiled as if I were now confirming something he had believed and tried to convince me of all along. I turned back to the diary.

" 'How come we haven't seen you before?' Ophelia asked me, stepping forward to dislodge herself from her admirers. They remained behind as if they understood that's where they were supposed to be. I must say I was amused by the hold she had over them.

" 'It's not easy for me to get away,' I replied. She turned a smile on me the way someone would turn a flashlight on a dark corner and searched my face for sincerity.

" 'Get away from what? Are you a convict?' she asked and checked to see if her disciples were still fastened to her every gesture, every word. Of course, they were and

they laughed in chorus along with her.

" *'I am a prisoner of sorts,' I replied. 'A prisoner of the theater.' I said it as if I were under some burden since birth, weighted down by the responsibilities and pressures.*

" *'Oh?' Her ridicule ended abruptly, as if I had uttered the magic words. I saw the sardonic expression in her face dwindle and then change to a more serious and even-tempered one. 'What do you mean by that?' she asked, stepping farther away from her tribe of admirers. I could see the disappointment in their faces as we moved beyond their hearing.*

" *'I'm an actor,' I declared in a tone of conclusion as if I expected she would understand what that meant, the burdens it implied. Her face brightened.*

" *'Really? So am I.'*

" *'Then you understand,' I said. By now we were fencing with our eyes—her gaze moving down my body in a single swipe, I countering with a slow slash across her breasts and then cutting to her hips. We both brought our eyes up so our visual duel would come to an end. Our gazes locked. I smiled and she made an obscene little gesture with the tip of her tongue that I must confess titillated me."*

"It sounds like he really appreciated her," my detective remarked.

"I never said she wasn't a very attractive girl. Richard's always been a connoisseur when it comes to women. That's only to be expected," I snapped.

"And you? Is it to be expected that you are a connoisseur of men?"

"Of course."

"Should I be flattered then?" He smiled with such smugness.

"Didn't you hear what Richard said at the start of

this section: Flattery is the poison with which assassins weaken their victims and get them to become careless and unprotected."

"Ooooo," he said with mock fear. He embraced his naked torso. "Am I unprotected?"

"Of course you are . . . when it comes to the Androgyne," I replied, my eyes as cold and dead as glass eyes on a mannequin. His smirk weakened. I returned to the diary.

" 'Where are you an actor?' she asked.

" 'I'm with a road company. That's why I haven't been around before,' I told her. Her eyes widened with appreciation. 'We call ourselves the Traveling Thespians of Stratford, even though no one is from Stratford,' I added with a smile. 'We perform Shakespeare obviously.'

" 'Obviously,' she said.

" 'Right now, we are preparing a new version of Romeo and Juliet. I play Romeo. I had a few days off and thought I would come to see Clea, a surprise visit. I guess I should have phoned first to be sure she was here, but I wanted to surprise her. Have you seen her?'

" 'Not in the last few hours. Actually,' she said giving it real thought, 'I haven't seen her since yesterday.'

" 'You say you are an actress? Are you active in the college theater?'

" 'Yes. Of course,' she added and brushed her hair back over her shoulder with a graceful sweep of her hand, exposing more of her soft white neck, which I must admit was as tempting to me as it would have been had I been a vampire. I quickly envisioned my lips pressed to that silky surface, luxuriating in the sweet scent of her body and the delicious taste I expected to find on her awaiting lips.

"I think Clea sensed how much I was stirred because I felt an ache deep within me, a rumbling that manifested itself in a feline growl or catlike hiss that reverberated *down the corridors of my heart and echoed maddeningly in my ears. I actually grimaced.*

" *'Are you all right?' Ophelia asked.*

" *'Yes, I was just feeling disappointed. I had hoped to find Clea so she could help me with my part, you see. I wanted her to read some Juliet to my Romeo. She's a very fine, perceptive young actress and when you rehearse with someone who has definite talent, it brings out the best in you. Being an actress yourself, I'm sure you would understand.'*

" *'Of course I do,' she said looking annoyed that there was even the slightest doubt.*

"I smiled warmly and took her arm to lead her farther away from our small audience.

" *'My name is Thomas,' I said.*

" *'I'm Ophelia Dell,' she replied, not without that arrogance Clea despised.*

" *'What a wonderful name,' I declared. 'Ophelia, have you ever worked with professional actors before?' I asked quickly, as if the idea had just occurred.*

" *'Yes. Often. My parents are professional actors.'*

" *'I should have known,' I said setting my trap of flattery. 'You've obviously inherited some of their talent, and you have a certain presence, a statuesque demeanor that suggests professional training. When I first walked into this lobby, I was immediately drawn to you. You're like a diamond surrounded by pieces of ordinary glass.'*

"Her eyes brightened. I sensed her lowering herself into my warm pool of adulation, submerging herself in my praise.

" *'People who have real talent stand out. Their talent gives them a certain glow, a light ordinary people don't have, don't you think?'*

" *'Of course.'*

" 'Have you ever been in a production of Romeo and Juliet?' I inquired.

" 'In high school, but the director was an English teacher who had little or no background in theater.'

" 'He didn't cast you as Juliet?' I asked, wide-eyed with amazement.

" 'No, and the one he did cast as Juliet was terrible. It took her ages to memorize her part. I was always feeding her lines in rehearsal and showing her how to recite them, but do you think the director noticed the differences between us, my superiority? No.'

" 'It takes people who have been around talented people to recognize them sometimes. When you are surrounded by mediocrity, you become mediocre.'

" 'Exactly,' she said.

" 'I know this is rather presumptuous of me to ask, but since you are tantamount to a professional actress and you are so familiar with Romeo and Juliet, do you think I could convince you to rehearse some of it with me? I'd be more than happy to take you out to dinner as a token of my appreciation.

" 'I don't mean to tear you away from anything important here,' I added quickly.

" 'There is nothing important going on here,' she replied with a disdainful glance at the girls watching television. 'Where would we rehearse?'

" 'Well, I've taken a room at the Courtyard, a pleasant little motel just outside of town and . . . '

" 'Yes, I know where it is.' She looked back at her girlfriends who were still looking our way with interest. Then she turned to me and smiled. 'Just give me a moment to change out of this.'

"She was wearing a plain gray sweatshirt and a pair of jeans with a pair of pink tennis sneakers and no socks.

" 'Oh, but you look perfect. It's the ideal outfit for rehearsal. I can bring you back to change for dinner. Maybe Clea will have returned by then and I can say hello before we go out.'

"I saw that the prospect of that pleased her. After all, she had stolen Clea's boyfriend away and she would bask in the pleasure that brought.

" 'Aren't you afraid she will be upset about you taking out another girl?'

"I shrugged. 'We go out but we are not obligated to each other. Children of the theater can't afford to tie themselves down like ordinary people do,' I added. 'Don't you agree?'

"I turned my most charming smile on her, making my eyes a bit impish.

" 'Yes,' she said. 'I do agree.'

" 'Then you will go?'

"She thought for a moment, looked back at her envious and curious girlfriends and nodded.

" 'Okay,' she said and we left.

"She didn't tell anyone where she was going. I asked her if she had to. She replied it was no one's business: a perfect example of arrogance.

"I drove her to the Courtyard, asking a stream of questions about her so our conversation would be concentrated solely on her. She told me about herself and Mark Bini. Of course, her version of the story was quite different and centered around her. Egotistical people like nothing better than talking about themselves. At the end of an evening's conversation, they will always tell you how much they enjoyed being with you, when in fact they haven't been with you—they've been only with themselves through you. It's as if they have gone out with a mirror and an echo.

"I had chosen the Courtyard Motel because of its secluded location on a rustic road branching off the main highway. The proprietors, an elderly couple, lived behind the office. I had checked in late the evening before, dressed in a jacket and tie. Today I wore a plaid flannel shirt, tight jeans and sneakers.

"The Courtyard consisted of rooms in a semicircular configuration with the exterior a freshly painted light blue. All the rooms had milk-white shutters and were clean, quaint and comfortable. Behind the motel was a thick wooded area. It was indeed a motel that offered a weary traveler a quiet, restful spot. My room was about midway between the office and the last unit. Only two other rooms were being rented at the time, but when we drove up, only one party was present, their car parked in front of their room.

"It was already late in the afternoon, the sun sinking behind some mountains and thin shadows beginning to emerge from corners and out from under overhangs. Even the trees began to take on ominous shapes, but if Ophelia felt any nervousness coming to a motel with a relative stranger, she didn't show it. I think she harbored some romantic belief that actors and actresses, anyone connected with the theater, were part of one great family . . . sort of like circus people. We couldn't be strangers and certainly had nothing to fear from each other.

"Smiling, I opened the door to my room and showed her in. The room had two twin beds, a television set, two dressers with a wall mirror above one, and a small table and two chairs. Awaiting on the table like cheese in a mousetrap was an opened copy of Romeo and Juliet. Ophelia was drawn directly to it once her eyes had set on it. She read a few lines and closed her eyes and drew *back her head as if she were savoring the sounds and digesting the poetry.*

"*What a ham, I thought. I could almost feel Clea cringe within me. But suddenly, she turned to me, her eyes fixed on me strangely. She sighed deeply and recited, projecting her voice as if she were on a stage.*

"*'... O gentle Romeo, if thou dost love, pronounce it faithfully: or if thou think'st I am too quickly won, I'll frown and be perverse and say thee nay so thou wilt woo; but else not for the world.'*

"*'That is very, very good,' I said. 'To walk in cold like that and pick up those words as though you had been rehearsing for hours and hours, as if you were on the stage and right in the middle of a performance ... simply wonderful.' I shook my head in admiration. I held my smile tightly because underneath it was Clea's disdainful smirk trying to emerge, but it was my words and smile that were needed.*

"*Ophelia's face glowed. I had fed her ego as one would feed a fire, and she had quickly consumed my words and become bright, hot, burning with excitement.*

"*Fortunately, I had memorized a piece and she had read from that opened page. I fell into Romeo's posture and demeanor and reached out for her hands.*

"*'Lady, by yonder blessed moon I swear that tips with silver all the fruit-tree tops—'*

"*'Oh swear not by the moon,' she cried, 'the inconstant moon ...'*

"*Clea slipped a laugh past me, nearly ruining everything.*

"*'What's so funny?' Ophelia demanded, pulling herself up haughtily.*

"*'I can't believe how lucky I am to have stumbled on you in that dorm.'*

" 'Oh.' She smiled. 'Am I better than Clea?'

"I felt a tightening in my stomach, but I was here to seduce this girl, was I not?

" 'Far better. Clea is good, yes, but you . . . you are that one in a million. They are very lucky to have you back at that college.'

" 'And yet Clea won the part of Desdemona over me,' she complained.

" 'Who's the fool who cast it?'

" 'The director, but how do you think she got the part?' she said.

" 'Oh?'

" 'Your girlfriend is not very faithful. In fact, she's a slut.'

" 'I was afraid of that. It's one of the reasons I came here,' I said.

" 'Well now you know not to waste any more time on her,' she said gleefully.

" 'That's for certain.'

"I approached her and reached down to turn the pages of the play script to arrive at that moment early in the play when Romeo and Juliet first meet and kiss.

" 'I'd like to try this with you,' I said. She gazed at the pages.

" 'Fine.' She turned to me, willing, ready, eager to prove how good she was.

" 'If I profane with my unworthiest hand this holy shrine, the gentle fine is this: my lips, two blushing pilgrims, ready stand to smooth that rough touch with a tender kiss.' I'm not half bad, I thought.

"She glanced at the book and then turned into me. We were so close the tips of her perky breasts grazed my chest.

" 'Good pilgrim, you do wrong your hand too much,

*which mannerly devotion shows in this; for saints have
hands that pilgrims' hands do touch, and palm to palm
is holy palmers' kiss.'*

"I skipped right to it, but she didn't mind or really
didn't know the difference.

" ' . . . thus from my lips, by yours, my sin is purged.'

"I kissed her, drawing her to me so tightly, she was
nearly off her feet. Never had I pressed my lips so firmly and demanded more from a single kiss than this. My
tongue latched to hers the way it would had I pressed it
up against a freezing windowpane. She gasped and began
to push against my shoulders, but she was already losing
her balance. I saw the way her eyes went back. She was
dizzy, overwhelmed. When I pulled my lips from hers,
she gasped.

"I brought my lips to her neck and sucked softly as
I lifted her in my arms and placed her gently on the
bed. She looked up at me startled by her own apparent
paralysis. My kiss had reached deeply into her, drawing
energy from her spine and stunning her as if I had shot
a tranquilizer into her or sent a jolt of electricity through
her body. She couldn't lift a finger; she could barely blink
an eye. She stared up at me, helpless, confused, but oh,
how sweet and beautiful she looked. I nearly lingered too
long, giving her time to recuperate. It was Clea, however,
deep inside me, chastising me and demanding action that
made me move on.

" 'Oh, Juliet,' I said, now mocking her, 'let's skip all
the bullshit and get right to it, shall we not?'

"Despite her paralysis, she expressed shock and surprise. I saw the struggle in her eyes, the great effort to
move her limbs, so she could get up and run out, but
all she could do was look up at me, terrified.

"Her expression of terror did more to excite me. Her

fear made my heart beat faster. I felt a rush. I was zooming down the steepest decline of a roller coaster, finding it hard to catch my breath myself. I closed my eyes and savored the sweet moment and then I lifted the sweatshirt off her. Her arms were like two disconnected limbs, just wobbling about as I pulled the shirt up and over her head. No longer supported by the effort, those arms fell beside her on the bed.

"She wasn't wearing a bra, but her full, milky white breasts were so firm, they barely spilled over the sides of her chest, and each nipple, a dark carrot shade, was turned sharply upward. On her left breast, she had a small birthmark just below the aureole. I touched it with the tip of my finger. She tried to look down to see what I was doing, but she couldn't see below her bosom.

"Her effort to scream and protest caused a slight quiver in her lips. There was a rippling effect down the sides of her jaw. I leaned over and kissed her softly on the mouth to lift that trembling from her. It was exquisite. How I relished the tiny, electric flutter as it traveled through my own lips and down the lines of my own jaw. Her eyes were as wide as they could be, her pupils bright. I brought my tongue to those eyes, forcing her to close her lids as I traced the eyeballs with the tip of my tongue. As I did so, I closed my own eyes and on the insides of my lids I saw what she saw.

"I expected to see a look of ecstasy in my face, but instead, I saw Clea gazing down at her with an expression of sadistic joy, and I realized that she was participating in this more than she had ever participated in anything I had done before. It was Clea who was driving me to toy with Ophelia; it was Clea who had turned my fingers and my lips into tiny knives, making my caresses painful and my kisses agonizing.

"I opened my eyes and sat back. For a moment Ophelia looked hopeful, but I shattered that optimism instantly when I unfastened her jeans and pulled them down her legs. I stopped at her ankles and ran my forefingers down the center of her stomach and over her bikini panties, hooking them at the crotch and tugging them off by lifting her lower body. Then I untied her sneakers and stripped her completely.

"I stood back, admiring her. Her beauty was so extraordinary, I had to offer her some solace.

" 'Think,' I said, 'think of the part you would most cherish, the role that you would seek with all your heart. Put yourself on the stage on Broadway. Imagine audiences giving you a standing ovation night after night; envision the lights, smell the makeup, listen for the swish of the curtains opening.

" 'If you are really as good as you think you are, you will carry yourself off and no longer be here suffering.'

"I could hear Clea scream: 'She didn't give Mark Bini any relief. Why are you giving her any?'

"I undressed and straddled her. When I looked down, into her eyes, I saw she had taken my advice. She had a far-off look. Her ears were filled with the sounds she wanted to hear.

"I dipped myself into her, first feeling as if I had lowered myself into a cold bath after being in the steam room. The chill made me shudder and I realized, the chill was coming from her. It was almost like making love to a corpse and for a moment, I nearly retreated; but I felt a pressure on my lower spine—Clea's hand pressing me down, demanding I do what I had come to do.

"Gradually, I went deeper and deeper into her until I reached her warmth, the essence of her life, that subterranean pool normally well protected, shielded from thirsty *predators, and I began to drink, drawing her life into me, absorbing her. The peach tint went out of her cheeks; the light dimmed in her eyes. Her breathing became labored; her heart clamored for richer blood, her brain screamed for oxygen. I could hear the alarms, feel the bedlam and the turmoil as all her organs cried out the danger. The frantic messages shot through her veins and arteries, every part of her demanding attention.*

"And then as incredible as it might seem, I thought I did hear a thunder of applause and shouts of 'Bravo, bravo, bravo.' The ovation trickled to a single pair of hands clapping sharply, until that final salvo ended and the stage went black. When I opened my eyes and looked at her, I saw that the gleam in her eyes was gone. Her lips went slack and fell away from her teeth. Her skin quickly turned cold, clammy, as if a sheet of thin ice had been drawn over her.

"I lifted myself from her, or rather, what had been she. The odor of death was already escaping through every pore, every orifice. A putrescent cloud of dying flesh settled over her. Without looking at her, I dressed quickly.

"It was at this point that I felt Clea take more control. Normally, I would have simply left the motel room and driven off to retreat within Clea, but Clea was more demanding. Justice and revenge had become too tightly entwined. She wanted more; she wanted some poetic irony.

"She made me dress Ophelia, which was something I had never done to a victim before. I hated every moment of it, hated the stiffness in her joints, the icy way her eyes glared accusingly in their death stare. As soon as that was completed, I went to the doorway and looked out. Darkness had begun to fall. Thin, murky shadows were

draped over the parking lot. It was as if some giant had thrown a grey veil over the world, but it was quiet, safe. There was no one around.

"I went out and opened the car door. Then I returned to the room, scooped Ophelia off the bed, as if she weighed no more than a pillow, and carried her out to the car. I sat her up in the front seat, keeping her firmly in position with the seat belt. Of course, her head drooped, but she appeared to be no more than someone dozing.

" 'Now let's see, what should we talk about now?' I asked the corpse as we drove off. I knew Clea enjoyed the humor. 'Should we still talk about you, or have we exhausted the subject? You do look somewhat exhausted.'

"Clea's laughter followed me all the way back to the college. By the time I had returned to the campus, the shadows had darkened and thickened. Night had taken a firm grip. Still in my Shakespearean mood, I thought it was truly the time of day when graveyards yawned. The dead did walk. I drove over the campus street slowly, my car moving like some ghost of a car, a dark spirit threading its horrific way through the darkness, hovering as close to shadows as it could, cowering away from the illumination of the streetlights as if the light had the power to destroy it instantly.

"Here and there students hurried across the lawns, some returning from late classes, most going to the dorm cafeterias. I drove around to the theater building and parked in the darkness. There I waited, the thump of my heart sounding like the beating of two hearts, Clea's pulse rushing over mine at times, just as Clea's thoughts invaded my own.

"I could feel my skin softening, my bosom aching as the breasts locked within began to throb like an incipient toothache. My penis tightened, retracted. Muscles through-

out my body were dwindling. My waist was constricting. There wasn't much time left. Clea was pounding on the door closed between us. She wanted to emerge and savor the moment, but she was being impatient. Just like a woman, I thought, expecting everything to be done the moment she wanted it done.

"I got out of the vehicle and went around to unbuckle the dead Ophelia and scooped her into my arms again. With Clea pressuring me to metamorphose, my superior strength began to diminish. I was practically as weak as an ordinary man and Ophelia was, after all, dead weight.

"Scurrying across the theater parking lot, I made my way to a side entrance. Fortunately it wasn't locked, for I didn't think I still had sufficient strength to yank it open. Once inside, I listened to be sure I was alone. Satisfied I was, I made my way down the corridor and entered the auditorium. I rushed down the aisle and placed Ophelia on the foot of the stage. Then I climbed onto the stage and opened the curtain.

"The stage was set up for The Zoo Story, *a one-act play taking place on a park bench. I put Ophelia's corpse on the bench, tilting her head back so her gaping mouth would be visible to the audience. Then I went to the costume and makeup room and got out the makeup kit. I returned to the stage and worked on her face until I had her looking like the mask of tragedy with two long black tears down her now-chalk-white face. I returned everything to the makeup and costume room and went up to the lighting panel. I found the light I wanted, a single spotlight placed to cut out the bench from the rest of the stage. I tightened the focus until all that was visible was her ghoulish face.*

"That done, I stepped out into the audience and

inspected my work. I could hear the clapping begin deep within me. It was Clea's clapping. It built in momentum and volume until it took over my arms and hands and I was clapping. Clea emerged more and more with each clap. I felt myself sinking inside her, and I felt her satisfaction. I retreated somewhere below the thunder of her applause. I would no longer resist metamorphosis.

"I had done what she had wanted."

I looked up slowly from the diary, aware that there were tears streaming down my cheeks. Whenever I read this section, I cried because it reminded me how much Richard loved me and how he would do anything to please me.

My detective simply stared, his head still propped up by his hand.

"And so," he finally said, "I assume that was the way Ophelia Dell was discovered?"

I nodded. "Early the next morning."

"No one checked on what time you girls arrived at night, or saw to it that you did arrive, so she wouldn't have been missed?"

"No. It was a fully liberated dorm. We could have men in our rooms; we could smoke, have alcoholic beverages. We came and went as we pleased."

"What happened next? Surely, there was an investigation that involved you."

"The custodian who found Ophelia's corpse on stage called the campus police. The story spread like a forest fire during a drought. Students flocked to the theater to see if they could catch a glimpse of the ghastly sight. You know how people are attracted to gore and death, how they slow down on the freeways to gape at an accident—their infatuation with the macabre."

"Uh-huh," he said dryly. "I know all about it."

"Some students actually got to see her before the body had been removed. And many who did exaggerated what they saw—there was a slash across her neck, her eyes had been gouged . . . stuff like that."

"But the police questioned you, of course."

"Oh yes. The girls who had been in the dorm lobby described Richard, and I was questioned about him. I told them no one of that description was familiar to me, and I had no boyfriend now or in the past called Thomas."

"They believed you?"

"What could they do? It appeared some psychopath was clever enough to use my name. Oh, it was hairy for a while—the scrutiny. They traced him to the motel and brought me a composite picture drawn by a police artist who had listened to the motel owner and some of the girls at the dorm. Naturally, I didn't recognize him."

"Weren't there any resemblances?"

"Nothing that they picked up on. Of course, I was very worried for a while and so was Richard. He made no effort to emerge for months afterward.

"And when Janice found out, she was very angry. She was going to pull me out of the school. I had to promise that nothing like that would ever occur again while I was there. After a while, the police investigation dwindled to nothing. We all went on with our lives."

"What was the cause of death?"

"Asphyxiation. Just like all the others."

"Did you have any regrets? Feel any remorse once time passed and you realized what you and Richard had done?"

"None whatsoever. She got what she deserved. I went on with my acting and received rave reviews, enough to

draw the attention of a theatrical agent—Freddy Bloom,
who came down from New York to see me."

"And that's how you got discovered?"

"Uh-huh."

I closed Richard's diary and leaned back on the pillow.
My detective continued to stare at me. I ran my fingers
through his hair.

"You have nice hair, healthy hair. They say you can
tell a person's state of health through the condition of
his or her hair."

"Goes all the way back to Samson and Delilah," he said.

"Yes." I laughed.

"When are you going to turn that diary over to me?"
he asked, nodding toward it on the nightstand.

"Soon. Are you anxious to get on with your investigation and rid yourself of me?"

"Just keeping my eyes on the prize."

"Can't you forget who and what you are for a while?"

"Can you?"

"Sometimes." He looked skeptical. "Especially when
I'm performing, assuming another identity."

"That's why you wanted to be an actress," he said
quickly. "It provides you with a means of escape."

I turned away. I certainly didn't expect he would be
so perceptive. It was a bit frightening. There were things
I didn't want him to know. Now I wondered if it would
be possible to reveal so much and not in the process
reveal it all.

"Why would I want to do that?"

"Something I picked up yesterday, something you said
about you and Richard being different from other Androgyne. There is a little too much of, what shall I say,
inferior blood in you. Perhaps somehow your family line
became diluted over the years."

"That's ridiculous. It can't happen. We don't mingle with inferiors. I told you—only Androgyne can propagate Androgyne."

"Maybe in your history there was some inbreeding, an accident."

"No."

"How else can you explain it?"

"Explain what?"

"You desire sometimes to be an inferior."

"I don't . . ."

"Sure you do. It's why you permitted yourself to fall in love with Michael," he said.

I turned to him sharply. His eyes were penetrating. Usually, I didn't underestimate an inferior male's abilities. Why had I underestimated his?

"I'm thirsty," I said. "Would you like something to drink?"

"Wouldn't mind," he replied shrugging. "What do you want? I'll get it."

"Just some orange juice on ice."

"Okay."

He rose from the bed. Naked, he walked out of the room. I lay back and closed my eyes. My heart began to pound. Richard was pulling himself up out of the darkness within me. I could feel his struggle. When I heard his voice now, it was softer, calmer, concerned.

"Let me come," he pleaded. "For both our sakes. Before it's too late. Please, Clea. Let me come. You have told this policeman too much. I have to end it. Now."

Perhaps he was right, I thought. Just thinking it permitted him a toehold. I could feel him pull himself up and out of the shadows. I didn't want him to emerge, but it was dangerously close to the point of no return, like going too far with a sexual embrace. The heat in the blood rushes over any hesitation and all restraint is quickly melted down.

My fingers tightened into a fist, my fingernails cutting into my palms until I felt the pain. My legs straightened and hardened. I felt a trembling in my bosom as my breasts became firmer. They were beginning to dissolve, the pectoral muscles beneath them enlarging. My shoulders started to thicken. When I ran my tongue over my upper lip, I could feel the emerging face hair. Soon, it would be too late to stop the metamorphosis. Richard would be waiting in this bed when the detective returned with my juice.

EIGHT

"ARE YOU ALL right?" my detective asked. He was standing at the side of the bed looking down at me, but I hadn't heard him return. I felt the beads of sweat on my forehead and when I looked up at him, I realized my vision had become blurry because his well-developed pectoral muscles looked like breasts.

"Here," he said when I didn't reply. "Drink some of this and you will feel better."

I didn't respond, so he brought the glass of juice to my lips, held my head and tilted the glass so the fluid would run in over my tongue. It was difficult to swallow, but I managed to ingest some. The cold juice was welcomed. My insides had become as blistering hot as the insides of a furnace. I knew my body was crimson and to my detective, it must look like a fire raged within, the flames just under my skin. I thought I would soon be consumed by the blaze and go up in smoke right before his eyes.

He put his palm on my forehead.

"You're feverish," he said. "Something's happening, isn't it?"

I could barely nod. I heard him rush into the bathroom and run water into the tub. Moments later, he returned and slipped his arms under me. I was surprised at the ease with which he lifted me and carried me toward the bathroom. When I rested my face against his chest, I thought the heat from my body would singe him, but he was oblivious to pain or discomfort. This close to me, he looked even more distorted. His lips were long and very red and his eyebrows were thin. His eyes were suddenly almond-shaped eyes and caught the light like crystal. I had to close my own eyes.

He lowered me slowly into the tub. The cold water was shocking. I tried to pull myself out, but he held me down, forcing me to endure the flow of the ice-cold water over my legs, my stomach, my torso. He dipped his hands into the water and anointed my head with it. I shivered and cried out, but he didn't stop. It was as if he knew it was Richard crying out, not me; for the cold bath was having its effect.

I felt Richard lose his firm grip on the rope of identity. His fingers slipped as if the water I was submerged in had run down the rope, turning it into a cord of ice. He held on but continued to slide. He sunk quickly into the dark pool of anonymity again. I heard his final cry of panic and defeat, and then, all was quiet within me. I lay back against the tile, numb.

My detective lifted me from the water and quickly brought me back to my bed where he wrapped me in bath towels. My body still quivered so he embraced me and held me to him, rocking me as if I were a baby as he rubbed my back in small circular caresses. Soon, I felt a surge of warmth returning. It crawled up my body, covering me with a pleasant afterglow.

I sighed. My clear vision returned; my heartbeat slowed; and I resumed normal breathing.

"How are you doing?" my detective asked. All the distortions in his face were gone.

"Better. Thank you. But how did you know to do that and so quickly?"

"Just basic first aid," he said nonchalantly as if he did something like it every day.

"Hardly basic. I doubt very much that anyone is taught how to stop a metamorphosis."

He laughed and stood up.

"I took a shot, hoping it would help. You looked like you were on fire and water puts out a fire," he said, shrugging. "Drink some more juice," he advised and gave me the glass. This time I could hold it myself. He watched me drink, his eyes intent, riveted, looking like the eyes of a physician who studied his patient.

"What happened? What brought it on?" he asked. "I hope it wasn't something I said," he added, smiling.

"Sometimes, it just happens," I replied, shifting my eyes away from him.

"But you usually have warning. Isn't that why you seduced me earlier?" he asked, his smile turning salacious.

"I let down my guard and Richard took advantage. It's as simple as that," I added quickly.

"Why?"

"Why did I let down my guard or why did he take advantage?"

"Both."

"I was careless, forgetful . . . perhaps because I had just finished reading his words."

"It didn't happen to you when you read his words before," he pursued. "Did it?"

"Oh, what's the difference. It's over."

"Why would he want to emerge now?"

"To rip off your head," I snapped. I glared up at him. "Satisfied?"

"So then I saved my life by coming up with the cold bath therapy, huh?"

"I'm sure you did. Perhaps you should go." I turned away from him and pulled the blanket over me.

"You want me to leave? After all that's happened to you?" he asked incredulously. I didn't reply. "What if someone tries to kill you again? What if Richard metamorphoses while you're asleep?"

"So then you will return and arrest him for the murder of Michael Barrington."

"I can't. I don't have enough evidence. All I have is your testimony and it will be a little difficult putting you on the witness stand, you have to admit."

"You will have the diary, Richard's own words."

"Can I take it with me now?" I didn't reply. It was one thing to plan on doing it—turning Richard's diary over to him, but it was another thing actually doing it. I wasn't ready.

"No, not yet." I turned back to him. "I just can't do it yet. Don't you see, I'm working myself up to this . . . this betrayal?"

He nodded, sympathetically.

"All right, but I don't know that I should leave you just yet. Why don't I lay beside you and let you talk yourself to sleep. Tell me more of your story."

I lay back on my pillow, and he took my hand and lay beside me. We were both looking up at the ceiling as if my story were about to be projected on it.

"All right," I said. I took a deep breath and began again. "After the incident with Ophelia Dell, I continued with college, performing in play after play. Whenever I returned home for holidays, Richard used the occasions to metamorphose and go on his hunts throughout Los Angeles and other parts of Southern California. I was home often enough for that to satisfy our needs.

"But eventually I started to give him other opportunities back East, especially whenever I visited Alison in New York. As was expected, she had done well in modeling school. In fact, she wasn't there six months before she had landed a job modeling clothing for some department stores and catalogues. Before she graduated, she made the cover of *Cosmopolitan* and then her career skyrocketed when she became the model for Infatuation, a new perfume and cologne."

"Oh, so that's who she was. I remember those advertisements. 'He can't help but become infatuated once you put on Infatuation.' "

"Exactly. Her face began appearing everywhere—on the backs of buses, in subway trains and stations, in every magazine and newspaper, and finally, she was in television commercials, making a small fortune doing these ridiculous things to make women believe sexual power was in this cologne. I didn't even like the scent."

"You sound as if you were jealous."

"Not jealous, just . . . impatient with my own career."

"That's the same thing."

"No it isn't. I told you—we're not jealous of each other. We don't have to be."

"Uh-huh."

I spun on him.

"You know you can be infuriating sometimes."

"I've been told that," he said nodding slowly. "So, Alison was becoming a celebrity, and you were still reciting lines in college theaters to a limited audience of faculty, students and friends. Then what?"

"I told you." Irritated, I folded my arms. "One night Freddy Bloom attended a performance at my school. The drama instructor had written to him, asking him to come, and he did. I was doing Nora in Ibsen's *A Doll's House*."

"Great play. Timely, especially today."

I turned to him.

"How do you know so much about literature, the arts?" I asked, narrowing my eyes suspiciously. Perhaps Richard and I knew less about him than we had first thought.

"Hey, just because I spend most of my life hunting down psychopaths and other riffraff doesn't mean I can't do worthwhile things with the rest of my time. So what was this Freddy Bloom like?"

I smiled, recalling Freddy's chubby face and friendly smile.

"He was nice, fatherly, old-fashioned. He liked to pick up a young artist and shape his or her career. He wasn't a money-hungry, hyped-up neurotic like so many Hollywood agents tend to be. He had a religious faith in talent, believing that eventually it will find its proper level.

"So he didn't feed me to the columnists and publicists. The first job he got me barely paid enough commission for him to buy postage stamps."

"The way the price of postage stamps is rising . . . that might not be so little."

"You know what I mean. He wanted to showcase me, get people talking about me slowly." I smiled at my memories of Freddy bringing people around to see me perform. He was more like a little old grandfather, proud. "Freddy used to compare his technique to an artist sculpturing. He was shaping me, carving, cutting away the rough places."

"*My Fair Lady?*"

"Not exactly. I wasn't unschooled raw material, you know."

"Right."

"Anyway, his strategy worked. It wasn't that long

before I landed a role in a Broadway show. Naturally, my performance stood out."

"Naturally."

"And the next time, I auditioned for the lead and got it. It was a revival of *The Glass Menagerie*. I received rave reviews.

"Actually, those days in New York were some of the happiest I can remember. Alison was making a lot of money then and had a large apartment on Riverside Drive. She invited me to move in with her. She had met a great many people who were involved in show business. Not only actors and actresses, but producers, directors, entertainment lawyers, entrepreneurs, artists, all great contacts. Her parties were wonderful events. Some of the brightest and most charming people in New York City were there. Those early days were rather exciting.

"Rich people in fine clothing and jewelry, celebrities, influential people from all walks of life. She had a grand piano in her apartment and there was always entertainment—someone from a Broadway show would appear to sing or some rock star would show up and perform his or her songs."

"What was it like for two young Androgyne to live together?" He laughed before I had a chance to respond. "I can just imagine the confusion with the toothbrushes, or did Richard share yours and Alison share Nicholas's?"

"Very funny. No, we didn't share anything. And there was more than one bathroom, you know."

"But there must have been some difficulties, some problems. Right?"

"Not between us."

"Meaning not between you and Alison. But what about Nicholas and Richard?"

I turned and glared at him.

"What? What did I say now that was so terrible?" he whined, his arms out in protest.

"How do you know what questions to ask?"

He shrugged.

"I'm a detective, aren't I? If I didn't know what questions to ask, what the hell good would I be? I have a detective's intuition," he said, pointing to his temple. "So there were problems then?"

"There were difficult situations because of the males, yes. As hard as it may be for you to believe, female Androgyne get along with each other far better than male Androgyne do. They don't have the insecurities."

"Uh-huh. Meaning?"

"Meaning we don't have to go around proving ourselves to each other all the time. Men always feel their masculinity challenged. They're afraid their women will see them as diminished whenever they confront a taller, stronger, more dynamic man."

"And women don't have this fear? They're not afraid their men will look elsewhere?"

"Not androgynous females." He looked skeptical. "Maybe it has something to do with the hunt," I admitted. "The male Androgyne has to prove himself all the time. Every time he metamorphoses, he's challenged. It's essentially the essence of his existence. If he fails, he doesn't provide, doesn't keep his androgynous being going, and don't forget," I reminded him, "he has more than himself to think about."

"But how can he fail?" he countered. "Look at all his advantages—his good looks, his charm, his superior intellect and physical strength. Not to mention centuries of wisdom when it comes to seducing women. I'm just quoting things Richard said and implied," he said when I reacted to the way he rattled off all of it.

"He can't fail exactly, but he can fail to choose as well as another, I guess, and not provide as well. The results will be visible in the female who has that much less quality to draw upon for her own vitality and beauty."

"So something of a competition developed between Nicholas and Richard, a competition in how well they were providing for you and Alison," he concluded.

"Yes."

"And it affected you and Alison, how you got along together?"

"Yes." I looked away. I didn't want him to see the tears in my eyes.

"You don't sound too eager to talk about it."

"It wasn't pleasant . . . for anyone, and we all still disagree as to whose fault it was."

"Well, if you tell me about it, maybe I can decide."

I couldn't help smirking at him.

"I know, I know," he said. "It's presumptuous of me to assume an inferior could possibly have more wisdom than one of you, but sometimes it takes an outsider, someone who can be objective."

That made sense, but he was being manipulative.

"You're a shrewd one," I told him.

"Comes with the territory. It's how I survive, how I provide for myself." He smiled coyly and leaned over to kiss me on the cheek. "I'm just teasing you. So?"

"You will have two viewpoints on all this—mine and Richard's. Whose do you want to hear first?"

"Yours," he said quickly.

"All right, but if I'm going to tell you about those days, I could use some coffee to stay awake. How about you?"

"I'm so comfortable," he cried.

"It will only take a few minutes," I said, getting out of the bed. "You don't have to move. I'll bring it in."

I didn't want the coffee as much as I wanted a chance to gather my thoughts. It wasn't going to be easy to tell this part of my story, our story, and I wasn't sure I had the strength to go through it. I was afraid of some of the memories, what reviving them would do.

What I had to do was reinforce my purpose and strengthen my resolve. I had nearly lost it just before he submerged me in cold water. I had to be careful. I wanted this confession to be complete.

While I was making the coffee, the phone rang. I wasn't going to answer it, but I was afraid the detective might, so I lifted the receiver. Even before I spoke, I knew who it had to be. Who else would phone this late at night? Actually, I didn't have a chance to say hello.

"Richard?" I heard Nicholas ask.

"No," I said.

"He was supposed to meet me tonight," Nicholas said sharply. I knew he was lying.

"Obviously, he doesn't think so."

"Clea, what are you doing?" he asked. "Do you know what you're doing?"

"Michael's dead," I said.

"So?"

"You knew how I felt about him, and you knew what Richard was going to do."

"So?" he repeated.

"Why didn't you stop him? I thought you cared more about me."

"Oh, don't be so . . . so . . ."

"Inferior?"

"Yes. You knew that sort of relationship would come to no good. I want to see you," he said quickly. "Now. Before all this goes too far."

"No, that's impossible. I can't go anywhere tonight."

"Someone's there. That detective is there."

I didn't reply.

"Someone tried to kill me," I said. "They shot at me when I returned home from dinner tonight. Do you know anything about that?"

"Of course not. Who would try to kill you? You certainly don't think it was one of us, do you?"

"I don't know what to think."

"That's ridiculous. Listen to me . . ."

"I don't want to talk about it right now."

"Clea," he said in a firm, heavy voice, "don't do anything you will regret forever. An Androgyne who is scorned by her own people is the loneliest creature on the face of the earth."

"Good night, Nicholas."

"I'm going to wait for Richard right where we were supposed to meet," he said.

"Suit yourself."

"Clea . . ."

I cradled the receiver and made the coffee. He didn't call back, but when I returned to the bedroom and looked at my detective, I saw immediately that he had been listening in on the phone by the bed. I could see it in his eyes, in his attempt to disguise it. However, I said nothing. I handed him his cup of coffee and sat beside him on the bed.

"Very good," he said after his first sip. "A French roast?"

"Yes."

"You were going to talk about the New York days," he reminded me when I sat sipping my coffee and staring blankly ahead.

"The New York days. Soon after I had moved in with Alison, I was in this off-Broadway musical, *The Bag*

Lady by Sue Cohen. She and the play got a big write-up in *Time* and that brought attention to me. I had a great part, an opportunity to show my musical comedy skills, but I had to arrive at the theater hours before the curtain opened because I needed this elaborate makeup to turn me into an elderly street lady."

"Were there other Androgyne in the theatrical world then?"

"Oh yes. There was and is a large community of Androgyne in New York City in all walks of life: doctors, dentists, lawyers, businessmen, brokers . . . you name it, Androgyne are part of it. Of course, they're very supportive of each other. I imagine that each and every one of them at one time or another saw me perform on the stage in New York.

"One of them owns a famous discotheque." I paused, hesitant to reveal the name. It suddenly occurred to me that the detective might have a wider purpose—perhaps hunting down all my people. I didn't want to hurt anyone but Richard and me. But my detective read the meaning of my pause.

"You needn't worry. I'm not taking notes. What happens in New York is the New York Police Department's problem, not mine. I'm interested only in what's been happening here in my jurisdiction."

"Yes. Anyway, even though Androgyne would frequent the disco, it was understood that no male Androgyne would ever go there to hunt. Frequent pickups in one place might bring attention to that place."

"Very clever."

"I told you there were Androgyne in the major police departments everywhere."

"Right." He sipped his coffee and waited.

"After a while it was just natural for Richard and

Nicholas to go out together to hunt. Living as closely as we did, Alison and I, Richard and Nicholas, we began to synchronize our metamorphosing. Actually, Alison and I would gaze into each other's eyes and sense how much they wanted to be together. It was like two lovers looking longingly at each other through glass walls, their heartbeats quickening as the blood rushed to the surface and their desire for each other became all encompassing, demanding.

"We might be sitting and having breakfast or just having a casual conversation and it would come over us. For both of us, it was a new kind of passion—more than a sexual craving. It was a lust for life itself, a desire to satisfy the appetite of muscles and senses; we had hungry eyes, hungry lips, hungry ears, hungry fingers. We thirsted for each other's male companionship, and suddenly Alison stood in the way of Richard and I stood in the way of Nicholas. They became more and more demanding. It was like an addiction beginning slowly and gradually taking over our very being."

"You were like Dr. Jekyll and Mr. Hyde?" my detective concluded quickly.

"Yes, and like the character in that wonderful story, Mr. Hyde began to absorb Dr. Jekyll until it became harder and harder for Dr. Jekyll to reappear. In short, Nicholas and Richard began to dominate us.

"It presented us with some logistical problems. A number of times Alison and I were late for appointments. Twice, I missed an audition. She missed three. Alison and I talked it over and decided we would try to resist what we Androgyne informally refer to as 'The Knocking on the Door.' "

"*Macbeth*," the detective said.

"Christ, what did you do, teach a course in literature?" He smiled a smile of self-satisfaction.

"Actually, I'm in training for *Jeopardy*. How successful were you two in preventing the metamorphosing?"

"Not successful at all. If Richard appeared, Nicholas wasn't far behind, and vice versa. Neither Alison nor I could resist very well. We pleaded, explained, warned, but they were both in a very selfish state of mind in those days. Eventually, however, it backfired."

"How so?"

"As I told you before, they became very competitive. At first their teaming up for hunts was novel and brought them more success. Most single women like to go out in pairs. Even in today's far more liberated society, it's more difficult for a single woman to go out on the town by herself than it is for a single man. It's only natural that a woman would have a sense of security when she went out with a friend. But you know what happens when one girl finds someone and the other doesn't . . . it makes it harder for her.

"So Richard and Nicholas would focus in on these helpless pairs of women seeking romance and excitement. In the early days, they didn't care who got whom. A kill was a kill, but also, as I told you before, there are kills that are better than others, quality kills.

"Alison claims it was me, but I know it was she who started it," I said sadly and sipped my coffee.

"Started what?"

"Comparing. Suddenly, my hair was richer, thicker, healthier than hers. My complexion was softer, my eyes brighter. I had more energy. All this explained why my career was suddenly exploding while hers seemed to have reached its plateau. She had tried a number of times to make the transition from modeling to acting, but she wasn't being very successful. Naturally, her perception filtered down to Nicholas.

"She was wrong, of course. Actually, I thought her hair was nicer and her complexion richer."

"So you complained too?"

"No, not exactly. Oh, I suppose merely thinking these things was the same as lodging a complaint. Richard sensed it, but Alison was the one who vocalized; she complained far more than I did, sulked, started to leave hints around the apartment: notes, evidence of new beauty creams, vitamins, et cetera."

"Hmmm. Sounds like you're not being honest about female Androgyne. They suffer jealousies of each other too."

"We weren't jealous; we were just upset with the way Nicholas and Richard were going about their hunts and how that was affecting us."

My detective smirked.

"It's not the same thing," I insisted.

"All right, all right. I'll take your word for it. So what did you do about it?"

"We didn't do anything. Once the message reached them, *they* eventually did something. They began to argue about the choices, who would get the prettier, more vivacious prey, and soon after they decided they would be better off going out on their own. When they began to do that, the synchronized metamorphosing came to an end."

"You sure you two weren't just jealous of the male bonding, like two wives envious of the good times their husbands had without them?"

"Typical male conclusion."

He laughed.

"Well, it doesn't sound like things became so terrible for you though. What were you implying before when you said things weren't so pleasant? There had to be more to it," he added, coaxing me to continue.

"The competitiveness didn't end when they ended their team hunts," I said.

"Oh?"

"They were like two cavemen eying each other's cave, coveting each other's results. The more beautiful I looked, the more jealous Nicholas was of Richard."

"And vice versa?"

"Yes."

"So what happened?"

When I didn't reply, he touched my hand and I looked up.

"You've told me this much, why not the rest?"

"Nicholas accused Richard of rape," I blurted, "but it wasn't Richard's fault; it was Alison's. She wanted it."

The detective sat back, nodding softly with understanding. "He made her pregnant."

"Yes."

"Let me see if I remember what you told me—when an Androgyne becomes pregnant, the male part of her is virtually imprisoned within for nine months?"

"It's longer than nine months because the mother breast-feeds."

"How long was it?"

"Just about a year," I said.

"During which time, Richard was free to metamorphose and hunt and Nicholas was incarcerated in Alison?"

"Yes."

"And when he finally metamorphosed, he accused Richard of doing this deliberately, to put him out of commission, so to speak?"

"Yes," I said. "Actually, Alison accused Richard of it first. That's why I said she claimed she was raped."

"Fascinating. Was she right?"

"You're the detective," I replied. We stared at each other a moment.

"Why didn't Alison have an abortion? Surely the pregnancy interfered with her career."

"Androgynous progeny are far more valuable than inferior progeny simply because there are far fewer of us. The importance of breeding our own kind is emphasized from the moment we can understand the meaning of the words. We don't get pregnant that easily. If Alison had had an abortion, she would have been ostracized."

Recalling Nicholas's words just spoken to me on the phone, I added, "And an Androgyne who is scorned by her own people is the loneliest creature on the face of the earth."

"Won't you be scorned by your own people?" he asked softly, "when they find out what you're doing here with me?"

"Yes, but I don't intend to remain on the face of the earth," I said.

We were both quiet for a long moment. My detective sat back thoughtfully, his hands behind his head, staring.

"Aren't you tired yet?" I finally asked.

"No."

"Do all detectives have your energy and perseverance?"

"Some, not all." He smiled. "Why, are you too tired to go on?"

"I didn't say that."

"Actually, you don't look sleepy. Your rosy complexion has returned and your eyes are bright. You look revived, as if relating all this invigorates you."

"Maybe it does." I finished my coffee and put the cup on the nightstand.

"Well, since you're up to it," he said, "I'd like to hear Richard's account of all this. Actually," he mumbled, "I'd like to hear Alison's and Nicholas's accounts as well."

"What?"

"Wouldn't it be something . . . the four of you: first you and Alison and then you both metamorphose, and I hear Richard and Nicholas."

I stared at him. He was beginning to worry me. Whenever I was in the midst of telling him the most serious things, he made jokes, and whenever I was being flippant, he looked serious. Perhaps all this was overwhelming for him, and in the end, he would be useless to me.

"Well you can't hear them," I said dryly.

"Just a thought."

I continued to stare at him.

"Tell me," I said, "what did you think when you first saw Michael's body?"

"Michael? Oh. I thought . . . shit . . . what the hell happened here? He looked like someone used his head for a baseball."

"And what else? Come on," I coaxed, "you saw the rest of him."

The detective squirmed.

"He had been castrated," he finally said.

"How? By now you have your reports. How?" I insisted.

"Human teeth."

I grimaced.

"Still think this is all so funny?"

"I never said it was funny. I . . ."

"The man who did that to him claimed to have loved him as much as a man can love another man, as much as an Androgyne can love an inferior."

"Love does things to you, tears you up sometimes."

I didn't laugh.

"Look," he said, "I have to be a little light-headed about all this. If I don't joke, it will destroy me. It's a madhouse out there, even without you and your kind. Human beings do the same horrible things to each other—they murder each other in hundreds of hideous ways and sometimes for no more reason than they didn't like the way the victim glanced at them.

"High drama almost doesn't exist in the streets. It used to be a police detective had a case of jealousy or greed or lust for power as the motive. He had something he could sink his teeth into. Nowadays the motives are as simple as 'he was in my parking space.'

"You find the good stuff only in mystery stories," he concluded so sadly I had to laugh.

"I feel sorry for you."

"You should. Anyway, now you can understand why I am so interested in what you have to say and what Richard has to say."

I nodded. He could be sincere when he wanted to be.

"All right," I said reaching for the diary on the nightstand beside me, "but some of what Richard has written is untrue. He's lying to cover up his own . . . selfishness," I said. "And for the Androgyne, selfishness is a cardinal sin."

"How do I know you're not the one who's lying and you're not the one who was selfish?"

"You keep telling me you're a detective," I said, "and it's your job to find the truth. So find it."

He laughed, but my heart had begun to pound again.

What if he was right? What if I was lying to myself as well as to him? What if I was confessing to the wrong crimes?

My fingers trembled as I turned the pages.

NINE

"*FROM THE BEGINNING I found New York City to be more exciting than any place I had been because of its tempo and cosmopolitan population. I discovered that all of us had a similar reaction. For the Androgyne, it was as if we were mountain lions slipped into a boxcar filled with sheep. Everywhere I turned there were attractive females. (I almost wrote nutritious instead of attractive, for that's what they were to me. They literally looked delicious, making my mouth water.) I found myself standing stupidly on street corners, turning this way and that to follow the feminine scents. I could close my eyes and taste their skin on my lips, feel their breasts in my hands. Every avenue, every block presented still more exotic delicacies.*

"*I would walk for hours on end just to peruse the selection, and whenever I stood on a corner to wait for the light to change and I was in the midst of a half dozen or so young women, I would feel my heart pound and my body stir in a way unlike it ever had before.*

"*In the beginning, before Nicholas and I emerged simultaneously, I often went out on a hunt and nearly failed to consummate it because every time I settled on a victim, I thought there just might be a better one around the corner. I would find myself wandering for hours without making a decision and suddenly I would realize I was going to let the night pass without a kill.*

"Nicholas told me he had had comparable experiences when he and Alison first arrived in New York. Only he had one additional reaction—like a child locked in a candy store, he became gluttonous, sometimes making two kills a night, one in one borough and one in another. Normally, there were a number of violent deaths in the city, so he didn't think his actions would matter, but his hunger drew the attention of other Androgyne, when one, who was a homicide detective, realized what was happening. They confronted him in a bar in Greenwich Village.

" 'Actually,' he told me, 'this detective seized my arm, showed me his badge and asked me to come out with him. There were two other Androgyne waiting in his car, both in tuxedos. They had just come from some party at Gracie Mansion and they were very angry. They told me I was putting the entire community in danger of being discovered and making it very difficult for others to hunt. They took me for a ride down to some deserted docks on the West Side and frightened me so much I retreated into Alison and remained submerged for weeks,' he said.

"By the time Clea and I had arrived in New York, Nicholas was calmer and more sophisticated. In fact, I was glad when he began to appear with me because he could show me around. He knew which bars and discos were frequented by single young women, which were mostly gay, and which catered to a much younger crowd. Occasionally, we both wanted a very young girl. They have a different sort of energy, what Nicholas sometimes referred to as a 'cleaner-burning fuel.'

"Nicholas believed, and I suppose there is some validity to that belief, that we are what we eat, or in our case, what we consume. In a real sense, we are the sum total of *all of our victims. Our prey become the building blocks with which we construct ourselves.*

"Sometimes, it was a question of variety. We sought diversity for its own sake. We are not incapable of boredom and just as there is a monotony in consuming the same old thing, there is a monotony in choosing the same old prey. And when it came to seeking variety, what better place to be than New York? Here we had a wonderful choice of black women, Oriental, East Europeans, Hispanic, etc., all within a relatively small area; and Nicholas, as I said, already knew where we could find what we wanted.

"So, we would begin our evenings by first deciding what each of us desired or perhaps needed. Usually, we were in agreement; our needs were remarkably similar, perhaps because Alison and Clea had similar needs; but occasionally one or the other had to compromise if we were to hunt together.

"I suppose we could say we benefited somewhat from Alison and Clea being so theatrical. Both Nicholas and I had inherited their dramatic tendencies. Before every hunt we would decide on roles to play. Sometimes we were brothers in business; sometimes he or I would be visiting from another country, usually a country that would be of interest to our prey. Occasionally, we passed ourselves off as models or actors. We loved affecting accents. Nicholas does this great Englishman, Lord Livingston. Whatever we decided to be, we found that young women were gullible. Few, if any, challenged us, and even those who did, did so with the air of nonchalance. They didn't really care. Everyone, in one way or another, was trying to be someone else anyway.

"She was a waitress who was really an actress; she was a legal secretary, but she expected to become a lawyer; she was a hostess, but she wanted to be an artist. On and *on it went—a world of dual identities. We fit right in.*

"Actually, there was never a question of our being successful; together we glided smoothly and easily over the hunting grounds, or what the inferiors disdainfully refer to as their 'watering holes.' How ironic. Just as a tiger or lion might go down to a 'watering hole' in the jungle and wait in the shadows, braced to pounce on its prey, we went to these bars and discotheques.

"Immediately after we made our entrances, we would stand and gaze out over the crowd of revelers and drink in the mixture of the hot, sweaty scents undetectable to them. We surveyed the panorama: a tableau of youth, vigor and energy. Their excited faces were made to look more so when they danced and bathed in the silver and blue, orange and pink flashing lights that dropped their rainbow of colors from dazzling ceilings filled with spinning silver balls and multicolored cubes—a veritable man-made galaxy of sensuous stars. It encouraged abandon. The loud music permeated through every pore of their bodies so that the incessant rhythms became kin with their very heartbeats.

" 'See,' Nicholas said, 'how even though they go onto the dance floor with a partner, they soon lose any bond and isolate themselves in their own private fantasy. Especially the women,' he added, probably because they were our primary concern.

"But it was true. Women, whom I would imagine to be mousy, shy types, withdrawn and cloistered within their conservative clothes and hairstyles, were out there gyrating, beckoning to some phantom of the disco, imagining themselves the center of his libidinous attention, desired, craved, about to be chosen for a night of ecstasy.

"Nicholas and I agreed—nothing in this modern soci-

ety trumpeted the self-centered nature of it as much as this frenzied dancing. It was almost as if we could hear them chanting: 'Me, me, me, look at me, me, me.' It made it all that much easier for us.

"We descended like two bats out of the darkness above them, directed toward our particular victims by our own special radar, a sensing in on the vulnerable, the sweet, the rich-blooded and ripe women longing to be held and wanted and stroked. We invaded dreams, honed in on the hungriest. Frustration hung over them like a cloud threatening to burst with the cold rain of disappointment. Satisfaction was eluding them yet again.

"We saw their desperation grow as the night wore on. Their eyes moved from one man to another hoping to find themselves discovered.

"But most drifted off, still unattached by the evening's end. They stopped dancing and retreated to what solace they could find with companions who had met a similar fate. They gathered at the bar, forced laughter, and punctuated their inane discussions with an occasional glance back at the lucky fish who had been hooked and were being reeled in.

" 'The world is a lonely place,' Nicholas said and then laughed. 'Fortunately, for us.'

"Of course, he was right. Wherever lust is married to loneliness, there is a wedding feast to which Androgyne have an open invitation.

"We plunged, moving like two dark shadows over the floor, our eyes riveted on our prey. Even before we arrived, they sensed our coming and were drawn to us. A smile, a query, a suggestion and they were snared easy as one, two, three.

"I can't recall the names or even a particular face. Now, whenever I think back to those days, the different young* *women meld into one. Even the different races, the black, the brown, the yellow and the white lose identity. I see a universal victim; I see beneath the skin, for whenever an Androgyne takes his prey, he draws from her essence, from deep down into her very being, and therefore the color of her eyes and hair, the color of her skin, her height, her weight is incidental.*

"It is as if we walked about with X-ray eyes. Inferior men, whose ken is limited, whose vision is shorter, whose senses are restricted, whose very being is circumscribed and fixed, would find no pleasure in our view. But that is why they would rather make love to a woman who has had a plastic surgeon reform her face, stuff her breasts with silicone, tighten her buttocks, suck fat out of her midsection than make love to many of the women we choose. And therefore, why we often have such good choices: the leftovers.

"All these nights were the same for Nicholas and me: We came, we saw, we conquered. In the beginning and for a while afterward, we simply let our instincts gravitate us to one or the other of the pair we targeted. If there were significant differences between one or the other and one of us had an advantage, we managed to compensate the next time out.

"But one night as we left the apartment to go on a hunt, Nicholas told me of Alison's displeasure. What surprised me was his agreement—she wasn't all wrong; he had been getting the short end of things too many times, not that we were keeping track.

"Despite my surprise, I didn't argue. When it came time to make our choices, I let him go first. He went first the next time out and the time after that as well.

"One night, I challenged his choice.

" 'You've taken the richest prize for some time now,

Nicholas,' I told him. 'Tonight should be my turn. I have felt Clea's concern, just as you felt Alison's.'

" *'But I had a lot to make up for,' he replied. When he grimaced and whined like that, I saw Alison's face flash in his.*

" *'That's not true,' I said softly. 'Even if there was some sort of imbalance, surely we have corrected it by now. I should take the girl on the right.'*

" *'No,' he said. 'If you want to take them together, I take the one on the right. Otherwise, we go after lone prey.'*

"This recalcitrance wasn't like him. He had had a bad metamorphosis, I concluded. If I had a propensity for the tongue in cheek, I would have said, he wasn't himself tonight.

" *'Then we'll have to go our separate ways tonight,'* I said. 'I'm sorry.'

" *'So be it,' Nicholas replied. I decided to let him have this entire watering hole and went off to another location. Soon after that, our synchronized metamorphosing came to an end, and we hunted in different parts of the city.*

"I can't say I didn't miss his companionship. Whenever I metamorphosed, I watched Alison carefully to see if she was on the verge of changing. I think she misunderstood my intentions, and I know that even Clea, when she reads this, might not believe me when I say, I did not expect or intend what happened next."

At mention of my name, I paused in the reading of the diary and took a deep breath. My coffee was cold, but I sipped it anyway. My detective stared at me without speaking.

"Are you all right?" he finally asked. I nodded, but closed my eyes.

.

"You know," I said, "that Nicholas knows you're here." I turned to him. "You listened in on my phone call before," I said accusingly.

"Couldn't help it," he said shaking his head. "I don't know whether I am a man who has become a detective, or a detective who just happens to be a man. I do so many things instinctively these days. Would you believe that two days ago I followed a man from Westwood to East L.A. because I thought he looked suspicious and might be involved in a cocaine ring dealing UCLA students? Turned out he was a shoe wholesaler. Yet I still wonder if there was something in the heels of those shoes . . . Anyway, I can't help myself. But I apologize. I shouldn't have done it."

"They're going to want to kill you even more now," I said.

"Oh? So maybe we can safely assume that bullet was meant for me."

"Maybe," I admitted.

"I'd better stay away from the windows."

"I wouldn't joke about it."

"I'm not. Anyway, it looks like I would be wise to remain here until morning." He put his hands behind his head and smiled.

"Isn't there anyone who will miss you, wonder where you are and what's happened to you?" I asked. "Family, friends, girlfriends?"

"Everyone close to me is used to my not showing up for days on end. I don't even have an answering machine anymore because the tapes run out, there are so many messages."

"You like this life?"

"I told you," he said. "It's who I am. Same as you in a sense . . . it's the hand I've been dealt."

"Hardly the same thing. You have alternatives."

"Apparently, so do you. Otherwise, I wouldn't be here right now listening to all this, right?"

"If you can consider suicide an alternative," I said.

"You sound like you're having second thoughts. Are you?"

I thought about Michael and about the agony of my existence.

"You began by telling me God had made your kind first; you were the chosen people."

"It's what we were told," I said.

"You don't believe it anymore?"

"I don't know. Let's just say, I have doubts."

"Isn't that blasphemy?"

"If thinking is blasphemy, if feeling deeply is blasphemy, if challenging and questioning is blasphemy, then yes, I am guilty of blasphemy," I replied.

"Jesus," he said, "when you get fired up like that, you are so beautiful, you make me crumble inside. I want to be putty in your hands." I nodded. "Typical inferior reaction, huh?" he asked, smirking.

"Yes."

"What's to become of us? Will we forever be prey for Androgyne, dust for worms?" He laughed at the expression on my face.

"The philosophical detective," I said. "You don't make love like a man with his mind in the clouds."

"I guess I know when to come down to earth." His gaze dropped hungrily to the diary in my hands. Or was he simply afraid of the look in my eyes? Anticipating what lay ahead in these pages, I felt myself stirred. I ran my tongue across my lips and pulled my shoulders back so my firm breasts would lift. But my detective didn't seem to notice; his mind was locked on one thing.

"You're right about yourself," I said dryly. "You are a detective who just happens to be a man."

He roared, and I turned back to the diary.

"Nicholas believes I tried to prevent his metamorphosing during those days in New York by seducing Alison so that she would fight his interfering emergence. The truth is Alison seduced me so that I would keep Clea from reappearing."

"I've heard that sort of defense before," my detective remarked. "Three out of four rapists have it imbedded in their brains: She was asking for it. Some juries buy it, especially the ones with frustrated spinsters complementing the angry men. Women are definitely at a disadvantage in this society, even androgynous ones."

I didn't look up from the diary. I let his words pass over me like an annoying wind.

"Sexual relations between two Androgyne are, on the surface, not much different from sexual relations between two inferiors. But when we are truly attracted to each other, we have the ability to see both of our dual personalities. Sporadically, Nicholas flashed in and out of Alison's face.

"I suppose the easiest way for an inferior to understand this would be for him or her to imagine his lover's sibling. Sometimes, brothers and sisters have such a close resemblance anyway.

"Essentially, what this means for us is the necessity of a compatibility, not only between the male and female Androgyne who happen to be metamorphosed at the time, but a compatibility between their submerged personalities as well. In essence four people fall in love or make love every time an androgynous female and an androgynous male do."

"Holy shit," the detective said. When I looked up at

him, I saw his eyes were wide and he was shaking his head. "Can you imagine the confusion on Valentine's Day."

"This concept is probably beyond your ability to understand," I replied dryly.

"I mean, it's hard enough nowadays for only two people to fall in love and maintain a relationship, but to have to have four independent personalities compatible . . . the divorce rate would double. Good business for marriage counselors, of course," he muttered.

"I wonder if I'm wasting my time with you," I said.

"Easy. I'm just trying to come to grips with all this. The line between tragedy and comedy is really a very thin one. What's tragic one day becomes absurdly comical after the passage of time."

"We happen to be in the present right now and right now, it's not comical to me."

"Okay, okay. Let me ask you this. If Nicholas didn't want Alison to fall in love with Richard and you didn't want Richard to fall in love with Alison, how could it happen? Given what you just read from Richard's diary, that is."

"If you will recall, I told you I found Nicholas quite attractive from the start and he . . . before his conversion . . . imagined himself kissing me, wanting me."

"Ah, so the seeds were always there?"

"Yes, but it's a little more complicated than all that. There is one aspect of our particular being that put us into jealous conflict. You inferiors suffer from Oedipal complexes and Electra complexes . . . sons jealous of mothers and their lovers, daughters jealous of fathers and theirs . . . we suffer from a Narcissistic jealousy— we can't help but resent it when our male or female counterparts fall in love with someone else."

"So no matter who Richard fell for, you would be jealous?"

"Exactly."

"And vice versa, which explains why he killed Michael Barrington," the detective concluded quickly.

"Yes," I said. I felt a tightening in my abdomen. It was as if a giant vise had been clamped down on my torso. I knew it was Richard's rage. His entire submerged being was closed into a red fist. The pain of my betrayal forced him to embrace himself with a male Androgyne's might. He was literally crushing himself to death within me. I had to take deep breaths.

My detective put his hand on my shoulder.

"Are you able to go on?"

"Yes," I said even though I was crying. "You see," I continued, "it was even worse because I had fallen in love with an inferior. Richard did all he could to destroy it, including seducing him."

My detective nodded, his eyes filled with sympathy.

"And in a way it all started with this mess between you and Alison, Richard and Nicholas?"

"Yes."

"Then let me hear the rest of it," he said. "If you're sure you can go on."

I nodded. A few deep breaths relieved the knotting within me and I was able to resume reading.

"Alison continued to pursue me in little ways: parading about half naked under the guise of wanting my opinion of this dress or that, asking me to massage her because she had a muscular ache here or there, coming in on me whenever I showered or dressed . . . on and on it went: the seduction. I tried to resist. I had other things to do, but she'd be there in the morning, bringing me a cup of coffee. Dressed in a diaphanous nightgown, she would

sit at the foot of my bed and peer alluringly at me over her own coffee cup.

"One night after I had emerged and I was preparing to go out on a hunt, she came to me in tears. She had auditioned for a commercial and not gotten it.

" 'I'm losing my uniqueness,' she cried. 'I'm not as beautiful as I was. Something terrible is happening.'

" 'Nonsense,' I told her. 'It's only in your mind. You're more beautiful than ever. I don't see how anyone can resist you.'

" 'You do,' she said. She denies saying these things and doing these things now, but she did.

" 'I don't resist you, I don't want to upset the balance we've all maintained so well.'

She pouted.

" 'If I can't be attractive to you, I must be losing it,' she insisted. She was crying now so I put my arm around her and kissed her to comfort her, trying to keep it brotherly."

"Oh brother," the detective quipped.

"But she misunderstood, deliberately misunderstood. She turned her lips to me. I tried closing my eyes so I wouldn't look into hers, and when I did so, she brought her lips to mine. It was the first time I had kissed an androgynous female passionately. For me it was as if I were an inferior male making love to a female for the first time, a willing, demanding, lustful female. Unfamiliar with this experience, I groped about awkwardly looking for a graceful way to restrain myself, but she continued to arouse me until I lost complete control.

"Before I knew it we were wrapped in each other's arms, our bodies naked. I heard Clea's cries, and I was sure Alison heard Nicholas's, but we were both beyond their influence, caught up in our own sexual roller coaster.

"I forgot about my hunt, forgot the real reason for my metamorphosis. We stayed with each other all that night and into the next morning. Every time I fell asleep, I saw Clea trying to begin her metamorphosis. It was like a recurrent nightmare, appearing each time in a different version of the same story: Clea trying to pry open a heavy dark door, getting it partially open only to have it slam shut on her fingers; Clea coming up through a manhole on a dark street, but just as she began to emerge, a heavy truck running over the lid and sending her falling back to the sewers; Clea in the Arctic Ocean under a ceiling of ice searching for an opening, but just after she found one, the ice closing, driving her under the water. Her cheeks were bursting; her eyes were bulging.

"I woke abruptly, the bad dreams forcing me to regress to childhood. Alison comforted me as would a mother comfort her infant. She embraced me and rocked me in her arms, kissing my cheeks and stroking my forehead until I felt safe again and could close my eyes.

"Making love to Alison was draining, as making love to an Androgyne would be for any other Androgyne because it's giving without drawing the needed energy. When I awoke late in the morning of the following day, I felt exhausted. Nothing she could give me to eat helped. We both knew I needed a victim desperately, but I was so tired, I didn't have the stamina to go out, and especially didn't look vigorous and attractive enough to attract prey. My image in the mirror looked pale, sickly."

"Why didn't the lovemaking have the same effect on Alison?" my detective asked.

"He's getting to that. Be patient," I told him and read on.

"Alison came to me and sat on the bed. She held my hand and stroked my hair affectionately.

" 'Poor Richard,' she said. 'And poor Clea.'

"I saw the tight, little smile in her face. She was enjoying the disadvantageous position Clea and I were in. Part of that was Nicholas's influence, of course, even though he was sinking deeply. I know Alison didn't realize it yet, but she should have. She should have felt more fatigue and needed Nicholas to metamorphose for a kill, as much as I needed to kill for Clea and myself.

"But something of me had combined with something of her and the fertilization had given her a healthy pregnant woman's vigor. Only she had yet to realize the reason for her vitality.

"I started to get up.

" 'Oh rest,' she said. She sighed deeply. Then she looked at me and laughed. 'I'll bring you breakfast in bed.'

"She pressed me back against the pillow and kissed my cheek. I knew what she meant.

"She was gone for a little more than an hour before returning with a teenage prostitute, some runaway surviving on what she could offer between her legs. I thought the girl was rather dim, like a lamp during a brownout. Her vibrancy had already dwindled. It wouldn't be anything close to a quality kill, but it would be sufficient to give me enough strength to stand on my own two feet.

" 'What's wrong with him?' the girl asked. She had thin red hair chopped short, a narrow face with a small mouth and a small nose. Her gray eyes looked more like two orbs with blotches of ash at their centers. There was a slight blush in her rather gaunt cheeks. She was small breasted, but she had a narrow waist and long, inviting legs. She wore a pair of jeans cut so the cheeks of her buttocks spilled out from under the jagged hems. Her *dark blue blouse was opened so that her shallow cleavage was visible.*

" 'Nothing's wrong with him,' Alison said. 'Except he's terribly depressed. His girlfriend left him for another man,' she said with an impish smile. I could feel Clea cringe within me.

" 'Oh,' the teenage prostitute laughed at that, her laughter sounding like the tinkle of broken glasses. She could understand and appreciate Alison's fabrication. Human misery was the trough from which she now fed herself and she felt more comfortable in the presence of other unlucky people. It made her feel less alone, less diminished.

" 'Can you cheer him up?' Alison asked her.

" 'Sure,' she said. She smiled at me and her toothy grin suddenly suggested the vicious grimace of a skeleton. Very portentous, I thought as she sauntered over to the side of the bed.

" 'You gonna watch?' she asked Alison. 'Cause that's another ten dollars if you do.'

"Alison considered it. She looked at me to see my reaction. I had none.

" 'All right,' she said pulling the vanity chair away from the vanity table and placing it at the other side of the bed. 'Another ten dollars.'

"The teenage prostitute looked happy about it. I thought she was as happy about having an audience as she was about getting another ten dollars.

" 'Hi there,' she said to me. She unbuttoned the remainder of her skimpy shirt and stripped it away. The flesh around her nipples quivered. Because I didn't move, because I simply lay there gazing up quietly, my eyes expressionless, she paused and looked at Alison.

" 'He ain't paralyzed or nothin', is he?'

" 'Paralyzed with depression,' Alison said. The teenage prostitute nodded as though she had come across this many, many times.

"For a moment I had the weird feeling I was about to be examined by a physician. Are prostitutes a kind of surgeon of the soul? I wondered. Could their sort of sex be considered a treatment, a remedy for frustration or loneliness?

"I looked at Alison, and I knew she was wondering something similar by the way she gazed at the young girl and at me.

"Amazingly, the young prostitute said, 'I can cure that.'

"She peeled away my blanket to find me naked beneath. I could see she was grateful for little favors—undressing her clients or patients, as it were, was more like menial labor. The real art work came afterward.

"She dropped her own shorts with a quick, almost invisible movement unfastening them. She wore nothing underneath. Her hip bones were very prominent and her small stomach looked sunken, in retreat. The path of pubic hair curled upward until it became a thin line to her bellybutton. She really wasn't very attractive, even to a desperately frustrated man, I thought. Surely Alison could have done better. The wry smile on her face told me she hadn't tried to; in fact, she might have sought just such a victim on purpose. She didn't want Clea's beauty nourished beyond her own.

"The teenage girl straddled me and stroked my genitals with a knowing hand. I was so disgusted, I was half tempted to resist, but hunger and need took control. When I was hard and erect, the victim lowered herself onto me, unknowingly, like a Roman soldier impaling himself on a stake. She slipped me into her and began her slow rise and fall.

"*I gazed at Alison who seemed genuinely absorbed in what was happening. Then I turned my attention to the victim and began to draw from her.*

"*Her eyes opened with surprise as I became more vigorous. She assumed she was performing well and doing what she had been brought here to do. She was, of course, but she was still unaware of it.*

"*Soon, however, something that had become perfunctory and routine to her took on a new significance. She who thought herself expert at arousing her customers, now found herself quite aroused. Her breathing quickened and so did her pace. The faster she drove herself at me, the faster I accepted and demanded more.*

"*The climax came quickly and I drew her life out of her in slow, long thrusts, siphoning the energy, the very essence of her fragile being. Her dim light that had brightened for a few ecstatic moments, dimmed rapidly again. Her ashen eyes darkened as blood drained from her lips and the surface of her skin. I felt her fold as if she were a paper doll. Her eyes went up and back into her head, her throat closed with a gurgle and her heart flattened and stopped as if it were a punctured bicycle tire. Then her thin, bony form fell softly to me and I threw off what was now the empty shell of her.*

"*I sat up quickly, revived. Alison rose without speaking and went out to get a garbage bag. While I dressed, she slipped the bag over the corpse and tied it neatly closed.*

"*'Can you drop this in the incinerator?' she asked. 'I have to get ready for an audition. I'm up for a network commercial.'*

"*'This was the best you could do,' I said disdainfully, pointing to the shrouded corpse. She was smiling with ugly self-satisfaction. I could feel Clea rising, her anger now creating stronger impetus for a metamorphosis.*

" 'On a moment's notice, yes. I would think you would be a little more appreciative,' she said, which only inflamed Clea's ire more.

"I seized the bag and lifted it off the bed with one hand.

" 'Will we have supper together?' Alison called, 'or will Clea be returning?'

" 'I don't know,' I said. I didn't. I only knew I had to go out and hunt for myself, for my hunger hadn't been satiated and Clea demanded more nourishment.

"Late that evening I did return, swollen, spry and strong. I had taken a beautiful young NYU co-ed in Washington Square Park, who happened to have been a drama student on scholarship. Her talent enriched both my and Clea's blood.

"The apartment was dark when I arrived. I was set to go to our room and retreat. Clea was gaining on me, her strength growing every moment.

"At first I thought neither Alison nor Nicholas was home, but when I flicked the light switch, I found Alison sitting in the darkness. She looked distraught, even somewhat dazed.

" 'What are you doing sitting there in the dark?' I asked. When she didn't reply, I thought I knew the answer. 'You didn't get the commercial?'

" 'I didn't even go to the audition,' she replied.

" 'Oh? and why not?'

" 'After you left I started to get ready. When I gazed at myself in the mirror, I sensed something different. There was something different about the way I was thinking . . . the sound of my thoughts . . . something different in my eyes . . . '

" 'Oh?'

" 'You know what I'm talking about. You knew before I left, didn't you?'

" 'No,' I lied.

" 'I'm pregnant. I didn't sense it before because I was so concerned about you, I didn't think about myself. But Nicholas . . . '

"She looked down, the tears streaming.

" 'Alison,' I said moving toward her. She cowered away.

" 'No!' she cried. 'Don't touch me.'

"Her eyes were wide, wild. I stood still, waiting. She began to sob.

" 'You did this to me, to us. Poor Nicholas,' she said shaking her head. 'When I close my eyes, I see him sleeping in a coffin.'

" 'Alison, you can't . . . you shouldn't blame me. You wanted it as much as I did; you were driven by the same passions. You neglected to take precautions.'

" 'You knew what you were doing; it was deliberate, planned . . . ' she said, her eyes red with accusation. I shook my head.

" 'You're rationalizing your own guilt,' I said, but I could see how it was and I didn't want to get into an argument. Besides, Clea was pounding on the door. My voice was up in pitch, my skin was tightening.

"I left her sitting there and retreated to the bedroom."

"What happened after that?" the detective asked as I was closing Richard's diary.

"In the morning when I emerged, Alison was already gone. She couldn't abort the child, but she wanted to make arrangements immediately for some other Androgyne to adopt it. She wasn't ready to be a mother. Actually, she's never been ready and never will."

"So where is the child . . . Richard's child?"

"I don't know. Alison wouldn't tell, and neither Richard nor I pursued."

"Richard would have no say in its disposition?"

"No."

My detective was thoughtful for a long moment.

"What happened afterward, when Nicholas could reappear?"

"I told you . . . he was angry; he accused Richard of rape. I had moved out of the apartment by then. My New York days were coming to an end. I had been seen in a play by a movie director, and he offered me a part in a film, a lead."

"*Playmates*. You played that woman imprisoned in the home of that mad family."

"You've seen that?"

"I've seen all of your films."

I studied him. I shouldn't have any reason to be suspicious of that, I thought. I had many fans who had seen every one of my films, but somehow, I had never expected so much devotion from him.

"Yes, well it wasn't my best performance by any means, but it had sufficient enough impact to start my career rolling."

"Rocketing would be more like it. And so you returned to La-La Land?"

"Yes, but it wasn't pleasant at first. For one thing there was my mother's unexpected death."

"Strange way to refer to murder," he said. I looked up sharply.

"It was officially labeled an accidental death."

He shook his head.

"A cover-up if I ever saw one. But now, after hearing all that you have told me, I have one question for you—

why did you and your people want to disguise a murder as an accident?"

"How did you know we did?"

"I didn't," he said smiling. "I only suspected someone had. Thanks for confirming it," he added and sat back with a smug smile of self-satisfaction smeared over his face.

"You bastard."

He shrugged.

"I told you—I'm a good detective. Now, will you tell me why?"

"Why should I?"

"I have a feeling you never approved of what they did; you never liked the cover-up, and that's part of why you came to me in the first place, part of why you are disgusted being what you are."

He really was a good detective. He was right, of course. I would tell him all of it.

TEN

I ROSE FROM the bed and went to the window, parting the curtains to gaze out and up. Santa Ana winds had swept the sky clean of clouds and the unobstructed stars blazed brightly, their light more magnified and clearer than ever. Such a sky always made me more aware of how insignificant we all were, even the Androgyne. That and the mention of my mother's death reminded me just how much I missed her. We had often had nights like this where she had lived in Pacific Palisades after she had retired from modeling and doing television commercials.

"Maybe you shouldn't stand by the window like that," the detective said softly. He, too, had risen from the bed and stood behind me. I felt his hands on my shoulders as he drew me back. "I'd hate to lose you before I heard your whole story."

"Thanks for your sincere concern."

He turned me to him and smiled.

"I'm just kidding. I'd hate to lose you, period." He brought his lips to mine, just grazing them at first and then pressing them harder and harder until I responded. I felt his erection build as he pressed it between my legs and for a moment, it felt like Richard's erection in the midst of a metamorphose. I gasped.

The detective began a slow descent down my body, kissing his way between my breasts. His hands traveled down my back and settled on my rear. He hovered over the small of my stomach and then pressed his lips against my pubic hair. His tongue moved like a small creature, groping until the tip of it settled comfortably inside me. I moaned again, surprised at how quickly my legs weakened, but delighted by the electric tingle that fanned out over the inside of my thighs.

His hands urged me down to the floor. Never retreating from the pocket between my legs, he manipulated me until I was on my back, my legs up and around his head. Then he appeared, his eyes luminous and he slithered in between my legs, drawing himself up and over my torso until his erection parked itself firmly within me. We moved slowly, building our rhythm in gentle, gradual increments like two experienced and talented musicians playing a duet.

I welcomed it. Sex had been a panacea for sadness and loneliness since time began. All the bad memories and melancholy moments were driven away by the rush of blood, the pounding of the heart and the quickening of breath. The explosive nature of passion brought so much light into me that all the shadows and pockets of darkness were washed out in an instant. Every climax was another eruption of light and heat. I was a volcano, spewing my hot lava over myself, cremating sorrow.

And it was my detective who was lighting me up. I clutched his hair and cried out. Never had a man, not even my beloved Michael, brought me to this peak of pure animal pleasure. I could hear his laughter, his damn male superior laughter, confident, egotistical, dominating. I wanted to get hold of myself and take control, but by that point control was beyond me.

On and on he thrust. My head began to spin. Before I passed out, I thought, this was what it must be like for an inferior female when a male Androgyne is taking her for prey. With a great climax raging through my body, I felt myself grow completely limp and then all went black.

I awoke on the bed, disoriented, unsure of the time of day. I felt the wet cloth on my forehead and started to sit up. My detective was seated at my desk scribbling on a pad. He wore his pants, but no shirt and no shoes.

"How are you doing?" he asked when he saw I had regained consciousness.

"I don't understand," I said, taking the wet cloth from my forehead. "This has never happened to me before."

He shrugged.

"There's a first time for everything," he remarked rather casually. He didn't seem impressed with his own ability to overwhelm me sexually. "I guess you were just tired . . . the strain of all this . . . reading the diary, telling your story, being shot at . . . all of it takes its toll."

"You don't look very tired." I gazed at the clock. "It's nearly morning."

"I have this reserve tank I run on when I'm deeply involved in an investigation," he said. "Afterward, it will hit me just like it hit you and I'll pass out too. I'll sleep for days."

"What are you writing there?"

"Just scribbling some notes so I can recall some of the things you told me." He sat back, his arms folded over his muscular chest. The muscles in his shoulders tightened, their definition sharpening.

"You're rather a good lover . . . for an inferior male," I added. He laughed.

"That's what you call a half-ass compliment, if I ever heard one."

I began to get out of bed.

"Why don't you try to sleep?"

"I'd rather take a shower and dress. I've got a lot to do today, including a meeting with the director of my new film."

" 'Winter of the Virgin Dead.' "

"How did you know that?"

"Hey," he said holding his arms out, "Hollywood is my beat, remember? I read it in one column or another. Surprised you took the part," he added.

"It's an above-average horror movie. Vampires are portrayed in an almost sympathetic light, portrayed as victims of themselves."

"I see. You saw something familiar in it."

"Precisely, and I like the director, who also wrote the script."

"He's not . . ."

"No, but the producer is," I said. He raised his eyebrows and nodded. "If you want to shower, you can use the guest room," I said.

"Not Richard's?" he teased. It was remarkable how despite everything I still had a need to protect the sanctity of Richard's quarters. How it would infuriate him if I ever permitted my detective to use his bathroom facilities. But why should that matter now? I wondered. Why worry about Richard being upset over something so trivial compared with the ultimate betrayal? The detective provided an answer. "Old habits die hard," he said. "I know. I know. I'll use the guest room. Thank you."

He rose and went out.

After I showered and dressed, I found him dressed and waiting in the kitchen. He had made us coffee. The sun was just coming up. Dawn had a special meaning for me. Not only did the morning light drive away the caverns of darkness in which the evil of the world dwelt and from which it watched and waited to pounce, but it stimulated a rebirth of hope and promise. Each day brought a new opportunity to confront each night successfully. Never had I felt this as much as I had been feeling it recently.

"You look revived," my detective said. "And very beautiful, like a flower opening its petals."

"You? Poetic?"

"Hey, what can I tell you? You inspire me." Trying to cheer me up, he got up and poured me a cup of coffee. He affected the pose of a short-order cook. "Ma'am. What'cha want for breakfast? We got grits and eggs and oatmeal and stuff."

I laughed.

"Don't tell me you add short-order cook to your list of talents," I said.

"What'cha think? Of course. I make a wicked omelette if you're hungry."

"Fine."

He proceeded. "While I'm doing this, tell me about your early Hollywood days. Did you live with your mother?"

"In the beginning, but only for a few months. She had moved to Pacific Palisades by then and was doing less and less modeling and commercial work. I took an apartment in the marina and not long after, I bought this house. But I always spent a great deal of time at her house. She still had parties often and there were always interesting people visiting. Sunday brunch was a ritual. I never missed one unless I was away on location. Time with my mother was precious to me."

"Was she happy to see you had returned so triumphantly from New York?"

"Oh yes, she was very proud of me. We were very

close, more like friends by then than mother and daughter. And she was very knowledgeable about the whole Hollywood scene. Between her and William, I couldn't have had better advisers in those days."

"Who was this William? I mean, what did he do?"

"In his female state, as Mary, he was a noted therapist with a long list of celebrity clients. What is it they say, 'In L.A. you're not normal unless you're in therapy, whereas everywhere else you're not in therapy unless you're not normal.' "

He laughed.

"She wasn't Mary Williard, was she?"

"Yes. You knew of her?"

"Only in reading about her. I never knew her personally. So, now she's in an old age home herself?"

"Yes, sadly."

"Does that happen often to androgynous females after they've passed their time?" he asked.

"Unfortunately, yes. Occupational disease," I said.

"Do they all go to any special place? I mean, a place run by your people?"

"Yes."

He nodded and flipped the omelette in the pan. It did smell very appetizing.

"But that wasn't your mother's fate," he said, moving to get two plates.

"No."

He put the omelettes on the plates and served them with toast and jelly.

"It looks delicious," I said.

"Dig in."

"Very good," I said chewing on a succulent morsel. "Maybe you should do this full time."

"I'm considering it. Less stress. So," he said, "not

long after your arrival on the scene, your mother went into retirement."

"Yes. Many of her accounts tried to talk her into returning. She was still strikingly attractive and looked nowhere near her true age, but she was tired of the spotlight and was quite satisfied living vicariously through my experiences, even the unpleasant ones."

"Producers trying to bed you down, trying to force you into crummy roles, jealousy of other new actresses, tension on the set . . ."

"You've got it."

"Tell me," he said, sitting back and sipping his coffee. "How did you get out of marrying Tony Patio? Everyone was convinced that was simply a matter of setting the date. It was the ideal Hollywood marriage—the glamour couple harking back to couples like Clark Gable and Carole Lombard, Humphrey Bogart and Lauren Bacall. The two of you were on just about every magazine cover, in every column, attended every important opening and premiere . . . did you finally have to tell him what you were?"

"Hardly," I said, laughing.

"I don't understand. You're not telling me Tony Patio was one of you."

"Hardly," I repeated, laughing harder. He waited. "Tony Patio was gay," I said.

"You're kidding. America's young heartthrob? All those hot and heavy love scenes . . . Patio, gay?"

"Terrified of women, too. He was seeing Mary because he had this phobia that if he put his precious pecker into a woman, she would clamp down on it and cut it off and swallow within her vaginal lips. Honest," I said, raising my hand like a witness to be sworn in.

"I suppose head was out of the question."

"Only if he would give it. I used to have fun teasing him. Terrifying him would be more like it, I suppose. You can't imagine how much he sweated under that makeup whenever I clung to him or kissed him and pressed my bosom to him."

"That had to be one of the best kept Hollywood secrets. But how . . . who were his male lovers?"

"He had only one constant lover . . . his brother."

"What? That's sick. Incest, too, and with a crippled man?"

"Mary said he was far less threatened because of that."

"And everyone thought how wonderful it was he looked after his less fortunate younger brother. I suppose his drug overdose had something to do with all this."

"Of course. Mary made it a point not to prescribe medication of any sort unless it was truly necessary, but she couldn't control the unscrupulous physicians who filled out orders for every upper and downer under the sun. Some of them should have been tried for murder."

"Dark days, yet you survived it and went on to win bigger and better roles until you played the mother in *Surrogate Child* and received a nomination. That scene when your husband was trying to get you to see that your foster child was evil . . . you were great, so convincing. You seemed so genuinely needy. Had it already started by then?"

"What?"

"Your aversion to what you are?"

I hesitated. Despite everything, it was still difficult to admit it to someone not of our race.

"Yes."

"Which explains why you were so good in that scene. Not that you're not a wonderful actress anyway," he added quickly. "There was just something special there."

"Detective, short-order cook, and now critic," I said. "In that order."

We stared at each other a moment. There was something different about my detective this morning, some new glint in his eye. How much more sophisticated and assured of himself than he had appeared when I had first walked into his office. It was as though he were growing along with my story, gaining confidence and wisdom through my relating events.

"Now you tell me something," I said. "What made you suspect my mother's death was not accidental?"

He fingered his coffee cup.

"In my early days here, I was understandably fascinated with celebrities and everything associated with them, especially police business. As one of the low men on the totem pole, I wasn't included in any of the bigger, more celebrated cases, but that didn't stop me from poking my nose in whenever I had an opportunity.

"Your mother's death made headlines of course, along with the usual rumors that trembled through the department. Curious, I got hold of some of the reports and began reading. I noticed that one report had been altered considerably. I pursued, searched for the original, and found a duplicate copy stuck away. That business about the bannister being defective was obviously manufactured. I realized your mother didn't lean against a faulty balustrade that gave way. She had to have been pushed.

"I never understood why the police were covering up and I knew if I asked questions, I could find myself walking a beat in East Los Angeles. I know you were and still are upset about the cover-up, but do you know why it happened?"

"Yes."

"The how is obvious to me now. One or more of your

kind is in the department. You've told me that. Do you know who they are?"

"Some of them."

"How many of them are there?"

"Not that many."

"Well, why did your people want your mother's murder changed to an accidental death?"

I hesitated. My heart was pounding so hard, I knew it was Richard's fear combined with my own. He was no longer simply screaming "no!" somewhere inside me. He was curled into a hot crimson ball of rage and terror, his eyes pools of dried blood, his teeth gnashing and cutting deeply into his own lips from which his liquefied bones had begun to pour—a starched, white putrescent drool. Frustration had distorted him. Twisted and turned, he squeezed the juices out of himself, each drop of blood and bone falling with the heat of boiling water, singeing my very soul. I could smell the scent of burning flesh in my nostrils.

My detective leaned forward, his eyes riveted on mine, his gaze penetrating and prying deeper and deeper until I felt myself opening like a clam shell in hot water, my softer, secret insides nearly exposed.

"Why?" he pursued. I tried looking away. His insistence felt like a knife being turned one more time, breaking the last vestige of resistance. I looked up at him, my face on fire.

"Because," I said in a gasp. "We knew who killed her."

I ran from the table and went into the nearest bathroom to splash cold water on my face and catch my breath. I could hear the chant of the Androgyne, the voices in the darkness around me warning me not to reveal certain secrets ever. A small candle burned in a holder placed between my naked legs. The flickering light made the eyes of the elders flicker like stars in a night sky without moonlight. The eyes were so similar, I couldn't distinguish my mother's from the others.

"Never tell them . . . never tell them . . . never tell them . . ."

I put my hands over my ears to drown out the memory, but the voices were inside me. It was only the detective's knocking on the bathroom door that drove the chanting back into the vaults of my mind.

"Are you all right? Clea?"

"Yes, yes. I'll be right out. It's okay."

I took a deep breath, wiped my face dry and fixed my hair. He was standing just outside, a look of confusion written over his face.

"I guess I misunderstood what you said back there. It sounded like you said you knew who killed your mother."

I returned to the kitchen, him trailing behind me like a persistent string of lint one couldn't shake off one's clothing. I said nothing, poured myself some fresh coffee and sipped it silently while staring out the window at the morning sunlight burning off the marine layer of clouds. Already, there were patches of blue sea visible. My patient detective hovered behind me, an arrogant shadow unafraid of the daylight or any abrupt movements on my part.

"You didn't misunderstand me," I finally confessed.

"I see. Was it . . . someone you loved, someone you trusted?"

"Hardly."

A peal of laughter emerging from places within myself I didn't know existed rippled between us. The detective smiled.

"Why is that funny?"

"I left something out of our mythology," I said. "We don't talk about it amongst ourselves, much less between ourselves and outsiders." He stared. "Mary once referred to it as our Evil Eye Syndrome and that title took hold. Just as there are things you fear, things you fear deep down in your very essence and don't like to talk about because the talk brings them to the forefront of your thoughts and reminds you of them, we don't like to talk about the Evil Eye Syndrome."

"And this Evil Eye," he said, turning his hand in the air as if he were modeling gloves, "whatever it is, is responsible for your mother's death?"

"Precisely." I sat down again.

He stared, smiled, started to laugh, and then thought again and grew serious.

"Well, can you tell me something about it? Do you see it as a ghost, a creature . . . what is it?"

"It's anything it wants to be at the time. It can be a he or a she. There are no definite pictures, conceptions of its actual form; there are only pictures of it in other forms with its particular evil glint.

"Simply put, the Evil Eye is our version of what you would call the devil and as such it can be any man, woman or child."

"I see." He sat down beside me, looking thoughtful.

"When I described our mythology, our version of creation, I deliberately left out our belief that after God had created us and then given us this divine mission, the devil who had corrupted Paradise was even more frustrated. Being we were destined to be the true army of God, he, the devil, set out to destroy us whenever he could."

"And how does he do that?"

"The same way he supposedly does it to you—by temptation, by winning our trust, by invading our deepest thoughts, by getting us to betray the things we love, the things that are sacred to us—blaspheming . . . the seven deadly sins. You name it."

The detective sat back nodding.

"So you believe the devil, as it were, killed your mother?"

"Yes."

"But why cover that up? I don't understand. Why make it look like an accident?"

"First, for obvious reasons we couldn't disclose any of what I've disclosed to you; and second, we carry on our own battle. We certainly couldn't come to you for aid in this. What would we ask you to do—put out an all points bulletin for the devil who hunts Androgyne because we have been commanded by God to punish humanity for its devilish lust?"

"I see." He looked up quickly. "Does your kind have any luck in this battle with the Evil Eye?"

"Yes and no. We've killed our devil many times in many ways," I said. "Just like it's impossible to eradicate evil forever, it's impossible to kill him forever. The key thing is to kill him in whatever form he has taken for the moment before he kills us. Do you understand?"

"Yes." He stared at me, his eyes intense, penetrating. I was surprised by their sharply analytical glint. "But why is it," he began, "that I feel there is something else, some other reason why you and your people covered up the true cause of your mother's death? Does it have something to do with how the devil gets to you?"

"You're getting too good at this," I replied acridly, my words like razors slicing the air between us. "Either you are a far better detective than you first appeared to be or some of my androgynous insight and perception is rubbing off."

"Maybe you willingly gave me something of yourself during our lovemaking," he suggested. "You have described how the Androgyne absorb their victims; perhaps you reversed the process and transferred some power into me."

"That's ridiculous," I said. The mere thought of such a thing frightened me. He shrugged.

"Not any more ridiculous on the surface than some of the things you've told me. But, all right," he conceded with a smile, "I'll confess to being a far better detective than I first appeared. What did you leave out about your mother?"

We heard the front door open and he looked up sharply, reaching for his pistol at the same time.

"It's all right," I said. "It's only Sylvia, my maid."

A moment later she appeared in the kitchen doorway.

"Good morning," she said. The detective scrutinized her quickly, obviously impressed with how nonchalantly she took his presence. What he didn't know was Sylvia was as inanimate, as unemotional as any form of higher life could be.

She was tall and exceedingly thin. Her clothing hung on her as if her shoulders were wire hangers. She had a lean, long face with big, dull brown eyes and a mouth with pencil-thin lips. She never wore any makeup. Her dark brown hair was kept short and neat, the bangs trimmed. No matter how she washed or treated it, it would always have a flat look to match her flat complexion: pale white skin that had the yellowish tint of age behind her ears, at the base of her neck, and over her hands and arms.

"Good morning, Sylvia. This is Detective Mayer." She nodded at him.

"Good morning," he said.

"You can begin with my room, Sylvia," I said. She turned abruptly and left us as if we hadn't been there, as if I had left a note with instructions for her on the refrigerator. Detective Mayer turned to me quizzically.

"She can't be one of you?"

"No, but she's not one of you either. Sylvia is . . . how should I put it? I'll put it the way William once put it: 'a sexual albino.' She's an anomaly. We have our birth defects too, thanks to the way you and your kind have polluted the environment, our water and food.

"Creatures like Sylvia have no place in your world and no place in ours, really. Yet we have to provide for them, so we find places for them in our lives. They're satisfied to the extent anything can satisfy them.

"They have no ambitions, no passions, no hope, no drive . . . nothing stirs them and conversely, nothing really upsets them either. They're not even upset about their condition. We call them the Stoics, for obvious reasons.

"When William was in a particularly bleak mood, he would look at one and predict we would all become like him or her in time, even you and your kind. He thought it would be the form the world would take when it came to an end—we would all meld into one lifeless species, all become Stoics and sleepwalk through our lives. Birth would be unremarkable, almost another form of excretion, and we would pass on to death just as we would pass through any other doorway—unconcerned, barely noticing any differences."

"That is bleak." He grimaced. For some reason, I enjoyed depressing him at this moment.

"Emotions would be reduced to nothing more than the stimulation of nerve endings—pleasure would be simplistic; love would drop out of the vocabulary, as well as hate. We would simply like and dislike, taste and spit, satiate our appetites and move off to sleep like dumb animals."

"All right," he said succumbing to my doom and gloom, "I get the point. Get back to my point. How did the Evil Eye get to your mother?"

"You're determined to force me into a depression, aren't you?"

"Don't worry, I have the antidote." His promiscuous smile left no doubt as to his meaning.

"My, you are a vigorous creature. All right." I sat back. "I told you Mother retired even though she was still an extraordinarily beautiful woman. Androgynous women don't look anywhere near their age either so she could have gone on modeling for years and years, but she began to suffer from the symptoms of premature change of life. It happens to us occasionally.

"In our case the symptoms take one particular ugly form: It becomes more and more difficult to metamorphose."

"Sort of like creeping impotency," my detective suggested.

"Yes, only the consequence isn't simply a denial of sexual satisfaction for us—it's life threatening to our male selves. It's difficult for you to understand how devoted we are to our second selves, how much we love our counterparts. I suppose the deepest, most complete form of love is self-love, narcissism is pure and uncompromising. By definition, survival depends on self-love. When we hate ourselves, hate who we are or what we've become, we kill ourselves.

"Since the male part of us is in a true sense half of who we are, we suffer extraordinary pain when we lose him. It's why, as I explained, so many of us end up babbling in an old age home, or . . ."

"Commit suicide?"

"Yes."

"Which is what you are now doing in a sense?"

"Yes, a very true sense. Although I'm doing it slowly, contriving it."

"Okay, but I don't understand. You said your mother was murdered by . . ." He turned smiling. "The Evil Eye, but now you're suggesting she committed suicide. Which is it?"

"Both," I said.

"Huh?" He shook his head.

"You ever see a movie entitled *The Roman Spring of Mrs. Stone*?"

"Of course. Tennessee Williams."

"Then you remember how that ended, how she tossed her key out the window to the gigolo she knew would ultimately kill her."

"Uh-huh."

"My mother did the same thing—only she invited the devil in. She could no longer live without Dimitri. I knew it was coming.

"She began to tell me how difficult it was becoming for her to resurrect him, how he cried out to her from within her. His cries kept her awake at night. Can you even begin to imagine what it must be like to be haunted from within yourself?"

"Like a schizophrenic who appears to be cured but who has succeeded in only subduing his second personality?"

"Yes. He still senses it, hears it, needs it, but it won't come back. So he is in perpetual agony.

"My mother cried Dimitri's tears as well as her own. She would spend hours and hours in his room touching his things, his clothing, his razor and brush. She would stare at his picture endlessly, hoping the eye contact would strengthen her dwindling androgynous powers, but all it did was intensify her torment.

"All of this began to take its toll on her physically. She started to look her age; her hair turned gray. There were even wrinkles in her skin. It got so I hated to visit with her for I was watching her die.

"And whenever I did visit, all she did was complain and mourn. Richard felt the same way. He stopped visiting altogether. She asked me about him repeatedly. Finally, I had to tell her. She knew it anyway.

" 'I'm beginning to disgust you, too,' she told me. 'Don't deny it. I see it in your face.'

" 'It's not that you disgust me,' I replied. 'I hate having to feel sorry for you. All my life I thought of you as strong and confident, someone I could turn to whenever I felt afraid or lost.' She hated me for saying these things."

"All children feel that about their parents," the detective said. "You weren't telling her anything out of the ordinary."

"Yes, but they don't say it to their parents' faces, not like that. I guess there was a bit of the Stoic in me already; already I was uncaring. It was a heartless thing to do.

" 'All right,' she said, smiling, 'I'll stop feeling sorry for myself. I'll put an end to it immediately. You're right, of course. I should face my fate and be strong.

"She stood up and clapped her hands together as though she were going to begin a new life right that moment. Of course, at the time, I didn't know what she intended."

"What did she do?"

"She fixed herself up—had her hair colored, had her chin tucked, did away with wrinkles. She battled back at age with a fury I mistook for a hunger for life. It turned out to be a hunger for death, however."

"Huh? Who makes herself look beautiful before committing suicide?"

"An Androgyne," I said. "Once she felt confident about her looks again, she went out on her own kind of hunt, roaming through singles bars, threading herself through the dingiest sections of Los Angeles, weaving her own shroud. She brought home one loser after another. I couldn't believe some of the scum she permitted into her bed. A number of times I received phone calls from other Androgyne who recognized her haunting some bar and I had to go retrieve her. If Richard received the call, he would metamorphose immediately so I would do it. He didn't have the stomach for it. It wasn't easy.

"Everyone came to me complaining, of course; and of course, I begged her to stop, to get off this course of self-destruction, but she was already mad by then. She told me she would never stop, she would search forever until she found Dimitri."

"Which was something she couldn't do."

"Right, but she did."

"What do you mean? Dimitri was her male self, right?"

"Yes." I looked out the window. Although it was still a very bright and promising morning, it suddenly looked all gray and dismal. I was looking out through my own tears.

"You've really got me confused now," the detective said.

"I told you earlier . . . about the Evil Eye . . . how it can take any form."

"You mean . . . it took Dimitri's form?" he concluded. I nodded.

"And she brought him home with her. She would never have done so otherwise, but he had gotten into her madness, you see. That's why I say she committed suicide. She wanted that to happen. She brought him home knowing he had to be the death of her."

"But to push her off a balcony . . . that's not very imaginative of him," the detective said. "Why take Dimitri's form just to do that? He could have snuck in and killed her anytime, I imagine. Perhaps it was just some thief she discovered or one of those lowlifes she brought home."

I turned to him. Was he playing with me? Could it be that he really didn't know all of it? His face had suddenly become an inscrutable mask. I was losing my confidence when it came to him and I didn't like it.

"That wasn't how she died. I thought you said you read the original report."

"Well . . . I did, but . . ."

"Did you or didn't you?"

He smiled.

"Maybe I just heard a little tidbit here and there."

I turned away from him.

"Come on. You've nearly told me all of it. Why not finish?"

"I thought you understood when I made reference to *The Roman Spring of Mrs. Stone*," I said. "He took her the way the Androgyne take women—he made love to her and drained her of her life energy.

"Then he threw her into the balcony so she would crash to the floor below.

"But by the time she landed, she was already decomposing. When we found her, she was merely bones and dried skin flaking off into dust. Her beautiful eyes had already disintegrated.

"Don't you see?" I cried. "That's how we knew she had been the victim of the Evil Eye!"

ELEVEN

WE SAT IN silence for a while, my sad memories falling like a dark curtain between me and the immediate present.

"How did Richard react to all this?" the detective asked softly. His voice was a gentle intrusion, soft fingers parting the heavy drapery tentatively, permitting only a slim ray of soft light to invade my melancholy reverie.

"He went from sorrow to anger and rage. You'll find pages and pages in the diary describing his rampages through the city, pursuing every shadow, following every distorted-looking, evil-appearing thing in hopes of trapping the Evil Eye. He went everywhere, driven by his mad energy—from the slums of East L.A. to the streets of Santa Monica. For some reason he thought the devil would take refuge in the body of a homeless person. Richard went charging down Ocean Avenue, pausing before every lost soul to search his or her eyes, probably leaving the poor soul thinking he or she had just looked into the face of hell, rather than vice versa.

"Finally, he calmed down long enough to return so I could metamorphose and properly mourn our mother's death with friends."

"How did you determine which of you would attend the funeral?"

"It wasn't hard; he was in no condition to be seen in public. Afterward, he went to her grave privately. He still goes there often. He suffers from guilt, believing he should have done more to protect her. He forgets how difficult it was for him even to spend time with her during those dark final days," I added, smirking as if he were sitting across from me and I were reminding him of how he had left me with the problems.

"It was a big funeral. I suppose just about every androgynous being in the city attended, huh?"

"Most did." I turned to him. "You sound like you were there. Were you?"

"I have to confess I was somewhat infatuated by celebrities in those days and attended in hopes of seeing movie stars."

"Many put in an appearance, as well as important politicians, businessmen."

"I remember seeing you," he added smiling. "And Alison. She was at your side and looked as upset as you were. I recall thinking you were sisters."

"Yes. My mother's death was the catalyst for our reunion. Actually, Alison was a great help to me, as was Nicholas. He and Richard patched things up as well.

"But," I said, "Richard was never the same after our mother's death. He became far more bitter and that bitterness found its expression in a nihilistic hedonism. He became gluttonous, lecherous, gorging himself on sex, no longer hunting simply to satisfy our biological needs. He would take any kill, make love on a whim, pursue any woman no matter how old or how young." I sighed, the horror of those days washing over me, weighing me down with bad memories. "And then came his many homosexual experiences.

"It's all in the diary," I added sadly, "including his

heavy use of cocaine, the orgies he attended, his disgusting ménages à trois."

"Didn't all this have a detrimental effect on you?"

"Eventually. I began to resist metamorphosing to keep him in check, but we couldn't go on like that indefinitely. Finally, after consulting with Mary, I left Los Angeles and went to an ashram. The meditation and simplicity brought us both the inner peace we needed.

"Is this a retreat solely attended by Androgyne?"

"Yes."

"In California?"

"No," I said. "In New York." I wasn't any more specific because it was still strongly in me to protect my kind, and I couldn't see why it mattered to my detective anyway.

"Well," he said, "it must have helped. You returned to Hollywood and became an even bigger star."

"Yes, for a while I thought of nothing but my acting. It was another refuge, although I never stopped missing Janice and Dimitri. I miss them terribly even now. I suppose one dramatic result of their death was my growing dependence on Richard and his growing dependence on me. As funny as it might sound to you, we became even closer, even more tuned in to each other's needs."

"More so for him, however."

"Why do you say that?"

"His reaction to your developing a relationship with an inferior man. He resented anything or anyone who would come between you, especially if, as you say, you fell in love with this man."

"Yes," I said, nodding. "Of course, you're right."

"How did that happen? I mean, how could you . . ."

"Fall in love with an inferior?" I smiled to myself. "Maybe Richard was right—maybe it was just another way of trying to deny my essence.

"Soon after I received my Academy Award nomination, my agent suggested I employ Michael as my publicist. He had an excellent reputation and was considered more of a quality performer's publicist, getting me seen in places and mentioned in columns that catered to a higher clientele.

"We spent a great deal of time together, first so Michael could get to know me and know how to publicize me, and then because we grew fond of each other's company. I found him a very sweet and gentle man. Despite the fact that he lived and worked in this mad, hyper world of glitzy glamour, he had an almost angelic peace about him, a quiet, religiously peaceful aura. He had a way of shutting out unpleasant static. Right from the beginning, I felt comfortable and relaxed with him.

"Even our lovemaking was different—we explored each other with soft eyes, always conscious of each other's needs, never selfish, never demanding."

"It's hard for me to believe that an animal lover like you would find that satisfying," my detective said suspiciously.

"I know. I suppose in a true sense, Michael became another refuge for me. I could go to him after making wild passionate love and fall asleep in his arms with nothing more than the exchange of a loving kiss, if that's all I wanted."

"Did he know you had come from making love with another man?"

"Yes."

"And he was not jealous or disgusted? He still cared for you?"

"He loved me, truly loved me. He was understanding, compassionate."

"I don't know if that's love," my detective mused aloud. "It sounds more like a form of therapy."

"Perhaps that's all love is."

He looked at me sharply.

"What do you mean by that?"

"Love is merely a bandage, an oasis in hell, a raft in a tempestuous sea. It keeps us from facing the truth."

"Which is?"

"That no matter who we are or what we are, we are all alone. Ultimately, we are all alone."

"Is that how you feel now?"

"Yes. Especially with my mother gone and Michael gone, and Richard . . ."

"Richard?"

"Richard almost gone."

The detective sat there staring at me, his face expressionless, no pity in his eyes, no warmth, a bland mask. I noted the time.

"I've got to get to my script meeting," I said rising.

"If the ultimate result of all this is your demise as well as Richard's, why are you . . ."

"Carrying on? I don't know," I said after a moment. "Maybe it's just like you said before—old habits die hard."

"Or maybe you don't know yourself and your intentions as well as you think you do."

"We'll just have to wait a little longer to find out," I said.

"Ooo. A cliff hanger." He pretended to be terrified and pressed his fists together at his chin.

"Good-bye, Detective Mayer. You can show yourself out."

"I'll be by later," he called as I turned away. "Dinner, perhaps? There is still more for you to tell me, I assume, and there is the matter of Richard's diary," he added when I paused and looked back.

"All right, dinner. I'll let you take me to one of your haunts this time. I feel like mixing with the plebeians, groveling in the masses, inhaling the sweat and the Aqua Velva."

I sauntered away from him quickly, his laughter in my wake. I couldn't keep the smile from my lips. Odd, I thought, how my seeing him, my confession, my telling of my story was turning out to be more than a catharsis. It was something of a resurrection as well.

Perhaps I could do it; perhaps I could die as an Androgyne and be reborn an inferior. Had my detective instilled this wild hope in me, a hope that was as much of a sin as a dream?

I wanted to beg for forgiveness. Forgive me, Mother; forgive me, Father.

But I couldn't utter the words with any sincerity. I didn't really want forgiveness; I didn't want to stop sinning. I was like a whore who had stepped into the confessional to cleanse her soul and the moment she opened her mouth to speak, broke into a fit of hysterics, the likes of which her confessor had not heard. In fact, it frightened him to the extent he believed the devil had stepped into the booth alongside her.

He flung holy water at her desperately.

I returned to my room to fetch my purse and check my hair and makeup one last time. Sylvia had just turned down the bed. She looked at me strangely, almost as if something had frightened her deeply.

"Is something wrong, Sylvia?" I asked.

She held up the old bed sheets.

"They're still very hot," she said. I had to laugh.

"Passion can sometimes linger and burn like hot coals

dying slowly against the dark." I knew she would understand the words, but since the experience was so alien to her, she would not appreciate their meaning.

She shook her head and repeated her statement as mechanically as she said anything.

"They're still very hot."

"Well, cool them down then," I said and sat at the vanity table. I heard the detective leave. Almost immediately, the phone rang.

It was Nicholas.

"Can I see you today?" he asked immediately.

"I have a full schedule," I said.

"I must see you. Alison won't metamorphose until I do."

"Ridiculous. She's trying to intimidate me with this . . . this identity strike. Who does she think she is performing this sort of protest, Ghandi?"

"She's determined," he replied firmly.

"Why doesn't she leave me alone?" I snapped.

"You know the answer to that," he said calmly. "You're in grave danger. She's concerned."

"She's concerned about Richard being in grave danger, not me."

"Since when is that different?" he asked quickly. I felt tears burning under my eyelids. I gazed at Sylvia, but she was already hypnotized by her menial labor. Her hands moved mechanically, her head following her own movements with a robotlike swing. She wasn't listening to my end of the conversation. I imagined her mind was like some empty tunnel shut up on both ends, perhaps the echo of the last thought bouncing from one side to the other.

"What do you want?"

"I want to talk with you. That's all, Clea. You've got

to talk to your own kind. We've got to care for each other."

I paused. His soft, sincere-sounding voice confused me. My breath grew short, labored.

"Funny way of showing you care—trying to shoot me."

"I told you: I don't know what you're talking about. None of us tried to shoot you."

"Or the detective?"

"None of us did," he insisted.

"I guess I imagined it all and there are no bullet holes in the doorway and walls."

"Clea," he said softly. "Give me five minutes. Don't we mean enough to each other for that at least?" His voice was full of pleading.

"All right," I said reluctantly. Perhaps we should have one final meeting, I thought. "I'll come to your house after my script meeting. Are you there now?"

"Yes."

"You'll come alone?"

"Of course."

"Is the detective still there?"

"He's gone, Nicholas. I was just on my way out when you called," I said petulantly. "I'm already going to be fashionably late; I don't want to be ridiculously late."

"I'll be waiting for you," he said. "Until then," he muttered and cradled the phone.

I did a last bit of primping, found my copy of the script, left some last minute orders for Sylvia and walked out of the house.

The sun was so bright that even my Polaroids seemed inadequate. There was a particularly sharp glint of light bouncing off the hood of my car. I had to turn away and gazed at Richard's Thunderbird. It looked abandoned. It drove a sword of ice through my heart to think that he would never drive it again; I knew how much he loved driving it, but I swallowed my sadness quickly and got into my car. The top was still down and I welcomed the rush of warm sunlight over my hair and face. I took a deep breath, started the car and drove out.

As I descended the hill, my fingers tightened on the steering wheel and my legs grew so heavy that moving my foot from the accelerator to the brake seemed to require a great effort. After I made the first turn, I felt the car speed up and I instinctively pressed down on the brake. I could hear Alison's laughter and ridicule. "I burn out a set of brakes just visiting you," she had said almost every time she came to visit.

The car did not slow down. I pressed down harder on the pedal, but the brakes did not respond. Instead, the car built up momentum and I nearly lost control going around the second turn. I pumped the pedal again and again, but still, I had no brakes. The car went faster and faster. I squealed around the next turn and felt the right wheels lift off the ground. My fingers were gripping the wheel so tightly, my wrists hurt. I needed Richard's strength desperately, but he remained dormant, buried too deeply in his own anger to offer any assistance.

"Richard!" I screamed.

In my mind's eye, I could see him sitting stiffly in the seat beside me, his arms crossed on his chest, his head unmoving, his eyes stubbornly fixed on the next turn.

"You think you can do everything yourself," he muttered in my illusion like a sulky child, "so handle it."

I screamed again and barely negotiated the turn, this time leaving the road and driving over a part of the hill. It had the effect of slowing me down some, so I turned the car off the road and permitted it to bounce and heave over rocks and through bushes. Fortunately, no one was coming up the hill when I returned to the road and I was able to use all of it.

Just around the next turn was a flat field. I steered onto it and was able to direct the car toward a slight incline, which slowed it down considerably. I turned off the engine and it rolled to a precarious stop near the edge of a precipice.

I didn't hesitate. The moment I could, I got out of the car. Suddenly it rolled back and spun around until it began to tip over the edge of the hill. The car tottered for one precarious moment and then went bouncing down the ravine, crashing into the rocks below. Finally, it came to rest in a cloud of moribund dust, reduced to an accordion of metal, leather and shattered glass. As I gazed down at what I knew someone had intended to be my coffin, my relief quickly changed to anger and rage.

Was this why Nicholas had asked me all those questions? Was I leaving now? Was the detective with me? Could it be that he and Alison had planned this with some of the others? Richard invaded my thoughts with the thought: One betrayal deserved another.

I turned and marched back up the hill, fueled by my wrath. When I finally arrived home, I phoned the studio to say I would not be coming in and told them about the accident. The assistant director was sympathetic and concerned.

Sylvia heard me talking on the phone and came out to see why I had returned.

"Did you happen to see Alison or Nicholas here earlier?" I asked.

"No."

"Anyone?"

"Just that detective," she said.

"I mean other than him." Her stupidity could be infuriating sometimes. She shook her head.

"Are you sure because I was nearly killed just now." I described what had happened, not sparing a single grisly detail. Even so, she nodded as if it was nothing unusual.

"I didn't see anyone else," she said and then went off to clean the kitchen.

My fury unabated, I went out and this time took Richard's Thunderbird, his precious toy. When they saw me driving up in this, I thought, they will know they have much more to contend with than they had ever dreamed.

Alison and Nicholas lived in Brentwood Park in a house that would be better characterized as an estate. It was a two-story brick Tudor with wooden cladding on the gables and the upper decorative chimney pots. All of the windows were tall and narrow with multipane glazing. On the roof were three shed dormers, their windows shaded and dark. The house had an arched doorway with a board-and-batten door. On it Alison had put a brass knocker in the form of a shapely woman. It was her one contribution to the decor.

Alison had bought their house as is, furniture included. All of the furnishings were nineteenth-century vintage Victorian—ornate, flowery carvings in dark woods with patterned upholstery. She didn't have to buy a single piece, not a vase, not a statue, not a painting, not even a knickknack. The house even came with linens and towels.

"All we had to do was steam clean the rugs," she had told me, "and of course scrub down the tiles and bath fixtures. The previous owner wanted to start with everything new."

They had bought it from a widow whose husband had made a fortune in West Side commercial real estate. She had remarried and purchased a relatively new house in Beverly Hills.

Alison always had wanted to live in Beverly Hills, but Nicholas preferred the more rustic and more isolated Brentwood Park. It made coming and going much easier and provided a great deal more privacy. When Alison discovered how many celebrities were living in the vicinity, she relented. A real estate agent, who was one of our kind, found them the property.

I had found the house much too dark for my taste. Beside the twelve-foot-high hedges that blocked it from street view, there were enough trees and bushes to keep the morning and afternoon sun almost completely away from the front windows. Only the rear of the house, where there was a free-form pool set in mauve flagstone and a cabana, got any real sunlight and then only for a short time in the afternoon.

Today the house looked murkier than ever to me. When I drove up, I found the front gate open, but the driveway looked more like a tunnel because of the thick, dark shadows cast by the trees that lined it. The unlit, somber windows reflected the gloom. The breeze turned the silhouettes of branches and leaves framed in the glass into tormented spirits struggling to free themselves of invisible chains.

Unlike most times when I had arrived at Alison and Nicholas's residence, there were no gardeners mucking about, no service people of any kind caring for the property. It had a deserted, lonely appearance, the look of a house that hadn't been lived in for years. Leaves blown loose of limbs performed a macabre dance freely on the slate walkways and the tile patio as well as the driveway.

The grounds were so strikingly desolate, I came to a stop about three-quarters of the way up the drive. Nicholas had presumably dismissed everyone so we could have our private, undisturbed talk.

I went to the front door and clapped the ridiculous knocker. The subsequent tap could be heard echoing through the vast and grand entryway toward the spiral staircase with its hand-carved mahogany balustrade. How Alison loved making an entrance descending the carpeted stairway when guests arrived, the hem of her long dress or skirt floating over the steps. I waited, listening keenly for Nicholas's footsteps, but I heard only the silvery sound of the breeze whistling through the trees and around the corners of the estate.

I knocked a second time, striking the plate harder this time. Again there was no answer, no sign of life within.

Of course, I thought, Nicholas never expected I would appear. He assumed by now I'd be flattened at the bottom of that ravine.

Suddenly enraged now, I cried out, "Nicholas!"

In my angry tone, my voice suddenly sounded more like Richard's than mine; it resonated that deeply. Frightened at the hint of a change, I placed my palm against my breast. My heart was pounding.

"Nicholas!"

Had he gone to my mountain road to see my wreckage?

I stepped to the left and peered through the window. There were no lights on in the sitting room within and no one visible.

"Damn you, damn you both," I muttered and stepped off the patio to go around the building. Every time I reached a window, I gazed in, but I saw no one until I reached the windows of the office. Although it was really too dark to be sure, it looked like someone was sitting in the winged back chair that faced the desk. There appeared to be an arm and a hand resting on the arm of the chair. Why didn't whoever it was come to the door?

I continued around until I reached a side entrance. I didn't have to wonder if it was unlocked; the door was slightly ajar. I stepped in quickly, finding myself just outside the pantry. There were no servants inside, no maids, no cooks, no one.

The corridor led me to the kitchen and then to the enormous dining room with its twin chandeliers, its fifteen-foot-long table and its gold-lined satin drapes. I entered the main downstairs hallway and walked quickly to the doorway of the office, which was open.

There was definitely someone in the chair.

"Nicholas?"

I looked around when there was no response. Everything looked in place; nothing I had seen in the house so far had been disturbed. The grandfather clock in the corner ticked with the regularity of a calm, mechanical heart. I gazed at the figure in the chair again and then stepped forward slowly. When I came around the chair, I saw it wasn't Nicholas after all. It was Alison drowned in Nicholas's clothing.

She was slumped over, her chin to her chest so that the bullet hole in the back of her head was clearly visible, the now dried trickle of blood drawing a maroon line down the back of her neck and disappearing within the collar of Nicholas's dark gray silk sports coat.

I gasped, involuntarily putting a hand to my mouth. I suddenly felt Richard nudge out of his sulk. Both sides of my nature were stirred by this grisly sight.

Before I knew what was happening, we were scream-

ing in unison. A caterwaul reverberated through the deep
well of our mutual essence until the spirit of all of our
ancestry joined in the cry.

The sorrow was horrendous. One of our own had been
taken. Vivid memories of our mother's gruesome death
returned. I felt Richard lash out inside me, his soul flaring
madly like a prisoner too long in solitary confinement,
precipitously beating on the walls of his prison until his
knuckles bled. I did all that I could to keep him contained.
I closed my eyes to shut out the view of poor Alison. For a
long moment, I saw nothing, heard nothing, felt nothing.

Richard's fury subsided like a passing storm, but his
clouds remained ominously on the horizon of my consciousness. After regaining my composure, I opened my
eyes again. Alison was dead in Nicholas's clothing which
could only mean one thing: whoever had fired the shot
had murdered Nicholas. Androgyne could die only in
their female state. A fatal blow, a deadly arrow would
trigger them into instant metamorphosis.

It occurred to me that Nicholas might very well have
been innocently awaiting my arrival. He may have called
me from the phone on that very desk. Whoever had killed
him had snuck up on him, shooting him before he had had
an opportunity to turn about. The killer must have moved
on air. Nicholas would have surely heard him otherwise.
Androgyne are keen; our senses are sharp; we are rarely
taken by surprise.

Could it be that some other Androgyne, angered by how
Alison and Nicholas were handling me, had done this?
But in that case why would they not warn me first?

And if Nicholas hadn't tampered with my brakes, then
who had?

I spun around. I heard a sound. There was someone
in the front of the house.

Richard began clamoring to come forth. I was not the strong one; I couldn't face an opponent. It was the role of the male to defend the female part of us, he reminded me.

What would I do? If I permitted him to metamorphose, he would go wild and do something to prevent me from returning.

I was positive I heard someone approaching slowly, the steps were ponderous, heavy, deliberate.

"It's the great Evil Eye," I whispered. Or was it Richard warning me?

I backed away from Alison's corpse. Poor Alison, I thought. Her complexion already wan, her skin drying, her beautiful eyes that had glittered so with life, with sexual energy, were now as dark as blown bulbs. In death, her features barely resembled those I had known. Without the blush in her cheeks, the ruby red in her lips, the softness in her skin and the sheen in her hair, she was mortal.

And then it occurred to me: In death we were no different from the inferiors. Death reminded us we were all of one family, a family at war with itself, but nevertheless, a family spawned of the same seed.

Why did God put us through this torment then? Why burden us with all these curses and weigh us down with the baggage of hate and fury, a luggage of wrath that was particularly His and not ours? We are as damned as the inferiors, I thought. Even the Androgyne become dust.

I turned and fled the way I had entered. Every time I stopped and listened, I heard those footsteps. Now they were following me, I was sure. I rushed on through the kitchen and past the pantry to the side door. When I emerged, I caught my breath and listened again. I heard nothing, but I hurried to the car and got in quickly.

Richard was crying, pleading, demanding I settle back

and let him take charge. He chastised me for fleeing. This was our chance to face the devil, our chance for revenge and I was running away from it. But I couldn't help myself; I had things yet to do.

I drove out quickly, not looking back until I reached the bottom of the driveway.

I was going to go directly home, but when I reached the Pacific Coast highway, I turned south toward Venice Beach. I needed advice; I needed help; I was afraid of being alone.

The streets were very busy. The slow-moving traffic irritated my already inflamed nerves. Impatient, I wove the Thunderbird in and out of traffic, threading it through openings barely wide enough to accommodate its width. Horns blared at me. Complacent faces turned furious as I lurched by, but I was lucky. I had no accidents and I didn't attract any police.

When I reached Washington Boulevard, I turned left and drove to a building with a clouded storefront window. The structure was a Pueblo revival with a flat roof and stuccoed walls. It had projecting wooden roof beams over the parapeted front entrance. The walls were gray and streaked with soot and pollutants now. Whatever it had been originally was lost in the smudged print fading on the window. Of course it was dark, but I knew that did not matter. Diana would be there. I sensed it and knew that she sensed when she was needed.

I parked and went to the door, but before I had a chance to knock, a handsome young man opened the door. His big, dark, piercing eyes, firm lips and almost Oriental bone structure immediately told me who he was. I couldn't forget what I had envisioned. This was Diana's daughter, Denise, the androgynous child Alison had brought to see me. She had gone through her first conversion.

His good looks nearly stole my breath. I saw the look of recognition in his eyes and in the tight, small smile at the corners of his mouth.

"My mother is waiting for you," he said. Then he widened his smile. "She anticipated your arrival. I'm sorry," he said extending his hand quickly, "I should introduce myself. I'm Thomas. You've met my sister."

"Yes." I took his hand and entered a small sitting room with a rattan sofa and settee and one rocker. There was a rectangular glass table in front of the sofa. At the center of the table was a large piece of jagged crystal set in a red clay leaf.

"Please, be seated. I'll tell her you are here."

"Thank you," I said and quickly sat on the settee. Moments later, Diana appeared alone. She was an ageless Androgyne who had long passed through her menopause. Although her hair had streaks of gray, it was still long and thick, falling to the middle of her back. She had deep blue, serious eyes. They were her most striking feature. I could gaze nowhere else but into those searching orbs that were themselves two small crystal balls. Centuries of our history spiraled within. How could I look away?

Afterward, I would have trouble recalling much about her. Perhaps she changed with her visitors—growing larger with some, smaller with others. In a sense she reflected whoever had come to see her. She became a mirror revealing that part of her visitor that she or he could never see for herself or himself.

"Alison is dead," I said quickly. She nodded, her eyes closing slowly, her face, for one fleeting moment, becoming the face of a corpse: Her lips were bland, her eyes shut as if by death, her skin yellow and parched.

When she opened her eyes again, I felt myself drawn

into them, falling through them. My screams trailed behind me like long, bone-white ribbons.

Down I descended, down through a tunnel of the dead. Their faces appeared around me, faces of Androgyne who had lived and died since time began for us. Each seemed trapped in some terrible agony. Suddenly, I saw my mother's face: her mouth twisted and distorted, her eyes leaking a grayish white ooze that turned into bright red blood as it passed over her pockmarked cheeks. Her chin was nothing but bone and tendons. The skin under the streams of blood was smoking as if my mother's blood itself was an acid scorching away whatever trace of beauty remained.

I screamed and reached out for her, but she was sucked back into the dark. I fell on, passing other faces in similar torment until I saw Alison. She was as beautiful as she had been in life; her eyes sparkled with that same joyful glint, that joie de vivre that had always set her apart. It brought me some relief until suddenly a spidery shadow appeared in her cheeks. Her skin began to sink into the shadow. I saw the pallid bones within, and then her eyes popped as easily as egg yolks. Maggots emerged and began to cover her forehead, consuming her skin, her eyebrows, tearing down her nose and feasting hungrily on her lips.

I cried out for her, but she, too, was drawn back into the darkness. I began to fall again until I reached a mirror and my descent ended.

"What do you see?" Diana asked.

"Myself."

"How do you look?"

"The same."

"Yes," she said, "but there is a place for you there, a place prepared."

Her words brought me back to the moment. I blinked and looked at her.

"Do you understand?" she asked. "You are in grave danger."

"Yes, I understand. But where was I?"

"You were in our hell," she said. "All those you saw, including your mother and Alison, were taken by him."

"He's waiting for me. And for Richard," I said. She nodded.

"I can't tell you where or when."

"It doesn't matter. I'm almost at the point where I would welcome him," I said.

"That's what he hopes."

"What should I do?" I lifted my eyes to hers.

"Find yourself again. Love yourself again. Find a way to stop denying who you are."

"What if I hate who I am?"

"Then you belong in the darkness, imprisoned in the place prepared for you."

"Why?"

"All of us must bear the burden of our own creation and find a way to turn that burden into a blessing."

"Even if it brings us pain?"

"Find a way to turn that pain into pleasure. You had it once. There are some things we must accept just as God had to accept that Man is imperfect."

She pulled herself back, her shoulders high, her face suddenly becoming radiant.

"We are the Androgyne," she said. "He chose us to help Him overcome His own pain."

I nodded. She reached out and touched me, and when I looked up again, I saw my mother's face in hers. It brought tears to my eyes.

"Thank you," I said and I left her, my mind in a turmoil. I felt carried off in a river of confusion. It seemed too hard to continue to swim and so easy to just stop and let myself be carried down.

But I had the sense that Richard was standing on the shore waiting for me, waiting to rescue me from myself.

TWELVE

I DON'T REMEMBER the ride home. Suddenly, I was pulling into my drive, and the day that had begun bright and warm had turned dismal and gray, a thick layer of marine clouds sliding in over the deep blue, resembling some infinite gray curtain God was drawing over the world. I felt shrouded in misery.

As soon as I passed through my gate, I saw the detective's car parked in front of the house. I recalled his saying he would return to take me to dinner, but he was here far too early. I found him seated comfortably on the sofa, his feet up on a hassock and Richard's diary in his hands. He had made himself a drink as well and looked quite at home. After all I had been through, his complacent demeanor annoyed me.

"Where's Sylvia?" I demanded. She knew better than to let him in without me.

"She's gone." He smiled. "There was no one here when I arrived."

"Gone? How did you get in here then?" I asked without disguising my displeasure. Despite the intimacy we had shared, I detested the presumption on his part.

"Police powers," he replied, that self-satisfied smirk embedded in his face. "Actually," he said, "I'm just as surprised seeing you as you are seeing me." He held up the diary. "I was expecting to see Richard come through that door."

"You had no right coming into this house without me, and you had no right to take that and read it until I had given it to you," I snapped. I wasn't in the mood for any of his humor.

"It's evidence now. Especially now," he said.

"What do you mean?"

"He killed Nicholas today, didn't he?" he said, not changing expression. "That's why I was expecting him and not you. Yes," he said in reply to my look of surprise, "I discovered what he had done, but I didn't call it in yet. I was hoping to wrap it all up tonight." He narrowed his eyes and scrutinized me.

"Why did you permit the metamorphose? Did you want him to kill Nicholas?" he asked.

I stood there, staring.

"And what is your car doing at the bottom of that gully? It's all tied together somehow, isn't it? You might as well come clean," he said. "There's no point in holding anything back now, no point in playing games with each other." He leaned forward. "How did you survive that automobile crash, anyway? Androgynous powers?"

"I was lucky. I didn't enjoy any assistance," I added, recalling Richard's stubbornness within me.

"What happened?"

"The brakes gave out as I was going downhill. I managed to turn the car off the road and slow it down. After I had stopped the car, I got out, but it rolled again and went over the hill."

He nodded.

"I see. Someone had tampered with your brakes. You put two and two together, realized Nicholas was behind it, and released Richard—sent him over there like some attack dog," he concluded.

"No! I told you—Androgyne don't kill their own."

"So why has Richard withdrawn again?" he asked, ignoring me. "He's doing what he's always done, is that it? Hide inside you after a kill?"

"He didn't kill Nicholas," I said.

He shook his head and returned his gaze to the diary. I could see he had gone through most if not all of it.

"From what I've been reading here, Richard was always jealous of Nicholas, jealous of the way you and Nicholas got along. I think it's clear he expected Nicholas would someday do to you what he had done to Alison. Am I right?"

"Richard didn't kill him," I repeated with more insistence.

"Do you know how Richard comes across in this?" he asked patting the diary. "Like a mad, jealous, incestuous brother. There's not a love affair of yours he approves of, whether it be with an Androgyne or an inferior. No one is good enough for you; no one should put a hand on you, and if you so much as indicate pleasure or happiness with someone else, he becomes enraged or mocks it. Incestuous madness," he repeated. "It's true and it's clear as can be in this letter, his final letter," he said pulling it out of his breast pocket.

"You shouldn't have taken that out of the diary!"

"Why not?" He smiled. "What you really mean is, I shouldn't have read it, right? You were never going to read this to me," he said unfolding the paper.

"Put it back," I insisted.

"*Dear Clea,*" he read, ignoring me.

"Stop." I put my hands over my ears.

"*I am writing this with bloodied hands and a blood-ied heart. I know you will hate me at first for what I have done, but in time, you will realize I did it for both of us. You know that I do nothing for myself anyway. Even when I experience ecstatic sexual pleasure, I am experiencing it for you as well as for me. Whenever I chose a victim, I always considered whether you would approve, whether you would be happy too.*

"*I know you wonder how I can expect you to appre-ciate and to approve of what I have done, but you know that the male side of us is the more androgynous and knows what is best for our race, our existence. You must depend on my instincts.*

"*I would have done this earlier and prevented things from growing as bad as they did, but I was afraid that you would hate me with the same passion with which you love me. Now, I understand that was a weakness on my part. An Androgyne must be strong enough to withstand any emotional pain and then convert that pain into a strength, into another section of armor with which to withstand what Shakespeare called, 'the slings and arrows of outrageous fortune.'*

"*The more you loved this man, the more you denied and hated who you were. In time I began to realize what was happening. You were being tormented, tempted to deny your essence. You were committing one of the worst sins we could commit: self-denial. It was then that I realized who Michael Barrington was, who he had become or more precisely, who had possessed his form to defeat you and thus me—that same horrendous creature who has haunted us since our time began, the same one who took our loving mother, who tempted her to the edge as well.*

"*Then I knew I had to save you, save us.*

"I live for the day you fully understand and forgive me. Love, Richard."

Even hearing the detective read the letter in his sarcastic, cruel tone of voice brought tears to my eyes.

"Love Richard," he said. "What drool. What paranoia. The great Evil Eye again . . . the truth is he had just butchered and mashed a human being to death, your lover, a lover he corrupted on his journey to destroy your romance because he couldn't stand your loving anyone, anything else but him."

"No!" I cried, even though in my heart I had felt that to be true.

"Yes." He held the letter up. "You skipped a lot of this when you read to me, didn't you?"

"I did nothing of the sort," I said, throwing my purse down and going to the bar. My heart felt as though it were growing thorns, the sharp ends of which were threatening to burst out of my chest.

"Of course, you did. You know what else I think?" he said, turning to me. "I think Richard killed your mother."

"Killed my mother? That's ridiculous. You don't know how ridiculous that is."

"She was beyond metamorphosis, no longer an Androgyne. She had become an embarrassment to you, so he killed her."

"Ridiculous," I repeated.

"But matricide, even for an Androgyne, is horrendous. He couldn't live with what he had done; that's why he went rampaging around. He wasn't looking for the great Evil Eye so he could kill him, take revenge; he wanted the great Evil Eye to do away with him instead; he wanted and needed punishment."

I had to laugh.

"You don't know how stupid that theory is. Stick to your simple street murders, detective."

I poured myself a glass of vodka and drank it straight.

"You knew it all along, but couldn't face it, denied it. Finally, you couldn't deny it any longer and that's when you decided to come to me to confess. Somehow, you expected this confession would ease the burden.

"Well, I'm no priest. I can assign you no penance. You must turn Richard over to me. That's the only solution."

I stared into my glass, swirled the vodka, and then downed the remainder. The heat in my chest was comforting.

"I really don't have time for you right now," I said. "I can't waste time humoring you and playing your stupid games. Your theories are wrong; you shouldn't have read the diary without me; you didn't understand what you read."

I turned to him.

"Now if you will be so kind as to put it on the table there and then leave . . ."

He shook his head.

"I can't leave without Richard, no matter how long it takes."

"It's not time," I said.

"What's the difference when I take him?" he responded quickly. "You came to me originally for that purpose, didn't you?

I glared at him.

"Didn't you?" he repeated when I didn't reply.

"Yes, but I can't do it just yet."

"Why not?" He waited. The walls of my house suddenly seemed so confining and the air was so oppressive, I felt trapped. The detective's words twirled around me and became the chains that held me fast. He lifted his arms, turning his palms toward me so that he resembled a volunteer for crucifixion. I felt Richard's desire to pound nails through his palms.

"I just can't."

He shook his head.

"I need him," I explained.

"Need him? I don't understand. My impression was he was more of a burden at this point. Your whole existence was a burden. After what's happened now—Nicholas gone, Alison gone, I just assumed you would want a quick end. It's beyond your control.

"Prolonging it by reading this diary to me won't help," he said. "It will go on forever. When you come to the end, you'll create another tale and another.

"You're like Scheherazade, looking for a reprieve through storytelling, hoping to hold off the inevitable. Well, you can't tell this tale forever. It must come to an end. Make peace with yourself."

"Why do you want me to end it now? I was under the impression you had grown fond of me." I tilted my head suspiciously.

He smiled.

"We had a good time, but good times by definition end. Otherwise, it would all be the same and we wouldn't know what was good and what wasn't."

"Still the philosophical detective."

"It's the effect you have on me. Look, there's been another murder, albeit the murder of an Androgyne, but my people won't know that. They will think another ordinary human being was killed. I'm on this investigation, but I can't be on it for the rest of my life," he protested.

"You know I'm right," he added softly. "You can't live with it anymore. Even people you cared for are being destroyed. What's left? It's over. Do the right thing."

I stared at him. Maybe he was right; maybe I was prolonging what I had known all along was inevitable.

"I've got to think."

"Don't think. The longer you think, the more you procrastinate and prolong the agony.

"Look," he said standing, "I'm not being completely honest. I can't stand this anymore myself. I'm falling in love with you and I can't let that happen."

I looked up at him curiously. How quickly his expressions changed. He was a chameleon—coldly realistic, hard, demanding at one moment, and then soft, loving, sensitive at another. Maybe we weren't so different, inferiors and Androgyne. Maybe we all had many separate identities and what God had done was simply exaggerate one aspect of humanity to create us.

"I haven't been able to think about anything or anyone else but you since you first entered my office," he said. "I know that doesn't surprise you; you think all inferior men are vulnerable to your charms, and maybe they are, but it comes as a surprise to me. Now, all I want to do is be the one who brings you some relief, does something good for you. I think that's the best way, the most significant way I can express my love for you. At least in a way you can appreciate," he added and took a deep breath. "You're too beautiful to suffer any more, Clea. I mean that."

"My detective," I said, smiling through my tears. "My philosophical detective."

He smiled and stepped forward. I ran my hand through his hair, and he closed his eyes. Then, we kissed. It was a long, passionate kiss, a good-bye kiss in which the lips refuse to obey the commands of the mind. They press on and on trying to deny the reality of what is to follow.

"I'd ask you to make love with me one more time," he whispered, still holding me closely, "but that would only do what I've accused you of doing: prolonging the inevitable, unraveling the day's weaving." He kissed the tip of my nose and backed away.

I nodded.

"All right," I said. "You're right; the time has come."

He grew serious.

"How do we do this?"

"I'll go to Richard's room and lie down in his bed. You wait here. I'll call to you when it begins and you will be there as it happens so you can take him by surprise, quickly, swiftly, without any struggles."

"All right." He stepped back and when he did so, his jacket opened sufficiently for me to see his pistol.

I placed my emptied glass on the bar and started down the corridor toward Richard's room. I was tempted to look back, but thought if I did, I might not be able to continue.

"You're only doing what you had intended," I told myself, "doing what you set out to do. If you weaken, think only of Michael's battered body."

I paused before Richard's bedroom door, took a deep breath, and then entered.

I hadn't been in Richard's bedroom since I had gone in to erase every remnant of him in a desperate attempt to reduce his hold over me. True, all of his personal things had been swept away—his clothing, his jewelry, his bathroom articles, down to his toothpaste, but the moment I stepped into his room, I felt his presence anyway.

When I moved farther in and gazed into the wall mirror, I did not see my own reflection; I saw Richard's, and suddenly, I felt myself looking at this room not as a visitor, but as its occupant. I understood that once the metamorphosis was begun, it would happen very quickly, perhaps too quickly to call the detective. I couldn't hesitate, not a second.

I closed and opened my eyes, forcing myself to see myself in the mirror, for I realized that this would be the very last time I would look upon myself, stare lovingly at my own image and feel a woman's vanity.

It occurred to me that all living things might very well enter the portal of death with the thought that it was merely a hibernation, a sleep and then an awakening. We are deceived and thus we surrender to it rather than, as Dylan Thomas urged his father, "rage against the dying of the light." We are given to believe that whatever pain and suffering we are experiencing at that moment will pass, will be diluted and eliminated by the great sleep, the panacea which cures us of all the agony associated with life itself.

I would, like some ancient Indian, set myself down on the funeral pyre and permit Death to embrace me. Perhaps I would even smile as he put his deceivingly warm arms around me to lift me into his bosom. Could I die to the beat of my own heart drumming in my ears?

I headed for Richard's bed and began to take off my clothing, but to my surprise, he didn't begin his approach. He didn't step up to the doorway of identity and hover with anticipation. He lingered in the shadows and spoke to me from the deepest depths of our androgynous being. Of course, he knew I was delivering him, delivering us both; but his reluctance had more cause.

I hesitated.

He was urging me to open my eyes as Clea, to remain as Clea a little longer so that I would understand.

But understand what?

As if he had stepped out of me to turn my shoulders, I spun around and looked toward the doorway, and suddenly, perhaps because he had directed me to, because he had cleared my brain and washed the mist from my window on reality, I smelled it—the raw, wild flavor of blood. How could I have missed it before? It trickled from my nose to my tongue and my stomach churned.

Quietly, I slipped out of Richard's room and, pausing first in the hallway to listen, continued down the corridor toward one of our guest suites. The door was shut, but like a bird that sensed something alien had been in its nest, I knew that other fingers, the hands of predators, had closed this door. My fingers fluttered about the knob, hesitant. It was Richard within me, insisting, pressing me forward, that finally made me grasp the knob and turn it. I opened the door and entered, moving quietly over the rug, moving slowly through the room, my eyes shifting from side to side, sweeping the furniture, the bed. The scent of fresh death was strong, putrescent. It drew me to the bathroom and I opened the door.

I entered and stood there, my heart pounding. Then I reached forward and pulled back the shower curtain.

There Sylvia lay in the tub, her arms twisted out of their joints, her legs turned so far to the right, they were obviously broken. A thin red line marked where her wrenched neck had been split. The bosom of her white uniform was splattered with the ruby red drops that had fallen from her mouth and nose. Her upper lip was lifted in a sneer, but other than that, Sylvia's face was unremarkable. Her dead eyes had the same bland, lifeless glint they had always had. She didn't look like someone who had been in any particular pain. She had died with the same lack of passion with which she had lived.

Richard came clamoring down the tunnel that separated us from each other. "Do you see?" he screamed. "Do you understand now? He's here! He's always been here!"

Confused, dizzy, I spun about and reached out for the sink to catch my balance. My detective had said that Sylvia wasn't here when he had arrived. Obviously, he hadn't searched the house or he would have found her. He probably went right for the diary and made himself comfortable, I thought quickly. I must go to him and explain the danger we are both in now.

"I must warn the detective," I muttered.

Richard's laughter was like fingernails drawn across a chalk blackboard. My spine cringed.

"You fool, you romantic, blind fool. Think, recall, replay his words," Richard urged me.

I gazed at Sylvia's corpse. I knew it had to be the workings of my terrified mind, the twisted machinations of a distorted imagination, but it appeared that Richard, in order to impress what was true on me, slipped from me to Sylvia.

Suddenly, her head moved and then turned on her broken neck. The twisting caused new blood to spurt from the thin incision and tiny, hairlike streams streaked down and under the blouse of her uniform. Her curled upper lip slid back over her teeth and her dead eyes blinked. Then she spoke to me in Richard's voice.

"He said Nicholas was dead, that I had killed him. But anyone who found the body would have found Alison not Nicholas. In death Nicholas changed instantly back to Alison. Only the killer could know it was originally Nicholas who had been shot."

Sylvia's corpse collapsed. I gasped and looked toward the doorway.

The detective? My detective?

I could hear my mother's warnings, a child's story, a fable, and then the lessons.

"Remember, Clea. He's always out there, waiting in the form we would least expect, waiting to take advantage of our weaknesses. He's patient; he has all the time in the world."

My God, I thought, I had told him so much and put so many of our kind in jeopardy.

"Of course," I muttered to myself as well as to Richard, who I felt waiting just under the surface of my being, "he was so perceptive; he seemed to know so much and knew the right questions. And his powers of lovemaking . . .

I had told Diana I was almost at the point where I would welcome him and she had said that was what he hoped for. She had told me to stop denying who I was, to stop hating myself or I would be his victim.

That's what had brought me to him in the first place; that's why he had possessed the detective. He knew I would come.

That's why he was out there now, waiting.

I stepped away from the sink and began my journey back.

As I walked down the corridor, I felt it begin. This time, because of my own anger and my own aggression, it was a far greater rush than it had ever been. It was as if Richard were emerging from beneath my feet, seeping up through my soles, absorbing, changing, molding as he climbed toward my heart. I sensed a thickening in my ankles and a tightening and stiffening in my calf muscles and thighs. As Richard's being overtook mine, I began the androgynous retreat to that limbo, the waiting room of souls in which we rested and prepared for our rebirth. I felt myself sliding back to the womb, curling up into a fetal position, welcoming the warmth, the security, the oblivious existence in which there was no turmoil. Never had I welcomed it with so much enthusiasm as I did now.

Richard rushed past me, his eyes passing through mine. His were fixed with the hunter's glare, focused intently on the kill. I could hear his quickened breath, feel his pulse thumping as his blood flowed over my own, hastening my retreat, pressing me back protectively as he clawed his way to the surface of our being. In seconds it was over and the darkness swept across my consciousness, closing off my immediate existence.

What followed came in the form of a dream, and as with many of my dreams, I was an observer standing on the threshold, more a witness than a participant.

The detective was sitting forward on the sofa, his pistol drawn. He was leaning on his thighs, staring down, waiting. Once in a while, the tip of his tongue moved over his lips. It looked like the head of a tiny snake peering out, exploring the surface of its nest and then quickly retreating. It didn't surprise me. Surely snakes and rats, vermin and reptiles of all sorts lived within the caverns of this horrendous creature, this tumor on the face of creation. The detective was merely the shell around it now.

As if to emphasize that very fact, the detective's head began to rise. I saw the skin on his neck stretch with the strain. Finally, the skin snapped. He didn't bleed. All of his blood had been sucked in to the feed the rodents and the reptiles. When he lowered his neck again, his head dropped off and shattered on the floor, the eyes rolling away like two marbles. Bones and teeth shattered to gray-white slivers.

Out of the opening in his neck emerged a raw, red, bullet-shaped glob of pulsating flesh embossed with green

and blue veins. It bubbled at the surface and began to
take form. Diamond-shaped bone-white eyes appeared.
Beneath them, the flesh sunk in two small circles to
form what looked to be a nose. The mouth came more
slowly as the flesh ripped apart. Strings of it held on
as if to keep it from forming. Gradually, they snapped
and the opening grew larger. Teeth appeared—long, very
white, yet not quite fangs. Within, the tongue curled and
twisted like a writhing worm that had had half of its
body crushed into the ground.

It was fitting that he would be this ugly, as ugly as
nightmares, as ugly as sin. Janice once told me he takes
so many different forms because he has no form he can
call his own; he is whatever we see him as, whatever
evil is within us—that's the evil we see, and since we
all have different sorts of evil and different amounts of
it, he is different to each of us.

He lifted his hands from his thighs and the ends of
his fingers popped off to make way for the emerging
gray nails, each looking sharper than the one before it. In
fact, everywhere the detective's skin was visible, it split
or peeled to make way for him. His hot body burned
through the possessed one. He no longer had reason to
keep himself hidden.

Steam rose from the shoulders of the detective's jacket
and out from under the cuffs in his pants. The air around
him simmered. The furniture and the floor began to smoke
as his blistering body singed and burned. He had brought a
piece of hell with him. It was as Janice had said: "Everywhere he goes, there is hell. It's his baggage; he carries
purgatory on his shoulders."

When he opened his mouth wider, I saw fires burning.
I could hear the screams of agony coming from the souls
he had captured and swallowed. I realized that with every

acquisition, he grew more powerful, more vibrant and more formidable. Fearful in my dream, I stepped back from the window. I was afraid he could see me and had the power even to reach through dreams to grasp souls.

But when Richard entered the room from behind him, he did not see him as I saw him. He saw him as the detective, just a man as vulnerable as any other man. I wanted to shout out to warn him, but it was better for Richard that he did not see him as I saw him. He experienced no fear, only anger.

Swiftly, he moved across the room and came up behind the detective. Just before he brought his arm around the detective's neck, the detective began to stand and turn. But Richard didn't hesitate. He caught him in a choke hold and drew him back quickly. The detective raised his pistol and fired blindly, missing. With his other hand, Richard seized the gun and the struggle centered on that first.

Richard's strength was far greater than the detective's, even with the devil possessing him. He turned the gun down and the next time it fired, the bullet shattered the detective's breast. His resistance waned. Richard tightened his choke hold, and the detective's eyes began to bulge. His face reddened, but he was able to manage a cry.

Pathetically, because the devil faced defeat and began to withdraw, my detective cried out my name.

"Clea!"

I covered my ears when he cried out again. My poor detective—charming, vulnerable, witty, strong—everything I had dreamed my lover should be. I wondered about that last kiss we had shared. Had it been the devil's or my poor detective's? I would never know for sure.

And I would never know love, not the way the inferiors knew it, I thought. It saddened me to understand even though it was that very same longing that had brought me to this point. Our dreams, our hopes were really our particular curses. Pain came only from what we longed for and could not have. If we longed for nothing, we would suffer nothing.

But then we would be like the Stoics, like Sylvia's kind, never unhappy, true; but never happy. The paradox was our curse, a curse we shared with the inferiors.

I laughed, a mad laugh. One of the greatest lovers on earth, I would never know love the way I longed to know it. My mother had come to realize the same thing, and when she had realized it, she had embraced death, choosing to live in eternal damnation for one moment of earthly love.

I turned from the window of my dream grateful for Richard, rejoicing now in what we were. I was stronger than my mother. I embraced myself instead of the phantom, the illusion of perfect love. Instead, I returned to self-love in the greatest form it could take. I returned to the Androgyne.

I awoke in my own bed. I felt invigorated, well rested. I had no idea how long I had been asleep after metamorphosis until I looked at the clock and realized it was the next day. After I showered and dressed, I went to Richard's room and found it had been restored. All his things were back in place and it was as neat and as clean as ever—the towels properly folded, his suits and pants pressed and clean. Even his toothpaste was as it had been. It was almost as if everything that had happened since I had come into this room and taken it apart was merely a dream.

I went to the guest bedroom and looked in the bathroom, but Sylvia's body was gone. There wasn't even a trace of blood on the tub.

Of course, there was no sign of the detective, nothing to indicate he had ever been there. Except . . . Richard's diary was on the table by the sofa where the detective had been reading it. The last letter was back in the diary.

I went to the front door and looked outside and saw my car had been replaced with one just like it. Richard's Thunderbird was parked alongside it. Everything seemed to be as it had been; everything in place, ready, waiting.

I looked up; it was a warm day. The sun was peeping through the haze, burning it off. It would be a wonderful day. I was filled with so much energy, so much eagerness to do things, go places.

There were dozens of people to see. I had to call the studio to let them know I would be in; I was all right. I couldn't wait to act again. Suddenly, the camera, the lights, the makeup and sets, all the illusions were more exciting than ever.

I closed the door and went back through the house, making a mental list of all the things I had to do today. I had to find someone, preferably another Stoic, to replace Sylvia, of course; that is, if Richard hadn't already. I suspected he might have. He seemed to have taken care of everything.

Sure enough, when I walked into the kitchen, I found a note on the kitchenette.

"I made some inquiries and interviewed a prospective replacement for Sylvia. Her name is Bianca and she appears to be quite adequate. She will be here this afternoon. Don't worry. She has a key."

The note was signed, "Love, Richard."

We would truly look after each other until time took him from me and me from him.

EPILOGUE

IN HER WILL Alison had chosen to leave me the most precious gift of all—she revealed the whereabouts of her and Richard's child. She lived in Manhattan Beach with an androgynous woman who was about my age: Adrian Raven, an attorney.

On a beautiful Saturday morning a little more than a month after Alison's funeral, I called Adrian before driving down for a visit. The child, now an adolescent on the verge of her conversion, was walking the beach. Adrian had told her I was coming to visit, but she hadn't told her much more.

"I didn't have to," she said. "It's why we named her Sage. She's a remarkable girl, precocious, wise, often clairvoyant, and, as you will soon see, quite beautiful. We're all very proud of her."

We spoke a little about Alison and Nicholas, as well as other Androgyne we knew. Adrian was a very bright and successful attorney. She had a beautiful beach house. Alison had placed the child well, I thought.

"What does she know? What have you told her?"

"I never told her she wasn't my daughter," Adrian said. "I didn't have to. One night just recently, while we were sitting out here after dinner, she turned to me and said it herself. Naturally, when I didn't deny it, she asked about her real mother and I told her the truth. I had the sense that she would discover it on her own anyway."

"How did she take it?"

"With that same quiet acceptance she takes nearly everything. It hasn't changed our love for each other. She hugged me to her and said I would always be her mother and she would always love me as much as she could love a mother.

"I'm very glad I adopted her," she continued. "It would break my heart to lose her."

"Oh, I'm not here to take her from you," I said. "You must not worry about that."

"I'm happy to hear it. She knows all about you. Instinctively, she has followed your career from the moment she could read."

"Really?" I looked to the beach. "Sage," I said.

"Yes. Why don't you go to her? She's waiting for you, I'm sure."

I thanked her and walked down to the beach. The water was rolling in gently, the whitecaps barely a foot high. At first I didn't see her, and then suddenly, there she was. She looked so much like Alison, she took my breath away. But as I drew closer, I saw she had Richard's eyes. It gave me the strangest, and yet most wonderful feeling. It was as if I were meeting Richard for the first time outside myself.

"Hello," I said.

"Hello. You're as beautiful in person as you are on the screen. More beautiful," she added.

"Thank you. You're becoming a very attractive young lady yourself. You look a lot like your mother."

"Did you know her well?"

"Oh yes. We were the best of friends. We grew up together, went to school together and lived together for a while in New York."

"I want to go to New York someday too," she said.

"You will, I'm sure."

"Adrian's taking me there for a visit next summer, but I think I want to live there."

"You're going to want to live in many places."

She laughed.

"I know. I feel that way already . . . about everything. Is it unnatural?"

"Oh no."

"I want to taste everything, see everything, do everything. Adrian laughs at me and says I flit about like a bird, but I can't help it. Sometimes, I wake up in the middle of the night and my heart is pounding for no reason."

I smiled.

"That's not unusual. It happened to me the same way."

"Did it? Adrian says that too, but . . ." She stared at me. "I've wanted to meet you for a long time. I'm so happy you've come."

"I'm happy I'm here."

"Will you tell me about my mother?"

"I'll tell you everything I can."

"Will we be good friends? Oh, I don't mean as friendly as all Androgyne are to each other. I mean special friends."

"Of course."

"Did you come now because it's almost my time?"

"I suppose, although to be honest, I didn't plan it."

"It's wonderful how things just happen for us sometimes, isn't it?"

"Yes," I said, and I had to laugh at her exuberance. How much she reminded me of myself now.

"Let's walk along the beach and talk. Will you hold my hand?"

"I'd love to," I said and took her soft hand into mine. Then I hugged her to me.

"Are you going to stay overnight?"

"Do you want me to?"

"Very much. I think . . . maybe it might happen tonight and I'd want you to be here to meet him."

"Yes."

"Do you know," she whispered, "I know something that Adrian says usually doesn't come until after the conversion."

"Really? What?"

"I know his name. It's just there; it's always been there like an egg waiting to hatch."

I laughed. "It could be."

"Oh, it is."

"What is his name?"

"Richard," she said. "Do you think I'm right?"

"Yes. I do."

"You know a lot, don't you? Will you tell me all you can? Will you?"

"I'll tell you everything."

"It is going to happen tonight," she stated firmly. "I'm sure now. And do you know," she said as we continued down the beach, "I'm not afraid . . . not anymore . . . now that you're here."

I hugged her to me again.

A tern swooped down before us, then soared toward a passing cloud. In the distance we could see a sailboat emerging on the horizon.

And suddenly I felt there was nothing as precious as life, and nothing as confusing.

A secret society of powerfully placed, embittered men dispenses its own brand of justice in Andrew Neiderman's terrifying new thriller

THE SOLOMON ORGANIZATION

Andrew Neiderman

After a flagrant affair and a burgeoning cocaine habit land him in divorce proceedings, Scott Lester thinks he's hit bottom. So when a sympathetic stranger offers the promise of a reprieve through the support of the shadowy Solomon Organization, Lester jumps at the chance.

But Lester's problems are only beginning, and he soon finds himself racing to track down the members of the Organization, whose Old Testament-style judgment sentenced him to this living nightmare.

Available in hardcover at bookstores everywhere.

G. P. Putnam's Sons
A member of The Putnam Berkley Group, Inc.